A Pure Double Cross

Book One of the
American Spy Trilogy
by

John Knoerle

This is a work of fiction.

Published By **Blue Steel Press**
Chicago, IL
bluesteelpress@aol.com
www.bluesteelpress.com

First edition – first printing 2008
Copyright ©2008 by John Knoerle.
All rights reserved.

Cover art and design by Katherine Bennett.

ISBN 978-0-9743199-1-9
Library of Congress 2008907387
Printed in the United States.

Also by John Knoerle:

"Crystal Meth Cowboys"
"The Violin Player"

And soon to come:

"A Despicable Profession"
"The Velvet Trench"

The author would like to thank the following for their help and support:

Kevin O'Donnell
Vern Morrison and the Cleveland Memory Project at the
    CSU Library
Joe and Anne Schram
Allan Guthrie and *Noir Originals*
Duff Kennedy
Mark A. Ward
Jeanne Jenkins
Barb Cooper
Robert Borchardt
Claudia Brown and the Kelleys Island Historical Assoc.
And Kate the barmaid at Otto Moser's

for JJ

"All a man can betray is his conscience."

-- Joseph Conrad

They're all lined up like little toy soldiers. Overturned shot glasses on the bar. I'm going to have to pace myself. Each overturned glass is another free drink in waiting bought and paid for by my adoring public.

I wasn't a hero after World War II. I am now. Here's how it happened.

Chapter One

The day was Thursday, November 29th, 1945 in *the best location in the nation*. So said the Cleveland Electric Illuminating Company billboards. T-bones were back. So were cooking oil, Friday fish fries and long Sunday drives with a full tank of gas and a dame wearing a white cotton blouse, a flared midcalf skirt and *silk stockings*. The war was over and Cleveland, Ohio, the smoke-belching colossus that smelted the ore and poured the heat and rolled the steel that won the peace, was feeling its oats.

My name is Hal Schroeder and I'm twenty-three years old. I walked from Mrs. Brennan's rooming house to the Detroit-Superior Bridge and jumped on the rattler. The bridge has two levels, cars and trucks on top, streetcars below. I wore a pea coat over my armored car uniform, an empty boodle bag stuffed in the coat pocket. I looked out the window as we crossed the Cuyahoga River to downtown.

From a distance The Flats looked just like the Ruhr Valley after a B-24 raid, mountains of oil black smoke rent by stalks of torchy flame. I wiped fog from the streetcar window and looked again. The long gray peak-roofed buildings along the riverbank were intact, ore trains steamed up slowly to their sidings, hoppers full to bursting. The oil black smoke poured from working stacks, the torchy flames from burn-off pipes. It wasn't oil black flesh-smelling defeat I was looking at, it was victory.

The rattler stopped at Public Square, Superior and Ontario. I got off and craned my neck at the Terminal Tower, the tallest building west of Manhattan and impressive as hell to a kid from Youngstown. The Society for Savings was a block north.

It was impressive too. One of those Greco-Roman-Gothic-Renaissance jobs with granite pillars and arches and red sandstone turrets.

I checked my watch. Five minutes to go.

I climbed the granite stairs to the Soldiers and Sailors Monument and hid my pea coat and my empty bag in the bronze sculpture of the Civil War cannoneers. The lake wind blew wicked cold as I crossed the street to the ten-story building in my spit-shined boots and gun belt, my cleaned and pressed uniform and my gold Brinks Armored Security badge.

The bank interior was a showstopper. A thirty-foot ceiling with a stained glass skylight, murals of pioneers yoking oxen and raising barns, acres of white marble and miles of polished brass. It had the desired effect, I felt small and insignificant, but what else is new?

I walked up to the banker's gate like I had a right to be there. They didn't buzz me in. I cleared my throat in an impatient manner. A lower down signaled for a higher up. The higher up stood on the other side of the gate and said he didn't know me.

"Pete's out sick," I said. I kept my yap shut after that and let my shiny gold badge do the talking. The higher up and the lower down had a whispered conversation. I tapped my foot and looked at my watch.

The higher up buzzed me in. I collected two bags of banded bills in large denominations, signed a receipt for $18,758 and got escorted to the entrance by a bank guard.

I entered the revolving door ahead of the guard, pushed through and jammed a rubber doorstop into the side of the door. The bank guard said, "Hey!"

I ran across the street and up the granite steps. I dumped the sacks of cash into the boodle bag and pulled on my pea coat.

The armored car pulled up to the bank right on schedule. The bank guard bellowed at them from his glass cage. I ran down the steps on the other side of the Soldiers and Sailors monument. A big black sedan was idling on Superior. I got in.

That night I put on coat and tie and hailed a cab. The cabbie told me all about the daring daylight heist at the Society for Savings. It was the headline story in the late edition of *The Cleveland Press*. We drove west to Lorain and Rocky River Road. They call it Kamm's Corners. I got out at the Green Light Tavern, paid the fare and added a dollar tip. What the hell, I was flush.

The Green Light looked like your standard issue beer and a bump dive. Sawdust on the floor, a jar of pickled pig's feet behind the bar. Only it wasn't. I ordered a local beer from the barkeep. It tasted like tap water. Two years in Europe will do that to you. I paid the barkeep and said "Double feature." He picked up the quarters and inclined his head.

The steel door was down a narrow hall, past the bathrooms, past the pay phone. It was partly open, held so by a gigantic man with a neatly trimmed white beard. He was Irish, had to be. "And you are?"

"Harold Schroeder, of the Gates Mills' Schroeders. Here to try my hand at a game of chance."

The giant's eyes narrowed.

"Perhaps a remuneration is customary," I said brightly, extending a sawbuck. The steel door opened wide.

I had never been inside a gambling parlor before but I'd seen pictures. Monte Carlo it wasn't. No icy blondes with upswept hair, no bored silver-haired gents playing baccarat. Just a bunch of working stiffs chewing green cigars and counting their chips at the table, plus a few loudmouths throwing dice at the craps table.

I sat in on a game of seven card stud and ordered a rye rocks from a waitress in fishnet hose. I lost two hands and ordered another round. I did it again.

This went on for quite a while. Along about the fourth watered down drink I threw down my cards, stood up and accused the dealer of using marked cards or dealing off the bottom, I forget which. The white-bearded giant scooped me up like a rag doll and headed for the back door.

"I'm Harold Schroeder, of the Gates Mills' Schroeders."

"Yeah, you said."

"And you are?"

The white-bearded giant kicked open the back door and tossed me into the alley. "Kelly," he grunted as he pulled the door shut.

I dusted myself off and walked around the front entrance. I parked myself at the bar once again and asked the barkeep if he had a bottle that wasn't half Lake Erie bilge water. He had to stand on tiptoe to nab a dusty fifth of Lighthouse Whisky, aged six years. I downed a shot, tipped him a deuce and said, "Tell Kelly that Harold Schroeder is here to kick his ass."

Kelly wasn't long in coming. He looked scary as hell with his neck veins bulging and his green eyes open wide as they would go. I had a moment's panic. But I got over it.

"You got a private room where we can do this?" I said. "I don't want to embarrass you in front of the patrons."

Kelly grabbed me by the coat collar and dragged me up a flight of stairs to an empty lounge outside a private office. I knew it was a private because it had a plaque on the door that said so. The door was closed but light shone underneath it. That was good.

Kelly moved some tables to make room. I took some deep breaths to get my heart quiet. Kelly rubbed his hands together and smiled. I assumed the position, arms relaxed, feet at ten and two. "You sure you're up to this gramps?"

He was on me in two strides. I had hoped to demonstrate my expertise at the double sleeve throw, or the complex reverse elbow arm bar. But it was simpler just to dart aside and trip him with my foot.

He was a spry old gent, give him that. He was up and turned around in a blink, his face a fiery red. "You're not gonna have a heart attack, are you?" I said. "I wouldn't want that."

Kelly flew at me, his fists high. I couldn't leverage his arm into a deft cross arm wristlock because I couldn't reach that high.

So I snap kicked his knee and spun to my right. He stumbled. I could have put him down with a rabbit punch just above the occipital bulge but that wasn't the point of this exercise. And I was starting to feel sorry for him.

Kelly got up and gathered himself. He advanced slowly, arms outstretched, grinning like a chimp. I no longer felt sorry for him.

There is one principle central to both espionage and ju jitsu. Avoid the head on collision of forces. My spy school ju jitsu instructor had not prepared me to counter a 280 lb. opponent willing to absorb a thumb to the eye and a knee to the groin in order to wrap me in a monstrous bear hug and squeeze my internal organs out through my windpipe.

I backed up a step, grabbed a chair and yelled. I smashed the chair against the floor and yelled some more.

The door to the private office opened. The man who stood in the doorway said, *"What?!"*

The man was half Kelly's size and twice as scary. Everything about him sloped downward, the shelf of brow, the beak nose, the frowning mouth and the chin like an ice-breaker's prow. He looked me up and down with his left eye. His right eye paid no attention. "What the motherhumping hell is this?"

"My name is Hal Schroeder and it's about a #10 envelope in my coat pocket," I said pleasantly. "And watch your mouth, you're in polite company."

The man's expression didn't change. It didn't have to, guy was born scowling.

"Throw him down the stairs," he said to Kelly and turned back to his private office.

I whipped out the heavy envelope from my coat pocket and threw it as hard as I could. Bob Feller would have been impressed. It hit the one-eyed thug square between the shoulder blades.

When he turned around he had a big nasty nickel-plated .45 in his mitt. He wanted to shoot me. He wanted to shoot me so bad you can't believe it but the contents of the envelope had spilled out onto the floor. Two stacks of crisp, bank-banded hundred dollar bills.

"Consider that my letter of introduction."

"To who?"

"The Schooler," I said. "Yes, it's from where you think it is and, no, it's not a set-up."

The man pointed his nickel-plated in my direction. I sighed.

"You're not going to use that thing. Not here. Now get on the horn and arrange a meet. You can shoot me later if The Schooler doesn't bite."

Slopehead trained his gat on my face and almost smiled. "Count on it."

My hands were bound with electrical tape. I was patted down and blindfolded and tossed into the back seat of a late model black Buick. Car doors slammed.

We drove a long way, no one in the front seat said a word. After about twenty minutes the hum of the tires got thin and I felt a jolt of cold air. We were crossing a bridge, headed east. Downtown.

We stopped a short time later. I was pulled from the back seat and stood up. The place smelled of creosote and old smoke. I was half-walked, half-carried for about fifty paces. The floor was slippery with oil and crunchy with metal shavings. Our footsteps echoed.

We stopped and waited. We waited some more. We waited some more after that.

"This must be a new form of interrogation. Third degree boredom."

Somebody slugged me in the stomach. I bent over and puked watered whisky all over my shiny black brogans. When I straightened up someone pulled down my blindfold and shined a flashlight in my eyes.

"Who are you and what do you want?" His voice was soft, fatherly.

I told him my name and said I wanted to talk to The Schooler. "Is that you?"

"Please continue," said the man.

"All right, I'll do that. Just as soon as you untape my wrists. I use a lot of gestures when I speak."

I braced for another haymaker but the man with the flashlight chuckled and gave the order. This was good, this was encouraging. If this guy was indeed The Schooler I might still be drawing breath after I finished saying what I had to say.

I massaged my wrists and took my time doing it.

"I robbed the Society for Savings this afternoon. $18,758. Not bad for a day's work but not good enough. I've got completely worked out heist plans in the six figures, all right here in Cleveland. But they're too big for one man, I'll need a crew."

The echoey room got quiet. I couldn't see diddly with that electric torch scorching my eyeballs so I shut my lids and enjoyed the silence. They were on my turf now.

"How did you pull off that job this afternoon?" said the soft-voiced man.

"I won't answer that question till I can see who I'm talking to."

The flashlight clicked off. A portly middle-aged gent took shape once the starbursts faded. I'd seen his picture. The Schooler.

"I didn't do the job by myself," I said. "I had an accomplice."

"Who?"

"The Federal Bureau of Investigation."

Chapter Two

It was a clambake that decided me. A Saturday afternoon clambake in Frankie Lemowski's backyard in Youngstown. All my neighborhood pals were there, back from Corregidor and Anzio and the Aleutian Islands, working at the mill or the hardware store, living in trailers and crackerbox apartments, the ink barely dry on the articles of surrender and most of them already hitched and half their wives in maternity smocks. Frankie and his wife lived in the basement of his parents' bungalow and counted themselves lucky.

My neighborhood pals are good guys, salt of the earth, shirt off their back. But they'd been reading too many of their own press clippings. They think they're heroes, still wearing their dress blues and oak leaf clusters to church on Sunday. They swapped their war stories and I listened. They gave me a hard time. 'Hal was busy sipping champagne with some Mata Hari in a French café.' Ha ha.

I was an undercover wireless agent parachuted behind enemy lines to provide intelligence on troop movements and potential bomb targets. I was recruited because I was the grandson of German immigrants and spoke *Deutsch*. That much they knew. I didn't fill my pals in on the gory details because I am prohibited by the Office of Strategic Services from doing so.

Cheesed me off. What I did was dangerous. So far as I know I'm the only behind-German-lines OSS agent who lived to tell about it. Only I couldn't.

My Case Officer would say I was alive because I shirked my duties but screw him. Had I followed his orders to the letter – fraternized with the *Wehrmacht* brass at the local *Biergarten*, infiltrated the nearby *Panzer* camp – my ability to dit dah valuable intel would have been severely compromised from being tied to a fencepost and used for bayonet practice.

So I'm no hero. Truth to tell neither were my pals. The real heroes, the ones who did what they didn't have to do, are all dead. Like Alfred and Frieda. They weren't awarded any medals and citations and nobody knows what they did except me. And I ain't talking.

The clambake got louder as night fell. Frankie sounded just like his old man when someone stole a sniff of the five-gallon pot of steaming clams, chicken, potatoes and corn on the cob. "Close the lid! Close the lid, you'll lose the flavor!"

Somewhere along in there I decided. I told Frankie I had taken a job in Cleveland, a job in a bank.

"Cleveland? Didn't Jeannie move up there?"

Jeannie was my high school sweetheart. We were plain crazy about one another. We would have been just two more dopey newlyweds at the clambake if Jeannie hadn't eloped while I was overseas.

"I don't know and I don't care," is what I said to Frankie.

Chapter Three

The FBI sent a registered letter to my address in Youngstown. It contained a roundtrip train ticket to Cleveland and a one-paragraph letter that invited me to a meeting, 2 November, 14:00 hours sharp, to discuss 'a matter of mutual interest.' It was signed by Chester Halladay, Special Agent in Charge.

It was not the sort of letter I got every day. Especially not from the FBI. The FBI and the OSS hated each other.

J. Edgar Hoover lobbied FDR to put the Bureau in charge of overseas espionage during the war. FDR tapped William Donovan to head the Office of Strategic Services instead. And Wild Bill did a passable job, if victory counts for anything. In 1944 Donovan secretly proposed making the OSS permanent. Someone leaked the proposal to a Washington newspaper columnist who dubbed it the "Super Gestapo Agency."

FDR shelved the proposal. Everyone from Wild Bill Donovan on down figured J. Edgar Hoover for the leaker.

Mind you I don't give a rat's patoot about the OSS. I signed on for a nine-month stint and was still humping my wireless set, dodging Yank P-51's and Russian shock troops, two years later. Then I came home in street clothes, shambling down the gangplank at Newport News after the uniformed GI's were greeted with popping flashbulbs and brass bands.

I didn't do as any self-respecting veteran of the Oh-So-Secret should have done. I didn't tear those train tickets in two. I had risked my neck for two years, I had been honorably discharged. I was going to play that for whatever it was worth. So I boarded the 11:47 to Cleveland the next day.

The Cleveland District Office of the Federal Bureau of Investigation is located on the 9th floor of the Standard

Building, corner of Ontario and St. Clair. The elevator operator
was an old man with a big Adam's apple. I asked him what the
'Standard' stood for.
    "Standard Trust, first labor bank in the country."
    "I didn't see a bank downstairs."
    "Went bust. President did eight years for crooked loans."
    "Was it the FBI who busted him?"
    The elevator operator spat tobacco juice into a brass spit-
toon and feathered the car to a stop on the ninth floor.
    I announced my name at the front desk and was swept
through a zigzag of corridors on a tide of smiles and bent back
doors until I came to rest in a dimpled leather club chair across
from the Special Agent in Charge. Chester Halladay stood up, I
shook his soft plump hand.
    I thought all G-men were jut-jawed tough guys who ate
nails and pissed rust but Chester Halladay, with his fleshy
jowls and wavy hair, looked more like a floor walker at
Higbee's. All he needed was a pink carnation.
    "How was your journey?" said Halladay when we had
settled back in our chairs. "The trains run on time?"
    I smiled and nodded. Nothing like a little Nazi humor to
break the ice. A file folder sat open on Halladay's desk. I
recognized the upside down picture. Yours truly. Halladay
leaned back in his spring-loaded chair and launched himself to
his feet. He walked over to the credenza on the far wall, turned
around and walked back.
    "Organized crime in the greater Cleveland area prospered
while you were busy making the world safe for democracy,
Mr. Schroeder. War rationing opened up a lucrative black market and they took full advantage, full advantage. But now,
they're hurting."
    Halladay walked over to the window above St. Clair Ave-
nue, turned around and walked back. A pink carnation was all
he needed.

"The mob doesn't do well in times of freedom and prosperity. Prohibition gave them bootlegging, the depression gave them loan sharking, war rations gave them the black market. But now, they're hurting."

Halladay leaned over and flattened his lunch hooks on the desk blotter which skidded forward, dumping an empty ashtray on the carpet. I bent down and picked it up. It bore the official seal of the Federal Bureau of Investigation.

"The mob can't make ends meet as racketeers these days," said the Special Agent. "So they've reverted to form, to what they truly are - gangsters. They've robbed four banks in as many weeks." Halladay fixed me with a meaningful look. "That's where you come in Mr. Schroeder. We want you to help them along."

This got my attention. I sat up straight in my dimpled chair.

The phone rang. Halladay answered, cupped his hand over the mouthpiece and said, "Assistant Special Agent Schram will give you the particulars."

I was whisked away to an adjoining office. Agent Richard Schram was more like it. Ropey and crew cut as a drill instructor. A crooked smile but straight teeth. The handshake we exchanged was just this side of Indian wrestling. He x-rayed me with a look. I got the feeling whatever cockamamie scheme I'd been summoned here for wasn't Richard Schram's idea.

"War hero are you?" said Schram through clenched teeth. Teeth, hell, the guy had clenched hair.

"No sir, I'm not a war hero."

"No?"

"No sir."

"What then?"

"I was an agent for the OSS sir. A spy."

"A spy!"

"Yes sir."

"Of course. That makes you a perfect fit."

"A perfect fit for what? Sir."

Agent Schram's eyes got sly. "You know."

"Just what the Special Agent told me sir."

"Which was?"

"That the mob was doing bank heists and he wanted me to help them along."

"And what did you say to that?"

"Nothing sir."

"Nothing?"

"No sir. Agent Halladay took a phone call before I could reply."

Agent Scram cranked up another crooked smile and held it for several seconds. I must have passed some kind of test. In any event the swollen vein in the middle of his forehead stopped pounding four beats to the bar and we got down to cases.

"We know who pulled those bank jobs," said Schram. "The Fulton Road Mob. They've been acting up lately."

"If you know they did it why don't you arrest them? Sir."

Agent Schram ground his teeth. "You are asking the wrong man that question."

"Yes sir."

"The plan, the *concept* is to insert pre-arranged heist plans, use them to ladder up the chain of command and bring down the mysterious Mr. Big."

"Mr. Big?"

"Theodore Briggslavski, a.k.a. Teddy Biggs. Now that he's the head magoo he's known as Mr. Big," said Schram. "The man's a phantom. All we have in his jacket is one grainy old photo."

Agent Schram handed me a file folder containing a picture of a tall pot-bellied man with a big mop of hair. I closed the folder and handed it back.

Schram's watery blue gaze turned inward. I kept my hands in my lap and my thoughts to myself. Someone in the Cleveland District office of the FBI would eventually get around to telling me what they wanted me to do. Wouldn't they?

A fire engine honked and wailed its way down Ontario. The sweep second hand on the electric wall clock rounded third and headed for home. The potted philodendron on the windowsill sprouted several flowering tendrils.

"Sir..."

"So what have you decided?" said Schram, snapping to.

"About what?"

"About signing on to become an undercover mob informant! I thought you were briefed?"

"No sir."

"*No* you're not interested?"

"*No* I wasn't briefed. Sir. But I am interested."

I don't know why I said that so quickly. I hated being a spy. But it opened my eyes. Good guys? Bad guys? Once the shitstorm starts there's not much difference. When I was behind German lines everyone was trying to kill me. What I wanted now was to get away, far away from the chest-beaters and the speechifiers before they found a way to start it all up again. Preferably to someplace warm. Preferably with Jeannie.

Hey, you never know.

So I was interested. Still, I couldn't resist twitting the Fan Belt Inspectors. "Why not get one of your own boys to do this job? Too dangerous?"

"Don't be ridiculous. We can't use our agents because they're known to the enemy."

"But why a broken down spy from the OSS?"

Agent Schram breathed deeply though his nostrils. He started to speak, cleared his throat and started again. "Because your training and experience," he said in a low voice, biting off the words, "make you uniquely qualified for this mission."

I smiled and thanked him and said I was in.

Chapter Four

People are so depressingly predictable. The guy from the gambling club, the scowling guy with the downsloped mug, yanked his nickel-plated .45 from his armpit holster when I mentioned that I was working for the FBI.

The barrel felt warm against my temple. I sniffed and made a face. "Your gun smells like BO."

He cocked the hammer.

"Jimmy," said The Schooler. The gun got holstered.

Jimmy? The name didn't fit somehow. I had Slopehead figured for a Rocco, or a Big Louie.

"Why should we trust you?" said The Schooler in his soft voice. A voice that didn't need to push or shout, a voice that was accustomed to being heeded.

"You shouldn't. You should trust the results. The feds are gee'd up to nab the head of your operation - Mr. Big they call him - and they've ponied up a fat wad of bait money to do it."

"And how does that work?"

"On the installment plan. Down payment, the C notes I gave to…Jimmy. Second payment, an armored car job courtesy of the FBI. Final payment, a six figure factory payroll heist where they plan to drop the hammer and spring the trap."

"And your proposal?"

"A pure double cross."

The Schooler looked amused. He chuckled in a mirthless way. *Heh heh heh. Heh heh heh.* He shined his flashlight at the ceiling. A rusted eyehook hung from a rolling track. I got the message and realized my mistake. I hadn't properly introduced myself. People care more about who you are than what you say.

"I'm not a G-man. The feds recruited me because I was a spy for the OSS."

"And why would a clean cut agent from the Office of Strategic Services want to turn to a life of crime?" said The Schooler, hiking his eyebrows.

I hiked mine back. "If I'm going to risk my life again I'd like to get paid what it's worth."

No response. My wit and charm weren't having their customary effect.

"The money's for real," I said. "The richer the prize, the higher the stake. It's the cardinal rule of undercover work. Mr. Big's a rich prize. To win his trust the feds have ponied up a huge fund of bait money."

Repeating myself, The Schooler inspecting that hook again and Jimmy's ragged hungry breath on the back of my neck. Not good, not good at all. Say something genius.

"Perhaps you're wondering how I plan to get away with this."

The Schooler's stolid face flickered to life for half a second. I gathered myself, weight on the balls of my feet. If this didn't work it was time to go.

"The Bureau won't try too terribly hard to find me," I said, breezily, hopefully. "J. Edgar's not going to want the world to know that a former OSS agent, and the Fulton Road Mob, played America's Bulwark of Freedom for suckers."

The Schooler liked that. What crook worth his salt doesn't want to put one over on the Bulldog?

"Let's take a walk."

He led me to a small room off the factory floor, a foreman's office. Jimmy stayed put and lit a cigarette against the darkness. There was a battered metal desk in the little room. The Schooler parked a haunch on a desk corner and set the flashlight upright like a candle. Mice scurried underfoot. The Schooler examined me for a good ten seconds. "I find you an interesting young man."

What was I supposed to say to that? And I find you an attractive older gentleman?

"It's an interesting proposition, what you suggest. Before I take it upstairs I want to set you straight on something. Even if everything you say checks out you'll still have to pay your dues."

"Meaning what?"

The Schooler shrugged. "You'll have to make the rounds, prove your loyalty."

This wasn't what I wanted to hear. I had already proved my loyalty, already made my rounds. Basel to Freiburg to Ulm to Karlsruhe. Spies do that, double agents don't have to. Double agents have superior knowledge.

"The Krauts inserted dozens of spies into England during the war," I said. "The Brits turned every one. But that's not the point, their..."

"How?"

"What's that?"

"How did the Brits turn them?"

"Uh, most were turned by capture, a few gave themselves up. And some just plain liked to play the game."

"What game is that?"

"The double cross game," I said. "But their Kraut spy-masters in Berlin never sniffed it out. They kept believing the horseshit troop movement and industrial production reports their agents sent back. Kept believing them right through Normandy, right up to VE Day."

The Schooler ran the back of his index finger across his cheek. "You said there was a point."

"Yeah. Loyalty is for saps."

There was a grimy window in the little room. The Schooler turned to look through it. Jimmy was playing with his lighter. His jagged profile lit up and went dark, lit up and went dark. "Then fake it," said The Schooler.

"What's that?"

"Loyalty. I'm riding herd on an itchy group of young men. They start thinking they can freelance and all hell breaks loose. Can you do that?"

Me? Pretend to be something I'm not? "Sure."

The Schooler didn't budge from his desk corner. He had something more to say. I watched Jimmy firing his lighter through the grimy window, the tongue of flame throwing lurid shadows on his face, making him look like Bela Lugosi. Or Lucifer.

"Which type are you?" said The Schooler. "The type who likes to play the game?"

"No sir, I'm a post-war double agent. I'm just looking for a payday."

Chapter Five

My digs are in what they call the Angle, a slice of west side real estate just below St. Malachi's Church and just above the river, corner of Winslow and West 25th. My room overlooks the ore docks and Whiskey Island. From what I've heard about the housing shortage I guess I'm lucky, if you can call a third floor walkup with a down-the-hall bathroom in Mrs. Brennan's rooming house - just *room, no* board - lucky.

Why not? Six months ago I didn't have a roof, a bed, clean clothes or steam heat.

I looked at the wall mirror where I'd stuck the creased and spattered photo I had carried through hell and back. It didn't do her justice. I told my pals in Youngstown that I didn't know where Jeannie was and didn't care but only the first part was true.

I could track her down. I knew her husband's name, Pappas. Old enough to be her father, so I was told. What the hell was she thinking? Those old country Greeks might come on 'all wool and a yard wide' but once the knot's tied it's back to the twelfth century. I could track Jeannie down, but what would be the point?

I clomped down two flights of stairs to the parlor, hoping to cadge a newspaper and a cup of tea. Mrs. Brennan always had a kettle on. She had a thriving business, Mrs. Brennan, a biblical number of freckle-faced kids, a kitchen that doubled as a laundry and a no-nonsense manner. Mr. Brennan was 'away.'

I leaned across the Dutch door to her kitchen. She was using a wooden paddle to haul sheets from an enormous pot of boiling water. "I'll take a cup of Bewley's and a corned beef sandwich."

Mrs. Brennan did not dignify me with a look. "You'll take a boot in the arse and like it."

I opened the Dutch door, walked over to her and took the wooden paddle firmly in hand. "This is not a suitable task for a woman of your quality."

Mrs. Brennan snorted. "Sure of yourself, aren't you?"

"Always," I smiled. "Now what am I supposed to do with this thing?"

"You're the smart one, you figure it out," said Mrs. B and went off to pour tea. She brewed it black and strong as any java. I yanked a soaking sheet from the pot with the wooden paddle and held it up. It weighed a ton. Now what?

"Twist it, twist it around."

I rotated the paddle so that the sheet wrapped around it.

"Hold it there and let it drip."

I did that too, shoulder muscles groaning.

It wasn't the precise moment I would have chosen to have Jimmy appear. Yet there he stood, hands resting on the ledge of the Dutch door, wearing a dark fedora and a smirk.

We drove down Lorain Avenue in the black Buick. Apparently I had passed muster with Mr. Big, though Jimmy hadn't said so. So far his end of the conversation consisted of "Let's go" and "Get in."

The neighborhood was old and well-established, red brick apartments above corner stores with striped awnings. Irish pubs, Hungarian restaurants, German *Bäckereis*. We stopped at every one and collected envelopes. The owners didn't say much and Jimmy said less, just fixed them with that Cyclops stare and put out his paw. I stood back with my hands crossed and felt like a heel.

We even stopped at a shoeshine stand. Who shakes down a shoeshine stand? But it wasn't like that. The stand was a sports book the mob bankrolled. Moe the owner had a bad weekend, something to do with the Cleveland Rams not covering the spread. Jimmy had to fork over a wad of bills. This put him in a foul mood.

We drove on. Jimmy pulled to the curb across from a block-long yellow brick building with a tall clock tower. WESTSI DE MARKET was spelled out in green letters along the roof-line. "Wait here," said Jimmy and crossed the street. I counted to ten and followed him inside.

The place was a riot of shoppers pressed cheek to jowl at arcades of stalls in every direction. If Jimmy was here to collect protection money it would take a week. I spotted him elbowing his way through the crush.

I threaded my way past Sielski Poultry, Barbo's Pies and The Pierogi Palace. The aromas made me weak with hunger. Jimmy pushed his way to the front of a stall named Baleah Meats. The man behind the counter greeted him like a long lost friend.

Jimmy nodded and spoke an entire sentence, maybe two. The man behind the counter hurried off and returned with a package wrapped in butcher paper. Jimmy paid him with one bill and didn't wait for change.

Well, well, Jimmy was human after all. Just another Cleveland ethnic with a taste for the old country. But what the heck kind of name was Baleah? Seemed like I'd heard it before.

I hustled back to the Buick. Jimmy returned and stashed his package in the trunk. His mood had improved, he hummed a little tune as he hung a U and drove west on Lorain. He picked up speed, honked his way through an intersection and sang the words to the tune he'd been humming, a kid's song from the '30s.

"When I grow up I wanna be a G-man, and go bang bang bang bang bang. A rough and tough and rugged he-man, and go bang bang bang bang bang."

Cute. I was about to join in when we screeched to the curb in front of Papa's Deli.

The place had a white porcelain deli case front to back, framed travel posters of *The Parthenon* and *The Blue Aegean* and no customers. A short swarthy man wearing a cheap hairpiece came running up.

"I don't wanna hear it," said Jimmy.

"But the people, they don't come!"

"Not my problem."

"But you said…"

"You signed the paper."

The man shook his head, fuming. "If my brothers were here they…"

"Shut up, Dimitri, your brothers aren't here. Your brothers are back on Mykonos, *fucking sheep!*"

The deli owner threw a right that caught Jimmy just below the cheekbone. Jimmy grinned and said, "Hold him up."

I hesitated. The man turned to run. Jimmy snatched him by the collar and dragged him back. Jimmy turned to face me. Both eyes seemed to focus, was that possible?

"Hold…him…up."

I did so. I'd done worse.

Jimmy worked the man's midsection methodically. The man's hairpiece flopped off and clung to the side of his head by a stubborn wad of spirit gum. The toupee twitched and jiggled with every blow. Eight, ten, twelve. I felt Dimitri's legs give. I dragged him back and laid him on the shiny blue and white tile.

"He's out."

And that would have been that if the dumb cantankerous son of a bitch hadn't groaned to life and sat up with a mouthful of very colorful curses. Jimmy whipped out a leather sap and waded in for the kill.

"Come on Jimmy," I said, circling wide, arms outstretched. "We don't need this headache. Leave this stupid gink be and…"

Jimmy brushed past me and raised his sap. I snagged his arm on the way down and roped his stroke into a two-handed wrist lock. The sap fell to the floor.

"Dimitri?" called a female voice from the back room.

"Time to go, Jimmy. Time to go."

Jimmy tried to twist around. I bent back on his wrist and drove him to one knee.

A young woman dashed out from the kitchen, looked down at Dimitri, looked up at me and put her hand to her mouth in shock.

It was Jeannie. I blinked and looked again. It was Jeannie, my Jeannie. We stared at one another, dumbstruck.

I released Jimmy's wrist. He swung around, raring to go. I snagged both his wrists and stood on his shoes. "Not now," I said, two inches from his face. "Not now, not here."

Jimmy bared his teeth. His breath was, of course, foul. I tightened my grip.

I imagine we looked pretty ridiculous, nose to nose in Papa's Deli, holding hands. God knows what Jeannie was thinking. This wasn't the romantic reunion I had dreamed about and pictured in my mind.

Jimmy grunted and closed his eyes. I took that for surrender and stepped back. Jimmy marched quickly for the door. I followed, with a look over my shoulder. Jeannie was bent over the deli owner, his head in her lap, soothing him.

Jimmy slammed the door of the Buick and gunned the engine. I had to hurry to jump in. Pappas Deli read the sign as we wheeled away. *Pappas* Deli, not *Papa's* Deli.

Well of course, numb nuts, what else? The swarthy man with the bad rug was Jeannie's husband.

Chapter Six

Jimmy gave me the silent treatment on the ride back. Not his usual dull silence, this was a barely breathing level of silence, a picturing revenge in gruesome detail level of silence. He stopped across from Mrs. Brennan's rooming house and drove off before I had both feet on the pavement. I bounced off the curb, dusted myself off and climbed two flights of stairs.

I hunted up my bar of soap and my boiled-in-a-pot and baked-in-the-oven towel. I kicked off my shoes and padded down the hall to the third floor shower bath. I showered, brushed my teeth, combed my hair, slapped some Bay Rum on my face and returned to my room. I put on a freshly laundered white shirt and my blue tie with the red clocks on it. I winked at the picture of Jeannie tucked in the mirror.

I took the rattler down to Public Square. The Terminal Tower's cathedral windows were hung with giant Christmas wreaths, Santa's elves hammered away in the windows of Higbee's Department Store. I took the escalator to the Men's Department and bought a vicuna topcoat for $90. I walked next door to the Hotel Cleveland for dinner, had steak tartare and a snifter of 20-year-old cognac. What the hell, I was flush.

I bought a pack of Camels from the cigarette girl, though I'd lost the habit overseas. I couldn't carry American cigarettes and Kraut cigs taste like pine tar. I paid my check, washed up in the men's room and straightened my tie in the mirror. I was ready.

I took the streetcar across the Detroit-Carnegie Bridge and hopped off at the corner of Lorain and 32nd. My wristwatch said 8:49. The window sign said that Pappas Deli closed at nine. Mr. Pappas would be recuperating with a hot water bottle and a tumbler of Ouzo. Jeannie would be alone.

I hid in a doorway across the street just in case.

The deli went dark promptly at nine. I crossed the street and waited two doors down. I unzipped the pack of Camels and parked one in my mush. My heart was pounding. The spark was still there, I'd felt it the second I saw her. Had Jeannie? That's what I was huddled in this dark doorway to find out.

Where was she? Had she gone out the back?

No, the red OPEN sign was still in the window. Maybe she forgot to turn it over? I went to peer through the window and almost knocked Jeannie down as she stepped through the door.

"Hal?"

"Dammit Jeannie, you've ruined everything."

"What do you...I don't..."

"Don't look at me," I said. "Just go back inside, count to three and come out again."

"Hal, what the..."

"Please."

Jeannie blew out a breath and did as I requested. I lipped a fresh butt, pulled a hank of hair across my forehead and leaned a shoulder against the doorway. Jeannie walked out. "Hey there, beautiful," I said. "Got a match?"

Jeannie looked me over coolly. "Your face and a donkey's bum."

We cracked up, just like always.

"It's good to see you."

"You too. What in the world are you doing here? In Cleveland? With that awful man?"

"It's complicated."

"I'm listening."

"Aww, shit, Jeannie I can't tell you. Not yet."

I expected to get her rubber-lipped eye-rolling look. Jeannie had more facial expressions than a rhesus monkey. But she regarded me with a plain sad face.

"Hal, I thought you were dead."

"Why would you think that?"

"Gee whiz, I wonder?"

"I know your girlfriends got letters once a month..."

"Once a week sometimes."

"I was *behind* enemy lines."

"Hal, you were a wireless agent, isn't that right? Your job was to send messages, isn't that right?"

"Sure, but personal stuff was strictly forbidden."

"Dammit Hal, you could at least have *tried*."

"I suppose. I didn't..."

Jeannie pressed her strong dainty finger to my lips. It smelled of mustard.

"It doesn't matter," she said, her eyes saying just the opposite.

I bent to kiss her. "Not here," she said, twisting away.

"Where then?"

She looked at me for a long time. "I'm a married woman now."

I watched her walk down the sidewalk, hugging herself for warmth, and enter her walk-up above the store. I trudged back toward Mrs. B's and thought things over. I didn't feel the cold.

Jeannie had a lot of questions she wanted answered and so did I. But she was right. It didn't matter now.

I approached Kiefer's German-American Tavern at the corner of Detroit and 25th. Rosy-cheeked couples spilled out onto the sidewalk, arm in arm. I wove my way through them. They looked sublimely happy and content.

The sons of bitches.

Chapter Seven

This is the best part of being a double agent I thought as I climbed the stone stairs to the Standard Building the next day. As a spy I risked my neck every time I wirelessed my case officer. The SD, Himmler's spy hunters, had high-frequency direction-finding receivers mounted on trucks. 'Huff Duffs' we called them. They drove around sounding the sky, trying to triangulate the location of covert transmitters. I had to keep it short, and never the same place twice. But now, look at me, walking up the front steps of FBI headquarters at high noon!

That's the best part. The worst part is the mission.

The mission of a spy is simple, gather information. The mission of a double agent is to gather information while sowing disinformation. Meaning you've got to lie your ass off in a convincing way. I could do that with the FBI. Problem was I hadn't stayed above the fray, I had come to the rescue of Jeannie's husband and humiliated Jimmy in front of a paying customer. Jimmy was now cheesed off. That was exceptionally stupid on my part because Jimmy had superior knowledge. One call to the feds and my cook was goosed.

Which is where the mission got complicated. I was going to have to turn the setup once more so that I, not Jimmy, had superior knowledge. And the feds weren't going to like it.

The receptionist escorted me through the maze of corridors to my twelve o'clock with Agent Schram. She tapped on his door and announced me.

"Come in," said Schram gruffly a short time later. He looked odd, standing behind his desk, his face flushed and covered with a scrim of sweat. I looked around. Had Assistant Special Agent Richard Schram been enjoying a nooner?

"Push ups," said Schram off my look. "I do fifty three times a day."

"Yes sir."

Schram dried off with a hand towel and tossed it to the receptionist. She held it between thumb and forefinger and left the office, closing the door behind her. "What do you have for me?"

I stuck out my chest, put my hands behind my back. "A positive report sir. I was able to penetrate the Fulton Road Mob using the bait money from the bank robbery. I met with the man they call The Schooler and presented my - our - heist plans and he carried them upstairs to Mr. Big. They're interested."

Agent Schram was rolling his head on his neck, all the way to the left, all the way to the right.

"They're waiting for the results of this meeting," I said. "For the detailed heist plan before they agree to proceed."

Agent Schram stopped his head in mid-roll and regarded me at a 45 degree angle. He licked his lips. "This meeting. You said *this meeting*."

"Yes sir."

"How do they know about this meeting?"

I hadn't said they did. But never underestimate the intuitive powers of a paranoid. "They don't sir. Not from me."

Schram leaned on his desk and mouthed the words 'Who then?'

"Sir to my knowledge the Fulton Road Mob *doesn't know* about this meeting."

Schram licked his lips in anticipation. I cleared my throat. What was it about this guy that made me so twitchy? "I *did* tell The Schooler I was working for the FBI."

Agent Schram liked this for about two seconds. He was right! Then he thrust out his canines and bit his lips white.

"I had no choice sir. I ran into someone, a classmate from Youngstown, who can make me."

Agent Schram charged around from behind his desk. "Make you as what?" he sputtered. "A *traitor*?"

I wiped his spray from my face, I kept a calm and confident demeanor. "Sir, the Fulton Road Mob thinks I'm working for them. I'm not. I'm working for you."

"You *say*."

"Agent Schram, if I was a turncoat..."

Schram jumped ahead. "You wouldn't have told me what you just told me. *Unless*..." He waited for me to complete the sentence.

I looked confused, took my time, Schram's watery blue eyes eating a hole in my forehead. "Unless I told you that I told the mob that I was working for the FBI in order to...what? Cover my ass in case you had another source inside the gang? Someone who could keep an eye on me?" I wiped my brow. "Whew. That's more thinking than I've done in a month."

I paused to see how my act was going over but it was hard to tell. Schram's watery blue eyes had gone glassy. "Sir?"

Schram came to. "How are you going to work your way up to Mr. Big if they know that's why we sent you?"

"I'll make myself indispensable. Mr. Big will come to me."

Agent Schram turned back to his desk and keyed the intercom. "Get Gilliam," he barked. "*With* the plans."

Schram sat down and shuffled through papers. This was it? The green light? At the very least I had expected to be braced by Chester Halladay about my unauthorized change in strategy. Not to mention the twelve grand I had left over after I bought myself a meeting with The Schooler.

Joe Gilliam announced himself from the other side of the door. I opened it on a corn-fed linebacker with a boyish face and thick reddish-blonde hair that came to a peak halfway down his forehead.

"Meet Harold Schroeder," said Schram from behind his desk. Gilliam's mitt swallowed mine whole. "Lay it out."

Agent Gilliam pulled diagrams and timetables from his briefcase and spread them out on a glass drafting table against the far wall. He turned a switch, the table lit up. Gilliam ran it down. The job was an armored car robbery, and not just any armored car, the armored car that collected citizen donations to the city's Help the Needy Christmas Fund!

"That ought to get the attention of the *Press* and *Plain-Dealer*," said Gilliam. Schram grunted from his desk.

Good Lord. My suspicion that the higher ups at the Cleveland District Office of the Federal Bureau of Investigation had bats in their belfry was, officially, confirmed. They wanted to conduct an undercover sting operation that garnered maximum publicity.

I should have walked out there and then. I didn't. Too stupid, too stubborn. I examined the documents on the light board instead. Someone had a done a lot of work. The diagrams were precisely drawn. But they ignored a key concern.

"And federal agents will be posing as the armored car guards?" I said to Gilliam.

"Of course. Didn't I make that clear?"

"Sure you did Joe, it's just this." I looked the question to Schram. He nodded curtly. "I told the mob I was working for the FBI." Joe Gilliam's bovine face froze in mid-grin. "It's okay, we're still in the driver's seat, but it gets complicated."

"How's that?"

"Well, on the face of it this armored car job should be a cakewalk. The crooks know the heist is FBI-approved, the FBI now knows that the crooks know. But - and here's the tricky part - the crooks *don't* know that the *FBI knows* that they know. The mob will think they have the advantage, but it's your agents who will have superior knowledge."

Joe Gilliam's eyeballs ping-ponged around the room, looking for answers. Agent Schram, who was busy wrestling a sprung paper clip back into proper alignment, ignored him.

"And I'm supposed to do what?" said Gilliam.

"Convince your guys to sell their roles," I said, patting his lamb shank forearm. "Because once they know that the *crooks* know that this heist is just a charade, your guys will want to leer at them, taunt them, pinch their cheeks. And then all hell will break loose." I patted Agent Gilliam again. "Got that?"

"Uh huh."

I unwound the maze of corridors, rode the lift to the lobby and walked down the stone steps of the Standard Building with a queasy feeling. Joe Gilliam was a good egg, he would do his best. It wasn't that.

My foot gave way on a patch of ice and I rode my duff down the final four steps to the plaza.

Ow.

I sat there a moment, contemplating the fates and rubbing my tailbone. It wasn't Joe Gilliam I was queasy about. The feds' misunderstanding of the nature of covert operations was troubling, but it was the quick, almost offhanded go-ahead I received from Agent Schram that was giving me the wim wams.

Chapter Eight

I'd lied to Assistant Special Agent Richard Schram, the Fulton Road Mob knew about my meeting with him. The Schooler was waiting at an undisclosed location to see the plans. I was to walk eight blocks to the corner of St. Clair and East 17th. If the coast was clear someone would pick me up. And I had a good idea who that someone would be.

The wind whipped down the concrete canyon of St. Clair Avenue, frosting my eyebrows. The women I passed wore fur hats. The younger ones, rabbit or beaver, the matrons, mink or sable. All the men wore felt fedoras, brims snapped low against the wind.

I must have looked like the Nickel Plate pulling into Union Terminal with the geyser of steam pouring off my dome. I have never gotten along with hats, was forever leaving them behind or chasing them down the sidewalk. But maybe it was time to buy a lid.

The street changed once I passed East 9th. Got colder too, if that's possible. The skyscrapers gave way to soot darkened brick buildings the color of dried blood. Lunch bucket guys in Elmer Fudd caps took the place of swanky dames in fur hats.

I cut across St. Clair, ducked down an alley behind a block long building that hummed with turbines and muffled shouts and hid behind a dumpster at the far end and waited. No one followed. Apparently Agent Schram had bought my story.

I went to the anointed corner and listened to my teeth chatter for ten minutes. Skimmer, hell, I was going to have to buy some long johns.

Jimmy's Buick pulled up a short time later. I climbed in and said, "You're late." Jimmy did not reply. "It's not that I mind freezing my yobs off in subzero temperatures you understand, nothing like that. It's just I felt a wee bit...*conspicuous* standing out there on the street corner."

Jimmy turned left on East 20th. "Hadda make sure you weren't tailed."

I removed my gloves and tried to rub some feeling back into my fingers. *No, you beak-nosed prick, you knew I had already made sure of that. What you wanted was for me to shiver on that street corner till the FBI tail car you expected after your anonymous ratting-me-out-to-the-feds phone call had tracked me down.*

That's what I wanted to say. What I did say was, "Sure." I had some fence-mending to do.

The Buick crossed the train tracks and turned west on Shoreway. The lake was a block of ice. We motored down the highway. The sky went dark in the shadow of Municipal Stadium, returned to dim winter light on the other side. Did I know for a fact that Jimmy had called the feds and peached me out?

No I did not. But something was sure going on in that simian skull. Jimmy was observing the speed limit, using his turn signals to change lanes, driving like your Great Aunt Bertha. Was he trying to figure out why the feds didn't roll up after his phone call and carry me off to the hoosegow? Or maybe he had puzzled that through and was worrying about what to do now. He couldn't very well tell The Schooler he had blown the whistle on me.

I flirted with the idea of coming clean, telling Jimmy that I had told the feds that I had told the mob I was an undercover agent because I knew Jimmy was hacked off and would rat me out. But what if he hadn't? He had, but what if he hadn't? Never tip your mitt till you have to, that's my motto.

We rolled across the big blue span known as the Main Avenue Bridge. I could see the lit-up cross atop St. Malachi's Church, a friendly beacon to homesick sailors on the lake.

Jimmy checked the rear view mirror for the tenth time and slowed to a crawl. Horns honked. The son of a bitch had definitely squealed.

The Buick slalomed its way down the icy exit way. Jimmy turned into the skids, kept the hood ornament straight as the back end swung and swayed. We looped back around to The Flats, the bottomland of the river and the arsenal of democracy. The steel plants were to the east along the serpentine Cuyahoga, the ship docks to the west.

Jimmy turned west. We drove down Elm Street, a block below Mrs. B's, and crossed a two lane cantilevered bridge to Whiskey Island. The Huletts, the towering one-armed ore unloaders, sat silently along the port channel, waiting for the spring thaw. We drove past them to the tip of the island.

Jimmy parked the Buick next to a wine red Packard big as a steam yacht. We climbed down the stairs at the head of a deserted pier and walked a few paces to the door of fishing shack. Jimmy gave out with a coded, top secret knock. *Shave and a haircut, two bits.* I followed him inside.

It was some shack. A paneled room with an upholstered chair and matching chesterfield, wood burning stove and a wet bar. The Schooler was sitting in the upholstered chair. Kelly the bouncer hoisted me up by the coat collar with one hand and patted me down with the other. Jimmy lipped a butt and thumbed his lighter. It was old home week on Whiskey Island.

Kelly dumped me on the chesterfield and crossed to the bar.

"What're you drinking?" said The Schooler.

"Rye rocks."

Kelly handed me a cut glass tumbler containing four ounces of liquor and two ice cubes. "I'm a man who hates to drink alone."

"From the same bottle," said The Schooler.

Kelly made another. The Schooler took a bite. I watched his Adam's apple bob up and down before I followed suit, and detailed the plan.

The armored car would be on its regular Friday run, picking up commercial deposits. The Wigman and East 7th location was selected because Wigman Place is a dead end. Armored car drivers are trained to drive off if their delivery guards are robbed at the collection point. This was why we would need a big truck, to block in the armored car.

"They're not gonna provide a truck?" said Kelly. "The G-men?"

"No," I said. "The G-men are not gonna provide a truck, a chauffeur driven getaway car or a box lunch. They're providing the money."

The Schooler coughed out a laugh that Jimmy echoed a moment later. Kelly grinned as if he had made a joke.

"We've got a truck," said The Schooler and looked to me. "Where are the buttons on this?"

I thought this a very odd thing to say. "Excuse me?"

"The buttons, the coppers, the *Cleveland Police Department*. Are they on board?"

"Oh. Yes and no. The cops will circumvent the vicinity of Wigman and East 7th but we don't get a free pass. If shots are fired we're on our own."

The Schooler wrinkled his brow ever so slightly.

I stretched out my legs and crossed my ankles. I made two ounces of whisky go away. I was going to have to take up smoking again. This was the perfect moment to take a drag and spew a long plume toward the ceiling. "It should be at least sixty grand."

The Schooler didn't exactly dance a jig but something approaching interest flickered across that impassive mug. "And what's your dib?"

"Fifty percent."

"Well, now we've got something to talk about."

"No we don't," I said, pleasantly. "This is a take it or leave it proposition."

Jimmy and Kelly muttered darkly. The Schooler's head rotated like a radar antenna. They clammed.

"I'll carry your offer upstairs," he said, then asked the question. "Will the armored car guards be federal agents?"

This was where deciding where to salt the lie with truth got tricky. The Fulton Road Mob wouldn't be tempted to misbehave if they thought the armored car guards were just dog-eared working stiffs. On the other hand they wouldn't be inclined to buy the FBI trusting a staged sixty grand heist to dog-eared working stiffs. I couldn't very well tell the Fulton Road Mob they'd be stealing Christmas donations to the poor. But I decided to give them this one.

"Yeah, the armored car guards will be FBI agents."

The Schooler smiled at me in a knowing way. "Of course they will."

We drank up and headed out. Jimmy and Kelly made for the Buick. The Schooler asked me if I knew how to drive.

"Sure."

He opened the door of the Packard touring sedan and handed me the keys. I climbed behind the wheel. It was more like a gentlemen's club than a car. The Schooler slid in on the passenger's side. I keyed the ignition and put my foot down on a clutch pedal that wasn't there.

"It's an automatic transmission."

"Of course."

"The shift is on the column."

"Of course."

The Schooler leaned over and put the Packard in reverse. We lurched back about ten feet. I found neutral and hit the brake. This was a serious beast. I eased into drive and wheeled down the road. "Where are we going?"

"For a drive," said The Schooler.

I crossed the two lane cantilevered Whiskey Island bridge and drove south on Riverbed, along the Cuyahoga. We passed a locomotive hauling flat cars of molten steel from the blast furnaces to the rolling mills. The plant stacks belched white clouds as the frigid air turned their smoke to steam.

"Vending machines," he said.

"Beg pardon?"

"Sports betting, loan sharking and vending machines. That's what we do now."

We passed an out-of-commission oil derrick on the flood plain. A reminder that this was all John D. Rockefeller territory once upon a time. "It pays money," I said.

"So does running a cigar store, ten hours a day, seven days a week, closed on Christmas, Easter and the Fourth of July. That's what my old man did for a living."

I wheeled the great beast under the concrete pylons of the Detroit-Superior Bridge. "My old man had to work on the Fourth of July."

The Schooler smiled. We drove on.

"Chester Halladay disagrees with you," I said. "Chester Halladay said you were hurting, said you *were* racketeers but now you're gangsters."

The Schooler told me to take a right on Franklin. I did so. He told me to take another right on West 25th. I did that too. We were headed back towards the Angle.

"Chester Halladay's an idiot," said The Schooler mildly. "What do you need from me?"

Huh? This was not a question I was accustomed to hearing from persons in authority.

"Well, I need you to tell Mr. Big the feds need an answer in twenty-four hours," I said. "And I need you to tell Jimmy not to get up on his hind legs and piss all over what might be the sweetest heist in the history of plunder."

The Schooler grunted his assent. We drove in silence to the corner of Winslow and West 25th.

Chapter Nine

Wigman and East 7th is in a downtown neighborhood they call The Haymarket, near the east end of the Detroit-Carnegie Bridge.

We were parked in a blind alley, in a souped-up Lincoln four-door, Jimmy and me in the front seat, and two young hoodlums with slicked back hair and striped shirts with white collars in back. One of them sported a pencil thin mustache. I forget their names. Another hood was behind the wheel of a box truck, idling on Wigman a block away.

I checked my watch and looked out the passenger's side window. Mr. Big had, to my surprise, agreed to a fifty-fifty split. We were ten minutes from H-Hour. A gaggle of stewbums huddled around an oil drum fire on the corner. The pomade twins in the back seat chattered nervously.

"This used to be Blinky Morgan's turf, down by here."

"Johnny Coughlin too."

"Yeah the coppers were crappin' their pants back den."

"You know it."

I peeled off a sawbuck and handed it to Pencil Mustache. "Go wish those boys a Merry Christmas." He jacked open the rear door. "And leave the shotgun here."

He put the gun down sheepishly and hurried off.

No one had asked me the obvious question, so far. Why was an armored car picking up a deposit from a St. Vincent de Paul Center? The FBI hadn't asked where we planned to go after the heist or what my share of the cush was. Jimmy was calm and quiet as a Hindu at the wheel of the Lincoln. Things were going far too well.

The ragged men around the oil drum grabbed the sawbuck and made for the nearest hooch house. Pencil Mustache scurried back down the alleyway. His pal breeched his shotgun for the umpteenth time. Jimmy keyed the ignition and laid his nickel-plated on his thigh. I had my liberated, Wehrmacht-issue, four-inch-barrel Walther P38 in a belt holster under my topcoat where I hoped it would remain.

Pencil Mustache climbed in the back seat. We all donned the black Zorro masks someone bought at a costume shop. It was time for my speech.

"Gentlemen, this job is a lead pipe cinch. Point your shotguns all you want but keep your fingers behind the trigger, against the trigger guard. The guards won't make any move against you so *don't* shoot them. Jimmy will be running the show, follow his lead. Any questions?"

"Yeah," said Pencil Mustache, "ain't that the armored car?"

I faced forward. The back end of a gray Regency Security Transport truck was blocking the alleyway.

Shit. The armored car was supposed to park further up the block. We were trapped in a blind alley off a one-way street. Jimmy fixed me with his evil eye.

"Relax," I said with a confidence I didn't feel. "They're just waiting for the parking space to clear."

Long seconds ticked off the clock. The truck pulled forward. I resumed breathing. "Okay, we wait till we see our box truck pull...."

"Shut up," said Jimmy, "I'm in charge now."

More long seconds. Somebody coughed, somebody passed gas.

Then the box truck rumbled past and we spun our tires on the icy asphalt and shot down the alley. Jimmy spun a donut on Wigman and backed the Lincoln up to the box truck, which was now wedged sideways across the dead end street, blockading the armored car.

The truck driver jumped down from the cab and got behind the wheel of the Lincoln four-door as planned. A couple passersby stood and gaped. They got scarce when they saw the shotguns.

We scrambled around the truck and converged on an armed guard carrying a canvas bag from the St. Vincent de Paul Center to the armored car, right on schedule.

Jimmy leveled his .45 and snarled, "Grab a cloud."

Good one Jimmy. Bet he'd been practicing in front of the mirror all week.

The armed guard dropped the canvas bag and raised his hands. The young hoods kept their fingers behind the triggers of their scatterguns. I grabbed up the canvas bag and backed away. So far, so good.

Jimmy indicated the rear door of the armored car. "Open it. *Now*."

The federal agent dressed as an armored car guard gave him a droll look and slow-footed toward the door. He fumbled in his pocket for the keys, whistling a little tune.

Jimmy switched his nickel-plated from his right hand to his left and slugged the agent in the kidney. The agent whirled, reaching for his piece. Jimmy shot him with his left hand. The agent crumpled to the street.

Jimmy yanked on the rear door. It opened. It opened on an FBI agent holding a Thompson submachine gun.

I had a big decision to make that I made before I even made it. I threw myself in between Jimmy and the machine gun, spread my arms and yelled, "*Don't!*"

No one fired.

The downed agent was wearing a flak jacket. I did an eyeball to eyeball with his Tommygun-wielding partner. "He's okay, he's gonna be fine. Let me grab the loot and we'll deal with these fuckheads later."

The agent edged forward and sneaked a peek to make sure his fallen comrade was still drawing breath. He was. The agent nodded and said, "No one else blinks!"

I helped myself to one of the four canvas bags in the rear compartment of the armored car. "Maintain your positions, do not fire," I said over and over as I dragged canvas bags to the curb. Sirens began to wail, many blocks off.

I surveyed the standoff with a jaundiced eye. The pomade twins with their itchy trigger fingers, Jimmy, his .45 on hot standby, all wearing those ridiculous Zorro masks. And the buzz cut number one son of J. Edgar Hoover compulsively training the muzzle of the Thompson from one target cluster to another.

It was almost funny. Christ, it *was* funny. I filled my lungs. "Put up your weapons you comical dipshits and do your god-damn jobs!"

Pencil Mustache and his pal snapped to it. They scooped up the canvas bags, tossed them into the trunk of the Lincoln and piled into the back seat. Jimmy and Mr. Tommygun continued their face off.

"Hey Zorro," I said, indicating our getaway car. "Care to join us?"

Jimmy didn't budge. I jumped into the back seat with the pomade twins and told the driver to get going. Jimmy, his .45 still trained on the FBI agent, backpedaled fast enough to jump on the Lincoln's running board as we took off. Mr. Tommygun co-operated by not cutting us to ribbons.

Our driver careened down the icy street, swung a wide slippery right on East 7th and headed south. The pomade twins dragged Jimmy in through the back window. Wailing squad cars flew by on Carnegie, headed east. We stopped and waited for them to pass. Either through incompetence or complicity the Cleveland PD was doing their bit.

"Well now," I said, leaning back with a sigh of relief, "that went okay."

It was the leaning back that saved me.

The right rear window exploded in a burst of machine gun fire. Our driver floored it, got clipped by an oncoming bus, shook it off, got the nose of the Lincoln pointed west down Carnegie and sped off, Jimmy's nickel-plated spitting lead out the window as high caliber Tommygun rounds stitched our rear end.

The machine gun fire came from an unmarked car carrying two men in gray suits. The FBI was in hot pursuit!

I felt warmth on my cheek, scratched and saw blood on my fingers. A good amount. In fact I was bleeding like a stuck pig. Superficial cuts from busted glass I figured as I performed a five-finger inventory of the right side of my face.

Then again maybe not. Something was missing. I patted the seat cushion, felt around on the floor mat with my hands and found it. The top half of my right ear.

We barreled across the Detroit-Carnegie Bridge and down Lorain. The unmarked car peeled off. I clamped my handkerchief against my head. It soaked through. Pencil Mustache handed me his. The bleeding slowed.

We hooked a left on Fulton Road, then a quick right on a narrow street, Cesco. Half a block down we slowed at H&R Manufacturing, a squat brick building with tarred windows that looked like any other Cleveland foundry or machine shop save for the coils of barbed wire atop the chain link fence.

The front gate rolled open by remote control. A big dog barked from somewhere close. We parked the Lincoln in a detached two-car garage. The big dog ran circles around us as we hurried to the back door. His name was Hector.

The Schooler, looking natty in a gray homburg and polka dot bowtie, was waiting for us in H&R Manufacturing's front office. A card table stood against a wall. A card table that held an ice bucket, bottles of tonic, soda, Coca Cola, bonded Scotch, rye, bourbon, vodka and gin. We went there. We stayed a long time.

I only remember two things for certain. Holding up my severed upper ear to great acclaim, and Jimmy leading the assembled in a stirring rendition of his favorite song.

"When I grow up I wanna be a G-man, and go *bang, bang, bang, bang, bang*. A rough and tough and rugged G-man, and go *bang, bang, bang, bang, bang*."

I had done it. Despite the snafus I had done it. No one was dead, I had won the tribute of the Fulton Road Mob, kept faith with the FBI and hauled off several canvas bags filled with negotiable currency.

Things were going far too well.

Chapter Ten

I reported to FBI headquarters the following day, feeling a little the worse for wear, looking it too. A mob doctor had showed up at some point during our bacchanal and dressed and bandaged my ear. I asked him if he could reattach the missing piece. I must have.

And he said no such luck. He must have. In any event the top half of my right ear was currently residing in my top dresser drawer in Mrs. Brennan's rooming house, wrapped in gauze. A precious keepsake of my first armored car job.

A moon-faced guy stood behind the counter, rummaging through the receptionist's drawers. So to speak. He filched two pencils and looked up.

"Who are you supposed to be? Leonardo da Vinci?"

"Huh?"

"Leonardo da Vinci, you know."

I said that I didn't.

The moon-faced guy rolled his eyes. "The guy who cut off his ear for the love of the Mona Lisa!"

There had to be a witty rejoinder to this idiotic remark but I was too busy keeping my head perfectly still to think of it. The receptionist rescued me a moment later. She escorted me through the maze of hallways to Agent Schram's office. My red badge of courage didn't win me any snappy salutes. The agents I passed all looked the other way.

Assistant Special Agent in Charge Richard Schram was waiting at his open door. Head Special Agent Chester Halladay was seated behind Agent Schram's desk. Uh oh.

"How bad is he?" I said, referring to the fallen agent disguised as an armored car guard.

"Three broken ribs," said Halladay.

Agent Schram closed the door behind me and stood to my right, hands clasped behind his back. I stood there, stone still, a rusty knife lodged in my frontal lobes, my severed ear throbbing with every pulse beat. "I'm sorry to hear that."

No reply. Well screw 'em.

"If the armored car guard had done as I suggested, instead of playing his part with a wink and a smirk, shots would not have been fired!"

Schram chewed his lips raw waiting for his boss to formulate a response. Halladay consulted an incident report, found what he was looking for. "Why didn't you return fire when the mobster fired upon our agent at point blank range?"

"He was wearing a flak jacket, I knew he'd survive. Why did your agents pursue us and rake us with machine gun fire?"

Agent Halladay looked to Agent Schram.

"You wanted a convincing performance, remember?"

I forced a smile. "Well, what's a few broken ribs and a severed ear in the big scheme of things? The good news is that the Fulton Road Mob is now sold on the program and ready for more."

Special Agent Halladay pulled a monogrammed hankie from his pocket and dabbed at his upper lip. Agent Schram kept still as a coiled snake. "And you know this from Mr. Big himself?" said Halladay.

"Indirectly," I said. Halladay winced. Wrong answer. "I'll get to him before the next go round."

Agent Halladay looked to Agent Schram. Agent Schram uncoiled.

"There won't be another go round. The Executive Assistant Director of Criminal Investigations in Washington has called a halt to this operation. Too dangerous."

I struggled to keep my voice in a lower register. "Agent Halladay, Agent Schram, we've dangled the bait but we haven't planted the hook. There is no, I repeat *no* way I can get to Mr. Big without the final heist!"

Special Agent in Charge Chester Halladay hove to his feet. Assistant Special Agent Richard Schram opened the office door.

"Stay in close contact," said Halladay. "Report any mob plans." He stopped to shake my hand and make meaningful eye contact. "I'll see what I can do." Halladay shot his cuffs and left the room.

Agent Schram and I faced one another, alone at last.

"Sir I believe I did good work out there, I put myself in harm's way to defuse a bloody firefight. I don't understand why the brass would call a successful operation 'too dangerous' when everyone involved in that operation is still in one piece." I flicked a hand across my bandaged ear. "Mostly."

Agent Schram jabbed his index finger into my chest. Hard. "*You're* the reason that Jimmy Streets shot our agent."

"I don't follow."

Schram angled his head away. "I thought you had it all figured out, Schroeder, knew all the angles, smooth operator like you." His lips peeled back in a grotesque parody of a grin.

"Guess not."

Schram bobbed his head side to side like a boxer. "No?"

"No sir."

Agent Schram continued to bob and weave, regarding me from several angles. I kept my face blank as plaster.

"You told Jimmy Streets you were working for the Bureau."

"Yes sir, I did."

Schram looked immensely pleased with himself. "You see it now? Pieces falling into place?"

"No sir, not really." Schram blinked several times, his eyes got milky. Christ, not this again. "The pieces are not falling into place and I have no idea what you're talking about. Sir."

Schram didn't seem to hear me. He turned to the window above St. Clair and went there and looked out. I waited a suitable time before I let myself out.

I wandered the maze of corridors and wondered what the hell was going on. I passed the moon-faced guy headed the other way. He walked with a limp. "Leonardo!" he said.

"Hey," I said and grabbed his arm. I nodded at the water cooler down the hall. "Buy you a drink?"

"Well, just one. I'm on duty." His hearty guffaw tripped depth charges deep inside my skull. I closed my eyes and waited for the explosions to subside. "Rough night, eh?"

"You could say that."

I walked to the cooler, he hobbled alongside. I introduced myself. His name was Wally. I handed him a paper cone of water.

"I'm hoping you can put me in the know. I just had a confab with Agent Schram and he seemed...distracted, kept staring off."

"You don't know?"

"Know what?"

"Richard Schram was a reserve Colonel in the 21st Infantry, called up in '44. He called the shots in the Leyte campaign, in the Philippines." Wally knocked back his water like a double shot. "Breakneck Ridge."

"Well, that would explain the thousand yard stare."

Wally nodded and limped off. I fought back an impulse to return to Schram's office and tell him I understood, tell him I knew what it was like.

But I didn't really. I had seen bloody chaos on a grand scale and in grotesque detail, from bombed out cities to a headless child floating in a ditch. But I had never had to do what Richard Schram did. I never had to order 19 year old kids, kids who looked to me for fatherly reassurance, to charge up razor-back spurs into the teeth of dug-in Jap snipers and machine gun nests. I had heard the story in some detail. A thousand GIs died taking the crest of Breakneck Ridge.

I wound my way back through the maze of corridors, down the elevator and the stone steps of the Standard Building. The arctic chill had moved east, bright winter sunlight assailed me. I closed my eyes and tried to think. What had Schram been trying to tell me? What did 'You're the reason Jimmy shot our agent' mean? My brain was in no mood to co-operate.

I walked two blocks to Public Square. It took days.

A group of just-home GIs spilled out of Terminal Tower trailing giddy wives, parents, cousins, nieces, nephews, Aunt Fanny and Uncle Scorch. The city of Cleveland was their oyster. They would stop at the War Service Center on the Square and pay tribute to the posted list of the honored dead. They would walk over to St. John's Canteen and accept the beer and blessings of the Archdiocese of Cleveland. And they would go home.

Home to a city untouched by buzz bombs and grass cutters, home to a city whose worst post-war problem was too much money in the pockets of six-shift war workers chasing too few big ticket Christmas gifts as Fisher Body and General Electric retooled from tanks and radar to Chevys and washer dryers.

I tried to be happy for them, going home and all, sweethearts on their arms. But I was jealous as a Turk.

Chapter Eleven

I took the Rapid Transit east to Shaker Heights. Nice ride, a high-class streetcar for a high-class burg. We sped past block after block of Tudor mansions with ribbon windows and arched double doors and more chimneys than a rolling mill. Just when you thought there couldn't be any more big houses, there were. And bigger. Where in the world did people get all that money?

I got off at Shaker Square. It was lined with shops selling Irish linen and Wedgwood china and Belgian chocolate. Not a Bohunk in sight. I looked around for street signs. I had an appointment to meet The Schooler at 2 p.m.

Shaker Boulevard was hard by Stouffer's Restaurant. I turned right and walked down the block to a neighborhood of apartment buildings that mimicked the Tudor and Georgian mansions nearby. They had separate addresses, the apartments in the Moreland Courts. I stood in the entryway and rang the bell for 2925. A smoky female voice on the buzz box said, "Yeah?"

I identified myself, the door buzzed open. I walked up the stairs and knocked. She took her time answering and it was worth the wait.

She had black black hair and white white skin. That was the first thing you noticed. That and the body that looked as if it had been poured, drop by drop, into her V-neck jade green Chinese silk dress. The eyes weren't bad either. Big as a cat's and the color of the Caribbean Sea.

"Henry will be here soon," she said and wandered off.

Henry. Yeah, that fit.

I crossed the threshold and glimmed the layout. Danish modern and Art Deco. Not the dark rumpled scatter you'd expect for an old gent like The Schooler. But then I hadn't expected a black-haired beauty with blue-green eyes. Was there a Mrs. Schooler? This the mistress in her *pied-a-terre*? The black-haired beauty returned, pushing a cocktail table on wheels.

"What're you drinking?"

"Whisky."

"Jim or Jack?"

"They're both good company."

She selected a bottle of Jack Daniels and poured it into a stainless steel cocktail shaker that looked like a Buck Rogers' rocket ship. She tonged in several ice cubes and added a dash of sweet vermouth. She shook it up. Perhaps a little bit longer than was absolutely necessary. She leaned down low to pour and said something I didn't hear, what with all the distractions. She said it again.

"So you're the G-man?"

"I am. What's your name?"

"Lizabeth, no *E*."

"Pleased to meet you."

Lizabeth poured herself a dram of Chambord and a splash of soda and sat down on a stiff S-shaped sofa. I parked my weary bones on a chair that had no arms.

"What's her name?"

"Who's that?"

"The woman you're pulling this crazy get-rich-quick scheme for."

"Why does there have to be a woman?"

Lizabeth lit a long black cigarette that smelled like French perfume. "Young men don't really care about money. They want power. Only women and old men really care about money."

I tipped the hat I didn't have. "I call her JJ."

Lizabeth crossed her legs, dangling a high-heeled slipper from her toes. I took a bite of cocktail. The spiked jibbet encasing my skull relaxed its grip.

"What's she like?"

"She's married."

"A lot of that going around."

She smoked. I drank. She was good. Sometimes silence is the most effective form of interrogation. I waited as long as I could.

"She's a wisenheimer. She's a wisenheimer and a tomboy and a choir girl and a sucker for puppies and old timey music and she's always, always up for a dare."

"The All-American girl next door," said Lizabeth, dryly.

"And then some."

She smoked. I drank.

"It must have been quite a shock to find yourself a member of the Brush-Off Club."

"I don't blame her. I was gone a long time."

Lizabeth gently, almost accidentally, kicked that high-heeled slipper right off her foot. She rubbed the sole of her foot absent-mindedly, sparing me the heavy artillery, keeping those aquamarine heaters on the far wall. "And you weren't worth the wait?"

I heard the scratch of a key in the door. I shot to my feet. The Schooler entered.

If he objected to the casual intimacy of the scene he didn't show it. He took off his gray homburg and his topcoat and hung them in the closet. Lizabeth replaced her shoe and shook up another Manhattan. She set it on the cocktail table and drifted away.

The Schooler took her place on the couch and slapped down a copy of *The Cleveland Press*.

"**Robbing the Poor Box!**" screamed the headline. "Time to call in the Bulldog?" was the sub-head, accompanied by a photo of J. Edgar Hoover. He really did look like a bulldog.

"You knew about this," said The Schooler. It wasn't a question. He draped his arm over the back of the couch and waited. "The feds want to make the Fulton Road Mob look as bad as possible so that when…"

"I understand that," said The Schooler. "Why didn't you tell me beforehand?"

I was too tired to lie. "Because you might have said no." The Schooler snorted and shook his head. "Not that it matters," I said. "The royal grand vizier of criminal ops in Washington has called a halt. Thanks to Jimmy Streets."

The Schooler showed no sign of surprise or disappointment. "I have spoken to Jimmy."

"When was that I wonder?" I polished off my drink and plunged ahead, drunk on exhaustion, Tennessee sippin' whisky and truth.

"My superior at the FBI said Jimmy shot the agent because Jimmy knew I worked for the feds. Yeah Jimmy knew, so what? I couldn't figure it at first, so obvious I couldn't see it. The *so what* is that Jimmy knew he could do whatever he damn well pleased. He knew the feds wouldn't arrest him and expose me and their undercover scheme before a packed courthouse. So long as I'm around," I said, thumbing my chest, "Jimmy thinks he's bulletproof."

"As you say, *so what?*"

I kept on. "But I wonder if shooting the guard *wasn't* Jimmy's idea. I wonder if maybe someone in authority told Jimmy to pull the trigger, to test my loyalty, to see if I'd shoot him in return."

I sat back in my armless chair, head spinning, waiting for the angry denial or confirmation I had baited.

The Schooler looked at his drink and didn't drink it. He shook his head sadly and said, "Such a mistrusting young man."

Was this how The Schooler kept his itchy young men in line? Posing as a stern father confessor, dispensing shame and blessings? It worked in my case. I felt like a kid caught filching from the poor box. Me!

"It took the FBI a lot of time and manpower to chart this course. They've invested a lot of money and prestige."

Was this a question? The Schooler encouraged me with his eyebrows. I riddled it out aloud.

"Let's see, the *Cleveland Press* is raising the roof about the heartless thieves who stole Christmas, the Cleveland PD is red-faced and cheesed off and...and if the feds call a halt right now the Fulton Road Mob makes off with sixty grand and the FBI is left holding the bag."

"Which means...?"

I liked the stern father confessor better. At least I didn't have to answer all these bloody questions. "It means that, uhh, we do nothing and wait for the feds to come around."

The Schooler inclined his head ever so slightly. "Would you like your money now?"

What a question.

The Schooler climbed to his feet. I resigned myself to another blindfolded ride to an abandoned factory but he returned a minute later carrying a fat pigskin satchel that he deposited at my feet, saying, "Thirty-two thousand six hundred and forty dollars."

I opened the satchel. The cash was neatly stacked and rubber-banded. It was more money than I had ever seen. But where the hell was I going to put it?

"Count it," said The Schooler.

"No need," I replied cheerily. "You're an honest crook."

The Schooler liked that. Leastwise he cracked a smile for the first time that afternoon.

"You'll want a cab," he said and went to make the call.

A tiny alarm bell sounded, barely tinkled, in the lower chambers of my skull. Something to do with The Schooler keeping a big wad of hot cash under his own roof. But I paid that tiny bell no mind. I was too busy zippering up my fat pigskin satchel.

I picked it up and looked around for Lizabeth. A faint wisp of perfumed cigarette smoke was the only trace of her.

A yellow cab was waiting at the curb when I bounded down the steps of the Moreland Courts, my fat pigskin satchel in hand. I scanned the four corners for a late model black Buick and climbed in the back seat. The hackie lowered the flag and asked me where to.

"East."

We set sail down Shaker Boulevard. I kept my eyes peeled for a bank. Some discreet Shaker Heights' establishment that would welcome a well-dressed young man with a fat pigskin satchel and no questions asked.

They say all good things come to those who wait but they, in my experience, are full of shit. There had to be a way to move the ball down the field. The FBI wasn't going to approve a big deal payroll heist so long as hothead Jimmy was in the picture. And the Fulton Road Mob wasn't going to bench Jimmy on my say so. Not yet anyway.

We passed a bank. I let the hackie drive another three blocks. "I need you to hang a U-turn at the next intersection," I said. "And use your turn signal."

No cars slowed, no cars followed. "Slow down a bit."

I looked out the back window. "Now speed up and turn right at the next street." I saw no sign of Jimmy's Buick, no sign of a plaster. "Stop here."

I paid the fare, gave the hackie a fat tip and lugged my pigskin satchel across Shaker Boulevard and into National City Bank to inquire about a safe deposit box.

Chapter Twelve

I tried to sneak out of Mrs. Brennan's rooming house the next morning, almost made it too. I was two steps down the stoop when I heard, "*Mister* Schroeder." My rent was paid in full, I was free, white and twenty-one. I could have continued on my way without a backward look. But I stopped short, the back of my neck all prickly.

"What is it Mrs. Brennan?"

"Turn around now." I did so. "Where's the rest of your ear? And your roughneck friend, come to mention?"

"Mrs. Brennan, listen, I..."

"*You* listen, boyo, I run a respectable rooming house."

"I understand that."

"Do you now?" said Mrs. B, meaty arms akimbo. "Then how do you explain yourself?"

This wasn't a question I got asked every day. I entertained several creative responses that withered and died under Mrs. Brennan's baleful eye.

"I can't explain myself just yet, Mrs. Brennan."

"Then you'll pack your grip. I've got GIs come in here every day, war heroes, looking for a place to hang their hats."

Ahh, *war heroes*. I marched up the steps. Mrs. B was about to get an earful. She didn't flinch as I approached, just lowered her head to butt me down the steps if I got out of line. I stopped and took a breath.

"Mrs. Brennan, there's a reason all these heroic GIs are swarming the burg right now as opposed to, say, blasting their way through fortified pillboxes outside Karlsruhe." I tapped my chest. "Agents of the OSS risked their necks behind enemy lines to commit acts of sabotage and target bombing runs that cleared many of those fortifications and paved the way for our heroic GIs to march to victory and free beer at St. John's Canteen. And if you..."

"You were a spy?"

"Yes ma'am."

She closed one baleful eye and examined me with the other. "That I can believe."

I walked up Winslow to St. Malachi's. Kids in parkas were chasing each other around the schoolyard. Three boys stood atop a mountain of plowed snow, shouting ferocious defiance, playing King of the Hill, preparing to defend the summit to the death against a dozen eager lads arrayed below. Why not? They were eight, nine or ten. For all of their conscious life the world had been at war.

I hoofed it west to Fulton Road and rode the rattler south to mob headquarters. I had a precise plan in mind, make myself indispensable and demand the ouster of Jimmy Streets. How to do that I would figure out when the time came.

I gave the conductor two dimes and jumped off at Clark. I walked a block south to Cesco and a half block west to H&R Manufacturing. I rang the bell at the front door. No answer. I knocked, hard. I saw an eyeball behind the peephole.

I mugged, I waved, I did jumping jacks. No response. I put the barrel of my 9 millimeter Walther to the peephole and the door swung open to reveal Pencil Mustache with a .22 pistol.

"Go shoot a squirrel," I said and pushed past. I worked my way through the cobwebbed lathes and drill presses on the shop floor, Pencil Mustache bobbing behind me like a toy balloon. I heard a guttural groan from somewhere. I followed it to a closed door.

"I wouldn't go in there I was you," said Pencil Mustache. "Jimmy's hacked off, The Schooler ragged him out bad."

"So I heard." Another groan from inside. "Who's he taking it out on?"

"A cop," said Pencil Mustache.

"A *cop*?"

"Dave Madsen. He's on our pad. Jimmy caught him double timing with the Bloody Corners Gang."

I opened the door on a big storeroom with bins of scrap metal and spools of welding cable stacked along one wall. The cop wasn't hard to spot. He was the one in the blue uniform tied to the chair. Jimmy was the beaknose slopehead standing over him.

Officer Madsen was in bad shape, head lolling, bloody mucus all down his front. Jimmy was wearing sap gloves, pouches of lead filings above the knuckles. He took a break from his exertions and looked over with his good eye.

"Get lost asshole."

"I was lost," I said. "I was lost but now I'm found."

Jimmy responded by slugging the cop in the midsection. He was a real champ when it came to guys who couldn't fight back. The cop coughed blood.

"Jimmy you're gonna kill the guy."

"What's it to ya?"

"It's a payday to me. Asshole. You kill a cop and you-know-who will definitely pull the plug on any future plans."

Jimmy grinned. "You're sayin' I shun't hit him no more?"

Officer Madsen, his eyes rolled back in his head, coughed, groaned, mewled like a kitten.

"That's what I'm saying."

"Okay then, maybe he's had enough." Jimmy grinned some more. We faced each other across twenty feet of dirty brown concrete. Jimmy made no move to go. A truck rumbled by on Cesco, making an empty rattling sound, hauling postholes.

I started forward. Jimmy grabbed the cop's limp wrist and bent it back. The cop didn't seem to notice. Jimmy increased the pressure. The cop blinked, shuddered and sat up straight. I stopped, ten feet away.

"Don't do it Jimmy. You snap the wrist he could die of shock."

I should have said the opposite maybe. Snap his wrist, I dare you. I should have known Jimmy Streets wasn't going to obey a direct order from Hal Schroeder.

Officer Madsen convulsed once in the desk chair when Jimmy did what I told him not to. Madsen's eyes went wide open as eyes can go. He died that way.

Chapter Thirteen

Jimmy was in big trouble. The Schooler had arrived with Kelly the bouncer and another goon I recognized from somewhere. He was fat and bald and big as a house. The Schooler called him Manny though mostly The Schooler didn't speak. He let his silence and his twin monsters do the talking for him. Jimmy was sweating bullets, standing over the dead cop's body, making excuses.

"I just gave him a goin' over, I din't mean to croak him."

I didn't volunteer the information about the wrist snap. I had superior knowledge on Jimmy Streets for the moment. And I intended to keep that shiv in my sock till the time was right.

"You dug this hole," said The Schooler to Jimmy. "You fill it in."

Kelly and Manny lumbered closer, Manny rotating his neck and shoulders as if about to climb into the ring. Shit a brick. He was Manny the Mauler, famed wrestler of yesteryear! Jimmy was in *big* trouble.

"Any ideas Jimmy?" said The Schooler calmly, menacingly.

"I'll take care of it," said Jimmy. "Dump the body in the lake."

"The lake's frozen."

"I got other places," said Jimmy, backing away as Kelly and Manny closed in, two flanks of a pincer movement.

"Madsen was a copper Jimmy, who worked for *us*. We need to dispose of more than the body." The Schooler's voice slid down to a whisper. "Any ideas?"

Jimmy didn't answer the question. The approaching six hundred pounds of beef distracted him maybe. If Kelly and

Manny twisted Jimmy into a pretzel and dropped him in the river the way would be cleared for the final heist.

But Kelly and Manny wouldn't. This was theater, complete with a sweaty old wrestler who took two breaths for every step. They were going to toss Jimmy back and forth like a beach ball for a few minutes then go out for steaks. The performance was for my benefit, I suppose. Or for Pencil Mustache and the group of young felons in training clustered by the open door.

Jimmy wasn't in on the joke. When the twin monsters had him backed up against the far wall he reached for his nickel-plated.

"Hold on gentlemen," I said. "I have an idea!"

Jimmy turned to look. Kelly ripped the nickel-plated from his grip as Manny pinned Jimmy to the wall with a big paw.

"Okay, the papers are screaming for a crackdown on racketeers and the cops are primed to take action. I see a way we can make chicken salad out of chicken shit."

Manny the Mauler thought this a very funny comment. He laughed himself into a coughing fit, his every spasm compressing Jimmy against the back wall.

"Madsen was playing three sides against the middle, the PD versus the Fulton Road Mob versus the Bloody Corners Gang. When you do that, and you get yourself bumped off, there are any number of crummy reasons why. We need to get ahead of the story."

I paused for dramatic effect. The Schooler's look said get on with it.

"We put a marker, one of our gambling chips, on the body and dump it behind the Green Light Tavern."

Manny grumbled and shook his great head. He didn't like me anymore.

"Why would you want to put *our* marker on the corpse?" asked The Schooler.

"Because the Cleveland Police Department wouldn't expect us to. Because the Cleveland Police Department, assuming they know that Madsen worked for us, will conclude that the Bloody Corners Gang is trying to set us up."

The Schooler pondered. "They might conclude that."

"They will."

"How can you be sure?"

"The cops will assume our rivals set us up because they don't believe we have the brains, or the balls, to play the double cross."

Chapter Fourteen

Jimmy turned into the alley behind the Green Light Tavern at 4:14 a.m. The bar was closed, the alley was deserted. I sat in the passenger's seat, hoping to hell I hadn't outfoxed myself with this clever gambit.

Jimmy put the Buick in park and left it running. We climbed out and popped the trunk. Officer Madsen was wrapped in a blanket. I took the shoulders, Jimmy the feet. He weighed a ton. The arctic chill had returned, our grunts of exertion became fat clouds of steam. We laid him out by the back door, the one Kelly had tossed me out of. I took the ten dollar chip from my pocket and stuck it in Officer Madsen's maw. Rigor had set in, it took a while.

"Hurry up," grumbled Jimmy from behind the wheel. I took a moment to mumble the Lord's Prayer and got back in the Buick. We drove down the alley and turned right on Lorain.

Jimmy was enormously silent at the wheel. Stay that way, I thought. *Do not speak a single syllable if you value your miserable life.*

We were headed east, toward the Angle, only I couldn't go there. Mrs. Brennan had a two o'clock curfew, doors barred and locked. The Warehouse District was just across the bridge. Had to be an all night joint there somewhere.

We stopped at a light. I winged open the door and got out. Jimmy tore through the intersection. The Buick's forward motion slammed the open door.

I walked across the Detroit-Superior Bridge, the lake wind slicing me clean in two. I told myself that the stupid cop deserved what he got, that you can't play three sides against the middle, that I, on the other hand, had both sides balanced like a see saw. I was golden no matter what happened. Why then did I find myself leaning against the railing of the Detroit-Superior Bridge wondering if I should pitch myself into the drink?

I shambled on. By the time I got to the other side of the bridge my shoes were frozen.

I shuffled around the Warehouse District on blistered feet, looking for a greasy spoon. Found one on Frankfort, Lulu's Place. Beef wasn't on the ration sheet anymore but no one had told Lulu. I ate an overcooked horseburger and drank three cups of joe. That killed an hour. A piece of vulcanized pie and three more cups got me to daybreak.

I lied about spending two years behind German lines. I was recalled to Switzerland every once in a while. Not even my CO thought I could survive two years in the world's most tightly controlled police state. So I came and went.

I hit the silk for the last time in January of '45, near Heilbronn. A downwind kicked up and I landed hard, broke an ankle. I hopped and crawled a mile to the farmhouse, knocked on the door, service revolver in one hand, L pill in the other. It looked like my designated safe house but you never know. Kindly old Alfred and Frieda took me in and nursed me back to health.

I was getting around okay on a cane two weeks later when a *Panzer* company rumbled up and commandeered the place. I could have hidden in the root cellar till they moved on. But I was young and dumb and full of patriotic fervor. I told Alfred and Frieda what I planned to do before I stumped out the back door and huddled in the orchard with my wireless set.

Alfred and Frieda remained inside for hours, deep into the night. I heard music, I heard laughter. I watched a lone B-24 returning from a run over Augsburg drop four incendiaries on the proper co-ordinates, just as I had instructed. I watched the farmhouse erupt in flames.

I spat a mouthful of bitter coffee back in my cup.

Chapter Fifteen

I wore my vicuna topcoat for my visit to mob headquarters the following evening, also my .25 caliber belly gun in case Jimmy got fresh. I left my boutonnière and matching wrist corsage at home.

The Schooler's office was paneled in knotty pine. Flintlock muskets were cross mounted on the wall, flanked by lots of framed photos of men holding up dead fish. I unfolded a late edition of the *Cleveland Press* and slapped it on his glass-topped desk.

A Clean Sweep! Screamed the headline above photos of portly mobsters being led away in handcuffs. Portly mobsters from the Bloody Corners Gang. The cops had been just smart enough to get themselves fooled.

"Well done," said The Schooler from his desk chair. "What do you want?"

Well. I hadn't expected a tickertape parade exactly but a hearty attaboy wouldn't have killed him. I closed the door to the office.

"Jimmy killed that cop deliberately," I said. "He snapped his wrist just because I told him not to. He's a half-wit and a hothead and I want him gone."

The Schooler nodded. "Yes, Jimmy's a hothead. But he's our hothead, loyal as a butcher's dog."

"And about as smart."

The Schooler smiled, thinly. "Smart is overrated."

"Then it's time to take this upstairs. I want to see the boss man."

"That's a possibility. When you have the final heist plans in hand."

"But I can't get the final heist plans with Jimmy still in the picture!"

"The FBI will come around eventually."

"Even if they do come around Jimmy will find a way to screw it up."

The Schooler didn't have a snappy comeback for that one. He'd spanked Jimmy for shooting the armored car guard. Jimmy responded by killing a cop.

"As I've said before I've got a group of itchy young men here. They respect Jimmy, he's their squad sergeant."

"Yeah, I imagine they were plenty impressed with Jimmy cowering against that wall."

The Schooler parked his chin on his fist. I shut my yap and waited for the great pearl of wisdom to come.

"You don't understand loyalty."

"Explain it to me."

The Schooler stroked his cheek with a knuckle. "Our itchy young men felt bad when they saw Jimmy backed up against the wall like that. They put themselves in his place."

I looked around the four corners. What was I missing here?

The Schooler answered before I could ask. "Then why did I call in the muscle?"

"Something like that."

"Because that's how it's done," said The Schooler, concludeing the conversation.

I made my way through H&R Manufacturing and out onto Cesco Road. The night was starry black, no moon, too cold for clouds. Perfect bombing weather. I one-two'd my way down to Fulton Road on blistered feet.

Loyalty again. You'd think a sharp guy like The Schooler would know better. And what the hell did 'that's how it's done' mean? It sounded like a perpetual motion machine. So long as you don't betray the tribe you can screw up all you like.

I had made myself indispensable and still Jimmy stayed.

It was time to get serious, past time. I would have to kill Jimmy by remote control. I was good at that. Get the word out to the Bloody Corners Gang, tell them who iced their dirty cop. Let them settle the account.

I hailed a cab on Fulton Road and said, "Short Vincent."

"Where else?" said the hackie. The cab drove there by itself.

Chapter Sixteen

Short Vincent was a five hundred foot block between E. 6th and E. 9th downtown. Five hundred feet of earthy pleasures, neon come-ons and bad memories poorly recalled.

I paid the hackie and climbed out. I pushed my way through the throng, past the French Quarter, featuring the Bare-ly Burlesque Revue, past Mickey's Show Bar, where dentists from Dayton shared bottles of bubbly with young women of negotiable affection. I pushed on till I reached it, the city's premier watering hole, Morris 'Mushy' Wexler's Theatrical Grill.

I was glad of my vicuna topcoat when the doorman opened the portals and permitted me entry. It was a rug joint. Waiters in tuxedos serving drinks, Oysters Rockefeller and more drinks to plushy upholstered booths crammed with movers and shakers. I goggled the first booth, the famed barrister's table. They were all buttoned down and Brooks Brother'ed save for two men in sharkskin suits, dark shirts and loud ties. Mob attorneys.

I looked deeper into the room. My plan was a hallucination sketched on tissue paper. All I knew for sure was it required the presence of Mushy Wexler. I'd read up on him. He'd retired from the rackets to become a snooty *restaurateur* but he'd made his pile running a horseracing syndicate and the head mucks of the Bloody Corners Gang weren't strangers to his table.

They wouldn't be dining with Mushy tonight of course. They were eating bologna sandwiches down at central lockup. Tee hee.

I spotted him, had to be. A dapper old gent alone in the elevated back booth, the one with the unobstructed view and the telephone on the table. He was inspecting a waiter's tray. The waiter did an about face and returned to the kitchen.

I checked my topcoat and parked myself at the enormous horseshoe-shaped bar. The barkeep plunked down a napkin-wrapped basket of salt sticks. "Fresh from our own bakery! What'll it be?"

Growing up in Youngstown gave me very limited experience with rug joints. I'd seen plenty of nightclub swells in the movies though. "Make it a Rob Roy."

"Yes sir, what's your flavor?"

"Excuse me?"

"What brand of Scotch do you prefer?"

Scotch, ugh. Old man hooch that smelled of peat bogs. "Whatever you recommend."

"And sweet vermouth, dry vermouth or 50-50?"

"Whatever you recommend."

The barkeep went to work, I tried not to look. Mushy Wexler hurried to greet an elderly man and a mink-draped matron who had shuffled in from the cold. "Your Honor" said Mushy above the din, or "Senator" or "Governor." One of those important *or* words.

My tissue paper plan curled up and blew away. I wasn't going to be able to drop a stray comment about the murdered cop to the barkeep, sit back and see who sidled up for a chat. The Theatrical wasn't a well-lubricated mob hangout. The Theatrical was formal as a church.

Or was it?

An otherworldly apparition appeared. A platform rose and locked into place several feet behind and above the horseshoe-shaped bar. On it sat a sloe-eyed bottle blonde in a sparkly dress and a slight Negro at a baby grand. The blonde sang, *"This town is full of guys, who think they're mighty wise, just because they know a thing or two..."*

The long-fingered pianist darted in and around her vocal. *"You can see 'em all the time, up and down old Vine, tellin' of the wonders they can do, hoo hoo hoooo..."*

I nibbled my Rob Roy. It tasted fine, if you liked peat moss.

"There's con men, boosters, card sharks, crap shooters, they congregate around the Metropol," sang the siren as three young men took seats at the bar, four stools down, closer to the door.

I rested the back of my head against my hand and looked them over. They made a great show of ignoring me. They wore off the rack J.C. Penney suits with hanger peaks in the shoulders and didn't know enough to remove their hats. Itchy young men, but none I recognized.

"But their name'd be mud, like a chump playin' stud, if they lost their old ace in the hole."

I was offended. Now that I was comfortably nestled onto a barstool, enjoying the musical stylings of Blondie and Longfingers, I wanted to hike my eyebrows at Mushy Wexler and have him 86 the riff raff. I pushed my Rob Roy into the bar gutter and ordered a rye rocks.

The punks drank beer from the bottle. I felt their darting looks on the side of my face. I was safe for now, they wouldn't try anything inside. The question was why they were here at all. Could be I wasn't as anonymous as I thought. Could be Mushy Wexler was quite the sharp-eyed *restaurateur*.

Nah, it didn't read right. Mushy Wexler wouldn't invite the punks inside the high temple. If he knew or cared who I was he'd tell the goons to wait for me outside.

The torch singer collected her applause on outstretched palms and launched into a sultry version of "East of the Sun." I ate a salt stick and ordered another rye.

Had I been tailed? I had got sloppy and didn't check, didn't take evasive action on Short Vincent, just plowed straight down the sidewalk. Dumb. But this didn't smell like Jimmy. Jimmy was a lone wolf.

I drank my drink and ate the ice cubes. 'You know what the enemy is planning by the questions he asks.' You knew the Krauts were planning a U-boat attack near the Orkney Islands because they were asking their agents for shipping schedules in that area. But that rule had a flip side. Note the questions the enemy doesn't ask.

The Schooler knew I was determined to get shed of Jimmy. He should have asked me what I planned to do next. He did not. Which might mean he had read me like a book and skipped ahead a few pages. The three loogans might be more of The Schooler's felons in training, sent to make sure I didn't tell any tales out of school. They weren't a hit squad.

I sat back, relaxed and didn't fall off the barstool. The rye was earning its keep and Blondie and Long-fingers were easing into something risqué, if their quicksilver grins were any indication. I was happy here. I wanted to live a good long life, die and be buried here.

The punks were digging into pockets, shagging for quarters. I considered offering to buy them a round of beers, thought better of it, made for the men's room and slipped out the back door, leaving my vicuna topcoat behind.

I know what I said about the punks not being a hit squad and all but I'm not always as brilliant as I think I am. I walked east down the alley, the warmth and jollity of the Theatrical carried off in one gust of icy wind. I heard quick following footsteps.

I pulled my belly gun and pivoted. A tipsy young couple stopped giggling and raised their hands. I put up my gun. The young couple ran the other way.

When I turned back around the three punks blocked my path. Their dukes were empty. I kept mine the same way.

"I surmise that you gentlemen have a matter of mutual concern about which you would care to confer."

They didn't know what this meant exactly, but they didn't like that I smiled when I said it. The oldest one, he had to be all of twenty, sneered like a B movie heavy and started forward, flanked by his two pals. No hardware came out. I was in no condition for hand to hand combat so I reached for my .25.

The oldest one was quick, on me in a blink, grabbing my gun hand.

I shot my left elbow at his solar plexus, missed and hit something hard with my funny bone. A gun butt in a shoulder holster. My arm went numb. The other two were on me now, punching my head and grabbing for the gun.

Shit. What a stupid way to die. I felt the .25 leave my grip. I braced myself for the *coup de grace.*

I heard a blast of gunfire, then another. Loud but not close. I felt intense stinging heat in my lower legs.

I looked up to see the three punks hotfooting it down the alley.

I looked the other direction. Jimmy Streets slow walked toward me, a pig snout sawed-off swinging at his side, spilling smoke. Wyatt Earp came to mind.

"Got a call you were in trouble," said Jimmy when he got close.

I was bent over, digging birdshot out of my calves. He must have fired a carom shot off the sidewalk.

"Thanks," I said. "I think."

Jimmy grunted and walked away.

Chapter Seventeen

I crept into Mrs. Brennan's rooming house before midnight and tiptoed up the stairs. I had returned to the Theatrical to retrieve my topcoat and see if my Lazarus act drew any stares from interested parties. It did not.

I went to my room, grabbed a pint of rye and my dop kit and went down the hall to the bathroom. I sat on the can and rolled up my pants legs, what was left of them. My blue socks were now purple. Four, six, eight, ten, *eleven* pieces of birdshot.

I rummaged in my dop kit. Best I could find was a nail file. I took a good yank, splashed rye on the file and set to work. I offered up the suffering as penance for my sins.

A drunken tugman in a watch cap stumbled in, hand on his fly. "Piss in the sink," I said. "I ain't moving."

He looked at me gouging tiny metal pellets from my calves and ankles with a nail file. He struggled to focus and get square on his feet. "*Ouch*," is what he said.

I laughed and passed him the pint. He passed it back. "You need it worse'n I do," he said and stumbled off.

I tried to puzzle it out for the umpteenth time. I was used to the sense of power that being a spy provided - you knew all about the enemy, they knew nothing about you. This was the reverse. Who were the three punks working for? How did they know who and where I was? How did they show up so quick? Who called Jimmy to say I was in trouble? And why did he care?

I soaked a towel in whiskey and swabbed my wounds. The cleansing sting felt good. I stood up and chanced a look at myself in the mirror. Purple fist marks on my cheeks and forehead, a yellowed bandage on my ear. I moved closer to the mirror.

There. That wasn't so bad. From neck to knees I was good as new.

I awoke the next morning to loud knocking. I got up and stood by the door in my boxer shorts. "Yeah?"

"Open up laddie."

Mrs. Brennan. I threw on some pants and did as I was told.

"Got shot last night did ya?"

"How do you figure?"

"I followed bloody footprints to your door. I don't know what it is you're doing, Mr. Schroeder, but it seems to me you're going about it the wrong way."

Well. Who could argue with that?

"I'll make you a nice breakfast and a cuppa tea," she said.

"You're too kind."

"Then you'll get down on your hands and knees and scrub the carpet. Clean."

I was halfway up the stairs with my scrub brush and bucket when I hit upon a plan. Find the mysterious Mr. Big my own damn self. He was the only one who could unclog this drain. I had lined his pockets with the armored car heist, I had engineered the cops' raid on his rival gang. Mr. Big would welcome me with open arms!

How to get to him was another matter. I scrubbed and pondered. The Schooler and his boss figured to have some elaborate communication routine involving pay phones, drop points and carrier pigeons. But what about the proceeds? Cash from gambling, extortion and vending machines. What crime boss worth his salt didn't want to stroke the fluted edges of those rubber-banded stacks of legal tender otherwise known as the weekly take? There had to be a point of transfer. And a delivery boy.

Jimmy collected the shakedown money, probably delivered it too. He and I had collected the merchant payoffs last Friday. Today was Thursday. I had one day to get with Agent Schram and set up a tag team shag.

I bent to my task, dunking and scrubbing. The blood spots went away. Mrs. Brennan had added a slug of peroxide to the bucket of suds. I wasn't the first boarder to bleed all over her carpet.

Chapter Eighteen

Friday, 5 p.m. My sophisticated tag team tail operation pulled up a block from Mrs. Brennan's rooming house right on time. Moon-faced Wally in a '39 Hudson. I climbed in and bumped my head on cold steel. The car had no headliner.

"You're it?"

"I'm it," said Wally.

I gave him the address. Wally ground the column shift into first gear and the Hudson bucked and snorted up Winslow to W. 25th.

I had not been able to get Schram on the line the previous day, the Assistant Special Agent was 'indisposed.' I'd talked to beefy linebacker Joe Gilliam instead, told him I might have a way to locate the quarry, the elusive Mr. Big. Agent Gilliam said what do you want and when do you want it. Wally the office boy in a '39 Hudson was the result.

"This heap have a second gear?" I asked as we crawled south on W. 25th.

"It's around here somewhere," said Wally. We lurched into gear and set sail down the street. Christ, guy even drove with a limp.

We turned west on Lorain. We passed the St. Ignatius High School baseball diamond. Dozens of kids in knit caps, scarves flying, were ice skating around the infield in the glimmering dusk.

"Fire department does that every year," said Wally. "Floods the field for a rink."

"Nice."

Wally blathered on. About how he loved ice-skating as a kid, where he went to school, how his mother made her famous five-way chili, how he loved baseball and who his favorite players were and how his bum leg kept him out of the service. This took about six blocks. When he came up for air I asked a question.

"What's the scuttlebutt around the office Wally? Is someone trying to put the squelch on this thing?" He turned south on Fulton Road. "Agent Schram for instance."

"Not him. They put him in the…you know." Wally pointed at his head and spun his finger.

"I'm sorry to hear that."

Wally drove, I puzzled. With Richard Schram out of the picture we should have had half the G-men in the Cleveland District lined up behind us in unmarked cars.

"If not Schram, who?"

Wally dawdled behind a double decker bus for two blocks. "Well, I heard something in the men's room. At HQ. I was on the crapper."

"Okay."

"Two agents at the pisser, or washing up. I'm not sure. I heard running water."

"What else did you hear?"

"The one guy says to the other guy, 'You know Mr. Big ain't who they say it is. It's not Teddy Biggs, it's Louis Seltzer.'"

Hokey smokes. Louis B. Seltzer. Editor-in-Chief of *The Cleveland Press*, the city's reigning power broker, Mr. Cleveland himself!

"And this is based on what?"

"Dunno," said Wally. "But the other agent, the one he said it to, he says, 'Tell me somethin' I don't know.'"

Moo oil. Gossip. Bullshit rumors that circulate through offices like forced air heat. Still, it had a wonderfully perverse logic. The owner of *The Cleveland Press* issuing fiery editorials demanding the arrest and conviction of himself.

I told Wally to turn right on Cesco. We approached H&R Manufacturing. "Better pull over here."

Wally curbed the Hudson. He turned his trusting moon face toward my mistrusting black and blue one and said, "The thing of it is, is that Louis Seltzer is short, like about five foot. They say he buys his suits in the boys' department at Higbee's. Why would they call him Mr. Big?"

I managed to keep a straight face. "I'm not sure Wally. Could be it's a joke."

Wally carefully considered this possibility. "You know, I'll bet that's it."

"I'm going in," I said. "Make a U and park in front of that dump truck. Best guess is he'll be headed east. If you see a big bruiser drive by in late model black Buick you're on your own."

Wally's chin trembled. "Whattaya mean?"

"I mean you take off and tail the Buick to its destination."

"Oh geeze."

"Don't sweat it, I'll be back soon." I climbed out, leaving poor Wally jacking his jaws like a just-caught fish.

I didn't know what to make of the Louis Seltzer rumor. If Special Agent in Charge Chester Halladay believed it was true he would stop at nothing to get Mr. Cleveland's head mounted on the wall behind his desk. Halladay would, but others above him might not. It was well known that J. Edgar prized favorable publicity above all. From what I'd read in *The Cleveland Press* Louis Seltzer was doing his bit.

Crap on toast, another Chinese angle to consider. I mushed my way through the sooty slush and pined for the clarity of war.

The front door to H&R Manufacturing swung open before I was halfway up the walk. No Pencil Mustache this time. His pomaded young partner from the armored car heist held the door open.

"Jimmy here?"

"Umm, I'm not sure."

"What's your name again?"

"Ricky."

"Try not to blink when you lie Ricky, it's a dead giveaway."

"But I tell you I don't..."

I stepped forward and clapped a mitt on his bony shoulder. "Don't lie to me Ricky," I said, giving him a moment to take in my gaudy beat-up mug. "I've suffered enough."

Ricky fought a nervous giggle to a standstill, then led me across the shop floor and down a corridor to a room in the southwest corner of the building. The Schooler's office door was closed. Ditto the door across the hall. "He's in there," said Ricky.

"Thanks, I'll take it from here." Ricky took off. I tippy tapped on the door in the most annoying way possible. I paused and did it some more. God forgive me but I did enjoy taunting this jerk.

Jimmy threw open the door with a purple face. "*What?*"

"Just a courtesy call Jimmy, to thank you again for saving my life."

Jimmy flared the nostrils of his great beak and his closed his good eye. Was this supposed to be scary? I gave his glass eye a cheesy grin and looked around. Manila envelopes spilling cash, three leather bound account ledgers, fat stacks of rubber banded fives, tens and twenties waiting to take their place in the three canvas bags below the counting table. The Fulton Road Mob'd had a good week.

"Need any help in here?"

Jimmy opened his good eye and came close, he reeked of garlic. Was Jimmy Italian?

"Get-the-fuck-*out*," he said and slammed the door in my face. I was right. Friday was delivery day.

A thought occurred as I made my way back down the corridor. Anonymous hoods were stalking me for unknown reasons. When I called for reinforcements the FBI sent Wally in a '39 Hudson. Time to take the money and run? The promised six-figure payroll heist looked like a pipe dream at this point. What was I waiting for?

I could ambush Jimmy as he loaded the canvas bags into the trunk of his Buick. Sap him down, shoot him in the kneecaps. Carry the cush down the alley to Fulton Road, hail a cab, go to National City Bank, collect the rest of my pile and disappear, apologies to The Schooler, Wally and the Federal Bureau of Investigation.

That's what I was thinking as I walked out the front door of H&R Manufacturing. What I did was slip behind a snowy evergreen at the corner of the building and train an eye on the detached two-car garage in the far corner. I was cold, hungry and happy as a clam, doing what I did best. Spying.

Chapter Nineteen

I waited behind the snowy evergreen at the right front corner of the building, waited for Jimmy to trundle those three canvas bags to the detached garage behind the building, whereupon I would leap into galvanized action.

A dog barked. A big dog, coming closer. Cripes, I'd forgotten about Hector the hound. He rounded the corner at full gallop, teeth bared. He dug his front paws into the snow and growled from tongue to tail. The fur around his neck stood to attention.

"Can it pal, I've dealt with tougher mugs than you."

The dog crept closer, head down, sniffing the ground, sniffing my socks, licking them. Of course. My shot up ankles were bleeding.

Jimmy marched across the snowy blacktop right about then, cash-filled bags in hand. He scanned right and left as he crossed the open area. I made myself small behind the evergreen. The Hound of the Baskervilles tore at my socks, shredding them. It hurt like hell.

Jimmy stopped in mid step at the sight of the dog's snout buried in a snowy evergreen. I lowered my socks, the great hound lapped eagerly at my oozing wounds. If ol' Slopehead came over to investigate I would take him down, grab the canvas bags and drive his Buick down the alley.

But Jimmy continued on to the two-car garage, apparently satisfied that Hector was masticating a rat. He wasn't half wrong.

Jimmy pushed open one garage door with a fluid muscular movement, then stood back to admire his effort. Ka-*bam* went the sliding door. I patted Hector's anvil skull and snickered at the sight of Jimmy showing off for himself.

So, Schroeder, you a rat or aren't ya? Jimmy's busy stowing loot in the trunk, his back is turned. Now's the time!

I told myself I should wait to see if I was right about Jimmy being the deliveryman. I told myself there was still a chance we could tail him to Teddy Biggs and collect on this cockeyed scheme. That's what I told myself. What I did was nothing.

Jimmy threw the canvas bags into the trunk of a car and slammed it shut. I'd blown my chance. I waited for Jimmy to back out and drive off.

But he stepped out of the garage, slid the door shut, yanked open the other garage door and backed his Buick onto the slushy blacktop. The razor-wired front gate rolled open by remote control. The Buick took a right on Cesco, headed east. Jimmy *wasn't* the Fulton Road Mob's delivery boy.

I raced toward the closing gate, didn't get there in time. I craned my neck to see the '39 Hudson pull away from the curb as Jimmy drove past. I flagged my arms and hollered but Wally didn't hear me. The Buick and the Hudson turned north on Fulton Road.

I had another opportunity now. One better suited to my cowardly nature. Pop open the trunk of the delivery vehicle, grab the weekly take and go. I was good with locks, Hector was my puppy now, he wouldn't object. It was a lead pipe cinch. And I couldn't make myself do it.

I didn't take any moral comfort in this you understand. I am definitely a rat, just not a very good one.

What now? I had to do something to redeem myself. I knew where the weekly take was stashed but had no way to follow it to Mr. Big. *Unless* I opened the trunk and climbed in, a foolproof plaster if ever there was. That I could do. Hiding took my kind of courage.

But that opportunity escaped me too. Hector, who had followed me to the gate, spun and bounded off, barking his fool head off. I darted back to the cover of the snowy evergreen as The Schooler stepped out a side door and stopped to ruffle Hector's fur.

The Schooler was the Fulton Road Mob's bagman. Of course he was. He was the mug in the middle, the buffer between Mr. Big and Jimmy and the itchy young men. So long as The Schooler was the one to lay treasure at the feet of the monarch his position was secure.

You should've doped this out earlier, Schroeder, should have thought it through. Maybe then you'd have a better vehicle for tailing the Packard to its destination than two bloody ankles on blistered feet.

The Schooler drove his Packard past the rolling gate and turned right. I managed to squeeze through the gate this time and watch the Packard turn south on Fulton Road. I slow-footed my way down to the streetcar stop, fumbling in my pockets for the fare home, hoping I still had some rye left in that pint.

I was waiting for the rattler when I saw the '39 Hudson nosing back down Fulton Road like a shot-up B-17 limping home to base. Wally saw my wave and pulled to the curb. I ran across the street and jumped in.

"I lost him, I'm sorry."

"Forget it, just get this heap in gear. Head south to...what's the next major east-west?"

"Uh, Denison."

"Take a left on Denison."

It was a long shot. The Schooler had a five minute head start to an unknown destination. But he'd be taking it slow and careful with all that cush on board and his Packard would be easy to spot. He figured to be headed in the direction that money headed in this town. East.

Wally drove south on Fulton, past Johnny's Bar and St. Rocco's Church. He waited for a slow moving truck to clear the intersection before turning left on Denison. I resisted the urge to push him out onto the pavement and grab the wheel.

Wally found third gear eventually and gave the '39 Hudson its head. Such as it was. We wove through traffic, we passed a cement truck, its rear end churning. We drove through a slump shouldered neighborhood of Cleveland doubles and three flats, crumbling mortar making their brown bricks look like rotting teeth. We approached fifty miles per hour.

"The guy in the Buick musta spotted me," said Wally, woefully. "He hung a U on Fulton, then he took off down an alleyway. By the time I got turned around he was gone."

"My fault, I had the wrong guy and the wrong car."

Wally's eyebrows crept up hopefully. "Yeah?"

"Yeah. Our pigeon is up ahead somewhere. Keep an eye peeled for a dark red Packard."

Wally stepped on the gas, whipped around a slow moving sedan, passed on the right, skidded on a patch of ice, got the chassis square and raced through the E. 71st intersection on the last wink of amber in the overhead traffic light.

"You said a red Packard, am I right?" said Wally.

"Uh huh."

"Well, I'm colorblind, but I know a Packard when I see one."

I followed his look. A wine red Packard was purring along in the #2 lane, fifty yards ahead.

"Get over," I said. "Close in." Wally did so. "Now back it down some. And don't hunch over the wheel, he'll see your face."

"Right," said Wally, settling back, on the job, in the hunt.

I eyeballed the Packard's trunk and reconsidered my plan. It had sounded plausible at the time. Find Mr. Big and convince the crime boss to sideline Jimmy so that the FBI would approve the final heist.

Now that reality was approaching at 40 mph I began to see some flaws. As in how to gain entry to a highly guarded compound and then win the confidence of a recluse whose hideout you have located by means of tailing his trusted first lieutenant?

A tough sell. And if Mr. Big really was Louis Seltzer, well, by this time tomorrow I'd be at the bottom of Lake Erie.

I eyeballed the Packard's trunk some more. I should have grabbed the geet when I had the chance.

A flat bed truck stacked with clattering wooden pallets pulled in between the Packard and us. I looked upstream. We were approaching another traffic light. I told Wally to swing into the #1 lane.

The traffic lamp turned amber. We were ten yards from the E. 93rd intersection, the Packard five yards ahead on our right, slowing down for the light. I slid down as we pulled alongside.

"Should I stop or go?"

"Stop," I said, sure that our tail was unmade.

We braked just as the Packard's V-12 roared to life. I sat up in the passenger's seat to watch The Schooler tear across the intersection just ahead of the cross traffic and disappear down the road.

Wally was looking woeful again as he pulled the Hudson up to Mrs. Brennan's rooming house. "What do I tell 'em? Downtown."

"Not a thing, I'll be in on Monday to file a report." I opened my door, clapped Wally on the shoulder and said, "We'll get 'em next time."

Wally nodded and drove off. I felt bad for him. It wasn't his fault he was paired with a numbskull. I also felt hungry enough to eat a horse. Thank God for small favors, horsemeat wouldn't be hard to find around here.

I let gravity take me down the hill. I kept my balance by flanging out my feet like a circus clown, crunching through the corn snow, skidding on ice. I managed to remain upright for

two blocks. To Elm Street, to a blue and white sign with a mermaid on it. *The Harbor Inn.*
   Valhalla.

Chapter Twenty

The Harbor Inn had a bar about a mile long. There were a million different beers lined up on a shelf above it, arranged alphabetically. By the time I reached the end of the bar I had devised a plan. I would start with a cold bottle of Anchor Steam and work my way down the line, concluding my evening with a frosty Zipfer Bier. An ambitious undertaking, no question, but I had a hog wallow of self pity to dive into.

The ruddy deckhands throwing darts and the sooty steelworkers wide-elbowed at the bar shot me sideways looks as I ambled by. The vicuna topcoat was inappropriate attire maybe. So I took a stool at the far end, dug out a Ulysses S. Grant and said those stirring words every barfly longs to say. "Drinks all around, on me."

What the hell, I was flush.

The barmaid palmed the fifty like this happened every day and started taking orders. The tugmen and steel smelters to my left had surprisingly refined tastes. The barmaid had to climb a stepstool to retrieve dusty bottles of Johnny Walker Black and Remy Martin VSOP. I got some *skol*'s and *prosit*'s, and one freckled rascal raised his glass with "May the best of your past be the worst of your future."

I smiled, nodded, and ordered an Anchor Steam. A waitress crossed behind me carrying something that smelled like heaven on a plate. I snagged her on the way back and ordered the same. She returned to the kitchen. I cleaned the bar with a drink napkin, it came up red. Ore dust.

You ever have one of those days when you're the butt of the joke and you don't know why? You've got a big piece of spinach in your grille maybe, or someone's pinned a 'kick me' sign to the back of your coat. That's the way it had been since I arrived in Cleveland. Everyone in on the joke but me.

Did The Schooler make us in the '39 Hudson or was he just performing standard evasive maneuvers? I didn't know.

Did Jimmy somehow stage manage my rescue outside the Theatrical or just catch a mystery call for help at the last second? I didn't know.

Did Special Agent in Charge Chester Halladay recruit me to infiltrate the Fulton Road Mob only to have his chain yanked by the Director because I was getting too close to Mr. Big, a.k.a. Louis Seltzer? I didn't know, didn't have a blessed clue.

I did know that the steaming platter of cabbage rolls and browned to perfection walleye perch that the waitress slung down on the bar in front of me was a thing of beauty. I admired it for half a second.

I was barely into the C's - Carling Red Cap Ale - when the barmaid asked me if I was Hal Schroeder.

"Who wants to know?"

"Some guy," she said, indicating the wall phone, its earpiece dangling.

I went over and picked it up. "Who's this?"

"Jimmy."

"How'd you find me?"

"Your landlady said you were out. I called the nearest bar."

"Smart boy. What do you want?"

"Thought we could have a little chitchat," said Jimmy and laughed, loudly.

I held the earpiece at arm's length. Jimmy laughing? I didn't figure he knew how. He was obviously deeper into the alphabet than I was. I heard him say something. I pressed the earpiece to my unbandaged ear. "Say again."

"Fats Navarro. Heard of him?"

"Yes I have." Every jazzhead in America had heard of Fats Navarro, hard bopping trumpeter extraordinaire.

"He's in town tonight, down on Central. Wanna go?"

There was only one answer this question. I wanted to find out what Jimmy was up to, sure, why he was making nice after I had taunted, humiliated and outfoxed him at every turn. But I *really* wanted to hear Fats Navarro in the flesh. "What's the name of the club, I'll meet you there."

Jimmy laughed again. Twice in one night!

"This isn't a grease job, G-man, it's a night on the town." His voice grew husky. "With a coupla very *friendly* young ladies."

"Jimmy I'm not..."

"Pick you up at nine," he said and rang off. I held the earpiece at arm's length and examined it carefully.

I stood at the curb in front of Mrs. Brennan's rooming house at 9 p.m. in subzero cold and wished for a hat. A scrim of ice was frosting my noggin like spun sugar. Jimmy's black Buick nosed down Elm Street five minutes later. I squared my shoulders for a strange night.

I climbed in, and mopped my forehead as I defrosted. I didn't look at the friendly young ladies in the back seat, I'd been with enough whores for one lifetime. Jimmy drove east across the Main Avenue Bridge. Nobody spoke. He turned south on E. 9th Street. Nobody spoke.

"The Pope die or something?" I said. Nobody laughed.

60th and Central was a smattering of storefront churches and chicken and catfish stands wedged between dimly lit row houses and tenements with tarpaper windows. Jimmy curbed the Buick in front of Jolly Jack's Lounge and Dance Parlor. A burly Negro opened his door and greeted him by name. I got out and opened the back door and almost had a heart attack.

Jeannie. The woman who had been sitting directly behind me on the ride over, the friendly young lady Jimmy had promised, was *Jeannie*!

Her wiseacre grin faded as she regarded my beat up face. I had no earthly idea what to say. What in the name of Christ and the Twelve Apostles was she doing in the company of a guy who had just beat the crap out of her husband?

Jimmy herded us inside. His date was a stacked blond in a fox fur who wrinkled her pert nose at the all black crowd. The seas parted for Jimmy as a light-skinned hostess escorted us through the bar to a table above the dance floor. She removed the *Reserved* card. Jimmy slipped her a folded bill.

We sat down and shivered. Despite the crush of bodies Jolly Jack's was icebox cold. Jimmy ordered a bottle of rum for the table. Also four cokes, a bucket of gizzards and "Plenty of *gris-gris*."

The waitress laughed.

Was Jimmy an octoroon? He seemed at home here. I entertained this asinine question in order to avoid trying to make sense of Jeannie sitting to my right, hair done, lips red, holding her hands in her lap and staring straight ahead.

The waitress poured four rum and cokes, no ice. Jimmy hoisted one. "Always glad to get two old friends back together."

What in the hell? He must have noticed our reaction to one another at Pappas Deli and asked her later. Jeannie's a terrible liar. She's also a smart cookie, she wouldn't have given him much else.

"Jeannie and I dated a few times in high school. Back in Youngstown."

"Umm hmm," said Jimmy, not buying it for a second. "You don't seem too thrilled to see her."

"She threw me over for a football player."

Jimmy's girl clucked, Jimmy smirked. Jeannie remained silent. I drank my rum and coke and tried not to look. It wasn't easy.

Jeannie had been girl-next-door pretty as a kid, all freckles and elbows. But she was a grown-up beauty now, composed, almost elegant. A grown-up beauty married to a bald Greek on a double date with a mobster, his moll and yours truly. What in the hell?

The waitress served a bucket of smoked gizzards, a wad of paper napkins and a bowl of shimmering hot sauce. "How did you peg me for a Fats Navarro fan?"

"Anyone who hates Glenn Miller can't be all bad," said Jimmy, hot sauce all down his chin.

I had never said I hated Glenn Miller. I *didn't* hate Glenn Miller. Hating Major Glenn Miller, whose single-engine Norseman disappeared over the English Channel in 1944, was tantamount to treason. I had merely groaned and turned down the volume when a Miller tune came on the car radio while we were make our shakedown rounds. "American Patrol" was a catchy little number built around drums and bugles that made patrol duty sound like bubble blowing night at the Trocadero.

Jimmy was nowhere near as dumb as he looked. He paid attention. Which meant he knew I had tried to have him tailed, and probably knew I'd tried to get him axed. The cops didn't much care what happened down here in Dingetown, especially after sunset. I rested the heel of my hand on the butt of my P38.

A man almost as wide as he was high stepped up on the bandstand and spread his arms. This would be Jolly Jack.

"Direct from Key West by way of New York City," he said in a thunderous baritone, "Jolly Jack's is mighty proud to present Mister Theodore 'Fats' Navarro and his Be-Bop Boys!"

The crowd erupted, the bassist, drummer and pianist dug into an up-tempo tune and Jolly Jack looked around for his star attraction. Jimmy and his girl did likewise.

I chanced a look at Jeannie. She met my eyes, cool as a cuke, and winked. I removed the heel of my hand from the butt of my gun. If Jeannie was jake with this sideways setup then I guess I was too.

The crowd stirred. The man of the hour made his way to the bandstand, slapping hands with the patrons, horn tucked under his arm. He was just a kid, a chubby-cheeked kid. He took center stage and waved away a curtain of green-gray smoke, some of it from cigarettes. The rhythm section backed into a standard 4/4.

"Let's warm this joint up," said Fats Navarro and swelled his cheeks like a fireplace bellows.

The resulting long-held low note rattled empties on the club tables. He picked up steam from there, always half a beat ahead, the crowd leaning forward, wondering if the piano, bass and drums could catch up.

Fats switched gears. His eyes got big and he began to talk through his trumpet. That's what it sounded like, I swear. The rhythm section kept up a backbeat as Fats Navarro gave out with his sermon, his soliloquy.

The audience pricked up their ears, this chubby-cheeked kid was saying things that needed to be said. I dug the jive-crazy intensity of it but, watching the dark rapt faces of the crowd, I also felt out of place, felt like a spy. Whatever message Fats Navarro was sending out through the bell of his trumpet wasn't meant for me.

He went on for a long time, whispering seductively, snarling in anger, finally winding down to an extended breathless pleading that froze the crowd in their seats and shamed the big talkers at the bar into silence. Fats gathered himself and concluded with a high C that had dogs howling all the way to Akron.

The crowd went nuts. Jimmy pointed at me with his cig, I nodded my appreciation. The light-skinned hostess huddled with Fats on the bandstand. He nodded and slipped something in his pocket.

"Special request from the congregation," said the young trumpet player with the almond eyes. Rumor had it his mother was Chinese. "A dance tune," he said and leaned into the microphone. "For two very special young lovers."

The crowd said *unh huhh huhh.*

My worst fears were realized after the first few bars. Even with Fats Navarro sliding up one note and down the next you couldn't help but recognize "I Dream of Jeannie with the Light Brown Hair."

Jeannie and I sat bolted to our chairs.

"Well *dance* with the young lady," said Jimmy. "Really," said his lady friend. The next table over muttered encouragement. A consensus had been reached.

I stood up and offered Jeannie my hand. Mine was hot and sticky, hers cool and dry. We made our way out onto the dance floor.

I was a so-so dancer under the best of circumstances. With the eyes of the crowd upon us and Fats Navarro beaming down from the bandstand I danced as if I had two clubfeet and a spastic colon. Jeannie didn't help. She smelled like a summer breeze that comes out of nowhere and cools you behind the ears. My head swam.

Jeannie drew me closer and squeezed my hand. "C'mon now," she murmured, "we know how to do this. Remember?"

I remembered. We danced a passable four step to Jeannie's signature song. Fats kept it slow and easy. Jeannie rested her cheek on my shoulder. The crowd went "Awwww."

Fats goosed the tempo a minute later. Other dancers took the floor. Young bucks in electric blue suits twirled giddy young girls in floral print dresses. The joint warmed up.

Jeannie backed up a step. I was grateful. Holding her body close to mine was pure torture.

We danced to the new beat, face to face. "What are you doing here?" I halfway shouted.

"Jimmy called and apologized about Dimitri, said he was just doing his job."

The thought of Jimmy apologizing made my skin itch.

"He said you wanted to see me but were afraid to ask."

"And that sounded like me to you?"

"I wanted to see you again!"

I lost a step in our swing and sway and just stood there and looked at her. Fats must have noticed because he changed the tempo from hard bop to slow waltz.

Jeannie and I came together again on the dance floor, wove and entwined ourselves till we could barely breathe. That's the way it had always been between us, rough and sweet in equal measure.

"And what are *you* doing here?" said Jeannie after a time, caressing my bandaged ear. "In Cleveland, with a hoodlum like Jimmy Streets?"

I gave her the best answer I could. "I can't answer that question right now."

Jeannie stepped back from my embrace. She looked cross. "You never could make a decision," she said and returned to the table.

Chapter Twenty-one

"I'll get out here," I said to Jimmy at the corner of Superior and E. 9th. It was 1:51 a.m. An odd mix of young revelers and men in overalls were marching up the steps to St. John's Cathedral.

"The church?" said Jimmy.

"Hey, it's Sunday morning."

I had been stupid to let Jimmy drag Jeannie into our blood feud. He wanted at me in any way he could. By showing him I still cared for Jeannie I'd made her a potential target. Fortunately Jeannie and I had reverted to form and had a spat. We hadn't spoken since we left the dance floor. Best to keep it that way.

"That's the Printers' Mass," said Jimmy's lady friend between hiccups. "Had an uncle worked at the Plain Dealer up the block. The pressmen they...they always...Gawd, I think I'm gonna be sick."

That was an exit line if ever I heard one.

I squeezed Jeannie's hand and said "Night all" before I opened the back door and stepped out onto Superior. I wouldn't be riding shotgun in Jimmy's Buick anytime soon, that was sure. His lady friend was hugging her ankles, retching rum, coke and chicken gizzards.

The Printers' Mass bore an eerie resemblance to Jolly Jack's Lounge. A loosey goosey atmosphere, dressed up couples strolling in, drunks in the choir loft noodling "Camptown Races" on the pipe organ. Something else too, whispered anticipation. I picked up bit and pieces on my way in.

"Father *Sullivan*?"..."I thought the Diocese"..."You're kidding"...

I stopped at the holy water font and dipped my fingers and made the sign of the cross. I sat in the last pew. I had no idea why I was here.

A priest with a meaty red face and a great deal of tightly curled gray hair lumbered out of the sacristy and surveyed the congregation from the front of the altar. He was wearing the purple vestments of Advent. Father Sullivan no doubt. Even from the last pew I could tell he was stewed to the gills.

He growled a blessing. *"In nomine Patris, et Filii, et Spiritus Sancti."*

"Amen."

Father Sullivan faced the altar and recited the Introit. The altar boys stood rather than kneeled below him, presumably to catch the good father if he pitched over backward. I bowed my head and listened to the soothing rhythm of the familiar words. I hadn't attended Mass in over two years.

Father Sullivan burrowed through the Introit, the Kyrie and the Epistle in fits and starts. The congregation grew restive, waiting on the sermon. Those who were still awake. Two uniformed pressmen to my right were happily sawing logs.

Father Sullivan clambered up to the pulpit at long last, the altar boys hovering nervously behind. He read from Paul's Letter to the Romans, Chapter 1. Recited actually, he never looked down. His rough-edged brogue woke the snoring pressmen.

"For the righteousness of God is revealed through faith for faith; as it is written. 'He who through faith is righteous, will live.'"

I had heard the passage many times. What it came down to was 'Take our word for it.'

Father Sullivan began his sermon. "You have to make up your mind to seek salvation," he growled. "Salvation will not seek you!"

He was right about that. Jeannie's last comment on the dance floor had been eating at me all night. *You never could make a decision.* It hadn't made sense at the time, it did now. She'd asked what I was doing here.

I'd said, *I can't answer that question right now.* Hell, I couldn't answer that question period.

Jeannie and I pledged our troth on my 21st birthday. Then I signed on for spy duty and didn't contact her for almost two years. I spent a little time in Switzerland between missions. I could've raised a stink, insisted that someone stuff my mash note in the diplomatic pouch. It was contrary to rules and regs but Jeannie was right, I could have *tried.*

I signed on with the FBI when I returned, determined to call the shots this time and make off with a pile. Yet I told the feds I had tipped my hand to the mob, just in case. I had a chance to grab canvas sacks crammed with loot but opted to wait and see. I was playing both sides against the middle, like that sad sack cop we dumped in the alley. It's tough to have superior knowledge when you don't know your own plan.

Father Sullivan said it better, spraying spittle four pews deep.

"Martin Luther nailed his ninety-five theses to the door of the Castle Church. He was righteously angry at the Church for selling letters of indulgence. And he was correct. He said that faith was of primary importance. He was right there too. Where he erred, and where his bastard spawn - the Calvinists and the bloody Anglicans - went wrong was the conviction that once grace was bestowed, once faith was embraced, salvation was sealed."

Father Sullivan took a moment to survey the congregation. They were his.

"Salvation is never sealed!" he thundered. "Salvation is *work.* Salvation is what you do when you leave these pews and get up tomorrow and tomorrow and, God willing, the day after that. Salvation," concluded Father Sullivan hoarsely, "is many choices well made!"

He was greeted with a chorus of raucous *Amen*'s.

Ushers passed the collection basket a short time later. It contained donation envelopes, a Thistledown racetrack ticket, a pearl earring and a pack of Lucky Strikes. I added a fin and passed it along.

It was time to make up my damn mind.

Mrs. Brennan extended the lockup hour till 3 a.m. on Saturday nights. I cabbed it back to the Angle with minutes to spare and marched up the stairs. I fished out my room key when I reached the door.

What was this? The keyhole had been gouged and scraped.

A dim light shone through the transom window but I had left a lamp lit. Never come home to a dark room. I pressed my good ear to the door and kept it there. I made out a muffled sound. Snoring.

Huh?

Only thing I could figure was Ricky and Pencil Mustache were lying in wait after I'd been lured away for a night on the town. It would explain Jimmy's sudden buddy-buddy. Come out and play, meet your long lost love, drink too much rum and stagger home drunk and preoccupied. Brilliant so far as it went. But my church detour messed with their timeline. They'd nodded off while waiting on me.

I got my Walther in hand and keyed open the door quiet as could be. I stepped in.

The three punks from the Theatrical were splayed about my room with their feet up. Two on the bed, one in the armchair to the right.

No iron came out but the one in the chair leapt to his feet. I took two quick steps and clocked him on the side of the head with my P38. He was out before he hit the floor.

"Hold up, hold up," yelled the oldest one from the bed, either to me or his playpal who was running headlong at me with malice aforethought. I liked it when they did that. I juked right and clotheslined him with my left arm.

He fell backward and bounced his skull off the hardwood. Two down, one to go.

I faced big brother. Not sure how I knew they were brothers exactly but they were. Big brother was perched on the edge of the bed, looking pained.

"This isn't what you think," he said.

"What is it?"

That's the last thing I remember. Apparently one of the young men I had dumped on the hardwood elected not to stay there.

Next thing I knew I was propped up on pillows, my right temple throbbing from a sap blow. One of the younger brothers was swabbing my face with a wet towel. I let him.

"I apologize," said big brother. "We just wanted to meet in private."

I moved my mouth but no words came out. "Why?" said big brother. "Is that what you're trying to say?" I nodded. "We want to join up."

It only hurt when I laughed.

"We're serious," said big brother. "The heat's on over at Bloody Corners. Not much shakin' for ambitious young men like Sean, Patrick and meself - we're the Mooney brothers by the way. We know you're the new boss of Fulton Road and we want to sign on."

I tried my vocal chords. They squeaked like a rusty hinge. Sean or Patrick proffered a flask. I took a yank. "Where'd you get that idea?"

"From Jimmy Streets."

My unhinged jaw asked the question for me.

"Guy calls up, won't say his name. Says our cop killer just walked into the Theatrical. He describes a mug looks like you. So we go on over to see what's what. We follow you out - we just wanted to ask a few questions, mind - and Jimmy comes outta nowhere with his sawed-off."

So Jimmy had stage managed the whole shebang. And big brother figured Jimmy wouldn't have bothered unless Hal Schroeder was a big cheese.

I guess. It was hard to think clearly with these apple-cheeked Irish loogans hovering over my bedded carcass, swabbing my head and administering anesthetic.

A thought occurred. These boys had been lied to and shot at by Jimmy Streets, they might come in handy somewhere down the line. But I'd seen their like by the hundreds overseas, fly blown and staring up at nothing, and I didn't feel like adding to the pile. Jimmy wouldn't kill easy.

"How about it?" said big brother. "You got a place for us?"

"G'wan home," I said. "Your mama's worried sick."

Big brother looked crestfallen. And here I was doing him a favor. "All right, all right. Give me a phone number. I need something, I'll call."

Big brother scrawled a number on a slip of paper. He would be named Seamus or Finn or...

"Ask for Ambrose," he said, handing me the note.

Ambrose?

The Mooney brothers tiptoed out, shutting the light and closing the door behind them, ever so gently.

I kicked off my shoes and tapped my foot to the thudding drumbeat in my right temple, thinking about holding Jeannie in my arms on the dance floor of Jolly Jack's Lounge and Dance Parlor. It had been some night on the town.

Chapter Twenty-two

"Jesus, Mary and Joseph," said Wally when I walked into FBI HQ on St. Clair the next afternoon sporting a lurid purple wraparound shiner that contrasted nicely with my yellow facial bruises and the grimy ocher bandage on my ear. "This Mona Lisa dame, I sure hope she's worth it."

"Oh she is, Wally, she is" I said with a painful wink. How can a wink be painful? I followed him through the labyrinth of corridors to Chester Halladay's office.

Security. That was why the office of the Special Agent in Charge was buried at the end of this Babylonian maze. Any assailant would have to run a gauntlet of junior G-men to get to Halladay.

Smart. If the assailant was dumb enough to mount a frontal attack. Not so smart if the assailant attacked from the rear. The Special Agent might find his escape route all bunged up. Safety bars aren't much help if a fire breaks out inside your house.

Wally and I arrived at our destination. I gathered myself before the great oaken door. Wally tugged at my sleeve and said, "Visiting hours are two to five."

Huh? I checked my watch, checked my memory. "But I have a one o'clock."

"And you're right on time," said Wally, tapping on the door. "But..."

"Enter and be recognized," said a smooth and hearty voice from the other side. I opened the door to see Chester Halladay and Agent Gilliam standing to greet me.

"*After* your meeting," said Wally, one hand ushering me inside, the other hand spinning at his temple.

"Oh, gotcha," I said and entered the Sanctum Sanctorum.

"What the hell happened to you Schroeder?" said Chester Halladay merrily.

"Just a little misunderstanding sir. Nothing serious."

Halladay resumed his seat. "What do you have to report?"

I told Halladay and Gilliam the truth. That the Fulton Road Mob's racketeering operations were thriving after the police raid on their rivals, that Wally and I had tailed The Schooler's Packard east on Harvard Road, hauling the weekly take, presumably to the palatial digs of the boss man. I told them we had lost contact due to my tactical mistake. And then I flat out lied.

"The Schooler is eager to get this final heist off the dime. He's agreed to bench Jimmy Streets if that's what it takes to get the green light."

Chester Halladay deputized his subordinate with a nod. Agent Gilliam said, "So we won't have to worry about Jimmy running amok with his scattergun?"

"Heard about that, did you?" I said. "Then you know he didn't shoot to kill."

"Yeah," said Gilliam. "Guy's a regular Florence Nightingale. Just ask that dirty cop he killed."

"Not that we care," said Chester Halladay. He said his words slowly, and looked at me as he said them. "He got what a traitor deserves."

I kept my face quiet despite the buffalo stampede thundering across my skull. Only Jimmy, The Schooler and I knew what really happened to that sad sack cop. The feds had made an educated guess based on how things played out. Bloody Corners Gang laying low, Fulton Road Mob raking it in. They were bluffing.

"Jimmy wanted to go to war when that cop's body was found. He didn't kill him!"

Halladay and Gilliam seemed to buy it. Leastwise they didn't bust out laughing.

"So Jimmy Street is out of the picture?" said Gilliam.

"Provided we get the go-ahead on the payroll job."

Chester Halladay spliced his hands together and used them as a pillow on which to rest his fat greasy head. "Teddy Biggs was going to come to you, you recall that?"

"Yes sir. I said Teddy Biggs would come to me because I would make myself indispensable. I've done my best, won acceptance without question. But I'm not indispensable without the go-ahead."

"I believe I can get you that go-ahead," yawned Halladay. "If you can assure me that you will present the final phase of the operation to Mr. Big and none other."

Gilliam stated the obvious. "We don't have a case unless you can testify that Mr. Big himself said go."

"Understood. I'll present the plan to the boss man or die trying," I said and, except for the dying part, meant it.

"Come back in two hours," said Chester Halladay with a plump wave.

Wally was waiting in the corridor.

The Army warehoused their shell shock casualties in a Quonset hut with chicken wire on the windows. Bunks in back, a day room with chairs, two couches, a radio and a card table in front. Crile Hospital, Parma, ten miles south of downtown.

Special Agent Richard Schram was sitting on a folding chair, his jaw working, dried egg caked at the corners of his mouth, his watery blue eyes furrowed as if trying to make out a distant figure.

"Agent Schram, it's Wallace Hirdahl again. How're you getting along?"

Something flickered across Schram's face. Momentary recognition? Distaste?

"Hal Schroeder came along too," said Wally, nudging me forward. "To pay his respects."

Cripes, the man wasn't *dead*. I studied Schram to see if the insult had registered. It had not. The only sign that Richard

Schram was still himself was his right hand. It was knotting itself into a fist, relaxing, knotting itself, relaxing.

I squatted down in front of Schram's folding chair and wedged my hand into his knotting fist. This got me a series of staccato blinks and a wicked left jab that landed just below my cheekbone.

I coughed and blinked water from my eyes. I felt moisture on my cheek. I checked Schram's left hand. It bore a service ring with pinprick diamonds, dripping blood.

I pressed my face close. I took both of Schram's hands in mine.

"Screw 'em all Richard. It's not your fault. You did your job and you did it right. It's not your fault. Don't let the bastards win. It's not your fault. You did your job and you did it right. Screw 'em all Richard, *screw 'em all.*"

Schram reclaimed his right hand and angled his head as if considering what I'd said. I thought for a moment that I'd gotten through, thought that Richard Schram was about to stand up, shake himself and march out of this makeshift dungeon. But it wasn't Harold Schroeder that Richard Schram was listening to on that folding chair.

Wally took my place. He placed a box of cough drops in the breast pocket of Schram's flannel bathrobe. "They're Luden's," he said softly. "Honey licorice."

Schram continued knotting his right fist, flexing his ropy forearm. I checked my watch. It was time to go.

"Good Lord, Schroeder," said Chester Halladay when I returned from the hospital, "we're going to have to get you a cut man."

Richard Schram's name was still on the door the of the office of the Assistant Special Agent in Charge, but Agent Gilliam's size 46 suit jacket hung from the coat rack. Gilliam stood to the right with his arms folded. Halladay sat behind the desk.

"Who'd you mix it up with this time?"

"Agent Schram."

Halladay's smirk drained to his chin. "I've been meaning to pay him a visit. How's he doing?"

"Lousy."

"I'll see to it that he gets the best of care," said Chester Halladay, solemnly.

Then he dropped a thick courier's pouch on the desk with a satisfying *whump*. "We got the go-ahead. But Jimmy Streets shows up and operational orders are shoot to kill."

"Yes sir."

Halladay ticked his chin at Gilliam. Gilliam removed a file from the pouch, unfolded a schematic diagram and laid it out on the light board against the far wall.

My heart skipped a beat when I saw the name on the precisely drafted blueprint that included room dimensions, width, length *and* height, rate of climb of the staircase, noted the total number of steps - noted, hell, each step was individually numbered - and depicted each and every desk and cabinet in the payroll department. Each and every desk and cabinet in the payroll department of Cleveland's largest employer, Republic Steel.

I listened to Agent Gilliam's recitation of the precise maneuvers that would comprise the largest armed robbery in Cleveland history. Special Agent in Charge Chester Halladay sat back and showed all thirty-two in a triumphant grin. It hurt to smile so I just nodded. That hurt too.

The ancient elevator operator with the oversized Adam's apple didn't blink at my battered mug when he opened the car door on the 9th floor.

"Lobby please." He closed the outer door and the sliding gate and cranked the brass knob. "How's your day going?" I said, the thick courier pouch tucked under my arm.

The old man muttered something I couldn't make out over the brass oompah band that had taken up residence above my right temple. The elevator car slowed and settled at floor #5. The bell rang as the door opened. No one there. We descended.

"Well my day's going quite well," I said to the back of the old man's head. His cap was sweat-stained tobacco brown and his yellow-white hair curled over his celluloid collar like ivy. The old man spat in the spittoon, cranked the brass knob and bounced the car to a halt. He drew open the safety gate and turned to face me.

"You'd best go home," he said and opened the outer door.

The bell sounded and I walked off.

Chapter Twenty-three

I hopped the rattler west, transferred at Fulton and Detroit and rode south to Cesco. I got off and hoofed it. It must have been cold, the folks I passed were turtled into coats and sweaters. But I had my courier pouch to keep me warm. I would have thrown my coat over my shoulder and skipped down the sidewalk were it not for that ancient elevator operator, pointing his craggy finger at me like Banquo's ghost and croaking, 'You'd best go home.'

Home. Where was that exactly?

I marched up the front walk to H&R Manufacturing and thumped on the door. No answer. I thumped some more. No answer. All that thumping gave me a headache so I kicked the door instead. "Open up!"

Jimmy did so. He looked annoyed for some reason.

"The Schooler in his office?"

Jimmy eyeballed the thick leather courier pouch I had tucked under my arm. He knew what it was. I knew that he knew, and he knew that I knew that he knew. We left it that way.

I followed him down the corridor. The door to The Schooler's office was open. He was on the phone. He looked up at Jimmy's knock on the doorframe, saw me, saw the thick courier's pouch and said, "I'll call you back."

"I have something of interest," I said, taking my rightful place in the center of the room, Jimmy scowling behind my back.

"Close the door," said The Schooler to Jimmy. Unfortunately he left off the 'on your way out' part.

"I need to speak with you alone," I said.

"I don't have any secrets from Jimmy."

"You will in a minute."

The Schooler hiked his eyebrows at this impertinence. I waited patiently.

"Give us a few minutes," said The Schooler.

Long seconds passed before the door swung shut. The Schooler sat back and looked droll. "Is that what I think it is?"

"If you're thinking it's the worked-out-to-the-last-detail diagram of the biggest heist in Cleveland history, yes sir."

"Why isn't it on my desk?"

I'd spent my time on the rattler hacking away at the underbrush. The Schooler hadn't made me tailing him in the '39 Hudson. Even if he made the Hudson he never saw me.

And Jimmy hadn't come clean to The Schooler about ratting out me to the FBI and the expected arrest that never came. Not a chance. That would've required Jimmy to beg the forgiveness of his superior on bended knee.

So far as I could tell The Schooler counted me a loyal soldier. Which meant I could probably say what I was about to say and not get plugged. "It's not on your desk, sir, because I will only present this plan to Mr. Big himself."

The Schooler steepled his fingers. "The FBI told you to say that."

"Yes they did. And for once I agree with them."

"Why is that?"

"Because I'm about to make a score that will either make me rich or make me dead. I would like to make the acquaintance of the man in charge."

I didn't want to meet Mr. Big to assess his trustworthiness. I wanted to meet Mr. Big to *insure* his trustworthiness. As in, I trust you not to ace me out of my dib because I now know who you are and will hunt you down like a dog if you do. That's the kind of trust a man can sink his teeth into.

The Schooler crossed an ankle over a knee. "We'll have to blindfold you."

"I understand."

"And bind your hands behind your back."

"Of course."

"And tie you to the back bumper and drag you down the highway for fifty miles."

"Sure," I said, running a finger down the lurid ruin that was the right side of my face. "What else is new?"

The Schooler chuckled. *Heh heh heh. Heh heh heh.*

A tiny alarm bell sounded, barely tinkled, in the lower chambers of my skull. Something to do with The Schooler's easy laughter, with his caving in without a fight. But I paid that tiny bell no attention. I was about to make the acquaintance of the shadowy and mysterious Mr. Big!

Chapter Twenty-four

Jimmy did the honors. Blindfolding me, binding my hands, confiscating my Walther, tossing me in the back seat of the Packard as The Schooler climbed behind the wheel. We meandered for a while but the icy chill and high hum of the Detroit-Superior Bridge told me what I wanted to know. We were headed east.

We drove a long time. The road got quiet. Nobody spoke. We passed Pepper Pike and Hunting Valley and Gates Mills. Had to.

I thought about stuff. Like how to turn the heist plan to our advantage. That was the easy part. The hard part was how to convince the boss man to sideline Jimmy Streets.

We drove on. I was half asleep by the time the Packard finally came to a stop. Jimmy got out, unlocked a chain and swung open a rusty-hinged gate. The Schooler nosed the Packard across the threshold. The rusty-hinged gate swung closed. Jimmy climbed back in and the Packard crunched its way up a long gravel drive. We rounded a bend and stopped. A circular driveway maybe. The front doors opened, the driver and the passenger got out.

"Wait here," said Jimmy. What a card.

My arms and wrists ached and my head pounded. I got to thinking morbid thoughts. As in once I explained my idea about how to turn the plan what the hell did Mr. Big need me for? Why not instruct Jimmy to take Mr. Schroeder for a nice long walk in the woods?

Tough shit. There are risks in every operation. And I had made up my mind.

My thoughts were interrupted by scratching and sniffing at the back door. What new hell was this? I smelled a sharp feral odor. Did they have bears out here? I heard a deep hungry rumbling growl that made Hector the guard dog sound like a Pekinese. I had been making halfhearted attempts to free my hands from the electrical tape. I increased those efforts now.

The beast let loose with a four-octave howl that put Fats Navarro to shame. I pried my thumbs into the electrical tape and dug down for all I was worth. This was a beast all right, a goddamn wolf.

Someone came running. Down steps, across gravel. "Shut up Kingdog," grunted Jimmy.

The howling continued, followed by a yelp of pain and canine whimpering. This was a *pet*?

Jimmy jacked open the car door and hauled me to my feet. He unwound my black tape ligature and yanked off my blindfold. He regarded me with a smug leer. My hero.

"You ready to meet the big boy?" said Jimmy. Kingdog was chewing on something a few yards away, something Jimmy had tossed him.

"Sure." I picked up the courier pouch from the floor of the Packard and dusted it off. We crossed the gravel drive and climbed the steps of an imposing three story brown brick building that looked more like a city hall than a rustic hideaway.

Mr. Big, here I come.

Kingdog bounded through the foyer and skidded left to the parlor. We followed. The parlor was a high-ceilinged walnut-paneled room with a stone fireplace you could roast an ox in. A fire was burning. A man and a woman were seated on an overstuffed divan, facing the fire, their backs to us.

Kingdog trotted over and put his great head on his master's knee. The woman was smoking a long dark cigarette.

We crossed the room and stood in front of the medieval fireplace and faced the lord and lady of the manor. Lizabeth, in a silvery satin dressing gown that reflected the firelight. And

The Schooler, lounging comfortably in a burgundy smoking jacket and slippers, a wolf at his knee, a snifter of cognac in one hand and a cigar the size of a hog's leg in the other.

"G-man, meet Mr. Big."

Well dip me in cornmeal and fry me in butterfat. The Schooler was Mr. Big! "But..."

"It's a long story," said The Schooler to my face full of questions.

"Very well done, brilliant. You had me fooled, the feds too. I guess what I'm wondering is, you know, *why*."

The Schooler feathered an ash from his foot long Corona into a crystal ashtray. "The Jews and the Sicilians ran the show in Cleveland during Prohibition. The Ginzos tried to corner the bathtub gin market. They used a lot of muscle, got a lot of press coverage, got busted or got dead. The Hebes ran bonded booze from Canada, stayed in the background, kept a low profile and got rich. I'm not Jewish or Sicilian but I learned the lesson."

"But you're not in the background. The feds and the coppers know who you are."

"Do they?"

Point taken. "But what happened to Teddy Biggs?"

The Schooler took another puff, took another sip. "I'll tell you all about it someday."

"Brilliant," I said again. "Which brings me to this." I held up the courier pouch. "The supremely detailed plan for the robbery of the payroll department of Republic Steel, scheduled for Friday, December 21st."

I paused for a round of applause and hearty huzzahs.

I continued. "Only we'll go this Friday, the 14th. Now that we have the layout it should be a snap."

Still no hearty huzzahs. Not even a polite smile on The Schooler's impassive mug. "Jimmy has something he'd like to tell you."

I turned around to see Jimmy standing beside the fireplace, smacking a new pack of butts against his palm. He removed the cellophane string with his teeth, peeled back the foil just so, squeezed the pack and smacked it with a blunt forefinger. One cigarette popped up.

Jimmy lipped the pill and thumbed his lighter, his good eye never leaving mine. I wasn't going to like whatever he had to tell me.

"I had an expert, a currency expert, check out the cash haul from the last two heists," said Jimmy, cool as cool can be. "It's all counterfeit."

I whirled around to Mr. Big. He nodded in grim agreement. The yellow-eyed wolf studied me hungrily.

Chapter Twenty-five

Shit a brick! How was this possible?

I was supposed to have superior knowledge, I was supposed to call the shots this time.

I was *not* supposed to be standing before Mr. Big like an organ grinder's monkey, dancing to Yankee Doodle Dandy. You know your enemy's plans by the questions they ask. And don't ask. *This* was why the feds gave me such a free hand, why they didn't ask for the heist money back.

It figured the Fan Belt Inspectors would get it wrong, they didn't know jack about espionage. A double agent is a liability before he's an asset. You have to invest in him before he pays off. The feds never ponied up a nickel.

"I didn't know that money was counterfeit," I said. "Swear to God on a stack of bibles."

The Schooler was silent. Jimmy snorted behind my back. I didn't have to look to know he had his nickel-plated ready. I could have tried explaining that it made no sense for me to get beat up and shot at for a satchel full of worthless money. But in the eyes of The Schooler I was either a traitor or an idiot. And neither one did him any good.

Wait a minute...

"We can still do this heist. We can! We're going in a week early. Republic Steel won't be handing out dummy dough a week before the heist. We can still make off with a pile, six figures easy!"

The Schooler curled his lips and raised his eyebrows, a screaming tirade by his standards. "The FBI's use of counterfeit money seems to indicate a certain lack of trust in you and this enterprise."

I waited. Jimmy, Lizabeth and Kingdog the wolf waited. Were we doing the Socratic dialogue routine again? The Schooler finally filled in the blanks.

"The FBI might hedge their bets. They might be waiting at Republic Steel in case you decide to show up for work a week early."

The sanctimonious son of a bitch was probably right about that. The rule of thumb in undercover ops was to get underway ASAP. The less time secret plans have to get unsecret the better. Republic Steel paid their workers every Friday. There was no good reason for the twelve-day lag between plan and execution.

"When we first met I asked why I should trust you," said The Schooler.

"Yes sir."

The Schooler leaned back, crossed his ankles and sent several fat gray smoke rings toward the ceiling. He was good, the rings were round and solid as a plumber's grommet. Apparently I was expected to humiliate myself without the courtesy of a prompting question.

"I said," I said glumly, "'Don't trust me, trust the results.'"

Touché said the twinkle in The Schooler's eye. The greatest armed robbery in the history of Greater Cleveland was *kapoot*.

Was I down the drain with it? I could feel the barrel of Jimmy's nickel-plated sighting up and down my back. I addressed myself to Lizabeth, who was smoking her perfumed black cigarette down to a nub.

"Could you get me a couple aspirin before Jimmy plugs me in the back? I've got a roaring headache."

A bilious cloud of expectation gathered in the high-ceilinged room as Lizabeth dredged up a tin of Bayer's from her purse and popped the corner with her thumb. Blood pounded in my ears.

The Schooler let me twist for a long minute before he said, "The feds aren't the only ones with heist plans."

He smiled when he said it. I exhaled to my ankles. Lizabeth leaned over and held out her hand. Four aspirin, smart girl. I thanked her and chewed them up, waiting to hear what The Schooler had up his sleeve.

"You ever notice that crooks always wait till the money is divvied up before they steal it?"

"I don't follow."

"They rob banks, they rob armored cars, local businesses," said The Schooler, gesturing with his Corona Corona. "Why not grab it at the source?"

"What? You want to knock off the Philadelphia Mint?"

"Not quite," said The Schooler, eyes alight, smile suppressed. "I want to knock off the Cleveland Branch of the Federal Reserve."

Well, so much for keeping a low profile. "Uhh, I don't know a great deal about the Federal Reserve Bank but I'm guessing it's a fort."

"Of course," said Mr. Big, cheerily. "The vault is underground. It's constructed of four-inch drill-proof steel plate with dual time-delay locks. The bank is guarded by the Federal Reserve Police, a rotating spit and polish crew of ten, heavily armed. And the Cleveland PD comes running at the push of a panic button."

I nodded, waiting for the other shoe to drop.

"And those twenty foot Greek statues by the front entrance on Sixth Street? They're hollow, connected by tunnels to the bank interior."

"Uh huh," I said. Still no shoe.

"The bank gets a delivery on December 13th from the Federal Bureau of Engraving, an extra large delivery due to the liquidity demands of the holidays."

"And you plan to hijack that shipment?"

The Schooler shook his head. "Too public, too many loose ends."

"O-kay."

The Schooler took his time, puffed on his cigar, played the moment. I stood still on shaky legs and listened to my head pound and my stomach growl.

"The Federal Reserve Bank is required to count deposits by hand before they're placed in the vault. Approximately one million dollars will be in the counting room of the Federal Reserve Bank on the night of Thursday, December 13th. And it won't be counterfeit."

Jimmy and Lizabeth reacted with surprise to this big revelation. Me personally, I got tired of waiting for that damn shoe.

"And you'd need an armored battalion to bust in."

"Not so," said Mr. Big, "all I need is you."

"Me?"

"You're my key to the front door."

I snorted. "Sir the Federal Reserve Police don't know me from Adam."

"They're feds. They play pinochle with the FBI every Friday night at Rohr's. They know all about you."

I put that in my pipe and smoked it. Maybe the Federal Reserve Police do know all about me. Sir. But they don't care, no more than the FBI does. I'm just a castoff agent of the hated Oh So Secret. Nothing I could do or say would convince them to lower the drawbridge.

That was what I wanted to say. But I didn't have the energy. Those four aspirin were burning a hole in my gut and my knees got wobbly when the oompah band that had set up shop above my right temple struck up a German beer hall polka. Somebody caught me before I hit the floor.

Must've been Jimmy. My hero.

Chapter Twenty-six

I woke up on a narrow bed in a small spare room with a crucifix on the wall. Someone had stripped me down to boxer shorts and covered me with a sheet and blanket. Had to be Lizabeth. Jimmy would gouge out his good eye before he'd undress me and tuck me in.

I looked out the window. Pink dawn painted the frosted panes as icy winds rattled them. I took inventory. My brass band headache was down to a dull roar, I had feeling and movement in my extremities, I knew my name, rank and serial number. And I was hungry, so hungry my stomach was attempting to digest itself.

I sat up in bed, saw stars and lay back down. There had to be something to eat in this brown brick mausoleum. I took a couple deep breaths and tried again, slowly. That seemed to work so I winched my feet out of bed and set them on the floor. Bare floor, cold floor. It felt good. I took a breath and stood up.

Ha! Who says Hal Schroeder can't stand on his own two feet? I took a step for the doorway and froze as the door swung open.

Lizabeth, carrying a tray, backed into the room. I sniffed the air hopefully. Bacon? Eggs? Rye toast slathered in butter? Lizabeth turned to face me and I slunk back to bed. All I smelled was Unguentene.

Lizabeth had her jet black hair pulled back. She wore black toreador pants and an untucked man's white dress shirt with the sleeves rolled up and the top two buttons undone.

"I went to nursing school a hundred years ago," she said as she plopped a thermometer in my mush and swabbed my face with cotton balls soaked in isopropyl. She gently uncurled the crusty bandage on my severed ear and clucked her tongue.

I enjoyed these ministrations, don't get me wrong. No feverish GI in no improvised field hospital ever fantasized a more fetching nurse. But I was about to expire from malnutrition. I tried explaining this with a mouth full of thermometer. Lizabeth shushed me.

"Breakfast is on the stove," she said. "We were all out of bacon so I fried up a T-bone with onions. That okay?"

Jeannie, please forgive me but I love this woman.

There is something about early morning that pierces the veil. It's tough to look tough in a breakfast nook wallpapered with pink primroses, early morning sunshine glancing off the snowy backyard and splashing through the louvered windows. I leaned back in my chair, having polished off a T-bone steak, four eggs, three pieces of toast and a mountain of cottage fries.

The Schooler sat across the table from me, head down, picking at his breakfast. He looked old.

Jimmy padded in in stocking feet, unshaven, sleepy-eyed, squinting against the sunlight and the pink wallpaper. He looked hungover.

Lizabeth bustled in from the kitchen wearing a black and white checkered apron. "Everybody happy?"

I raised my hand. The Schooler grunted. Jimmy poured coffee into a blue and white speckled mug and left the room. I loosened my belt and pushed my chair away from the table. America's most unlikely homemaker slid me a sideways glance before she returned to the kitchen.

The Federal Reserve job was still two days away. The Schooler wasn't going to let me return home for a hot shower and a change of clothes. He looked up from his half-eaten breakfast and read my mind.

"Razor and toothbrush in the bathroom upstairs. Couple clean shirts in the closet."

I nodded and got up to go. Lizabeth returned from the kitchen carrying a roaster pan. More grub? She stood by the door to the back stairs. I opened it for her.

Kingdog the wolf came galloping through the snow. Lizabeth stood on the top step and dumped the contents of the pan, a raw five-pound capon suitable for Sunday dinner at Grandma's, into the snow. The wolf attacked it as if it were still alive.

I went upstairs to shower up, any thoughts of attempting to slip out the door and sneak down the drive banished from my mind.

"We'll give Hal a gun and send him up the front steps on 6th Street," said The Schooler to Jimmy and me couple hours later. We were sitting around a burled walnut dining table in a room with a matching sideboard. A small statue of the Virgin Mary looked down upon us from a corner cabinet and a crucifix hung from the back wall.

Odd. I hadn't figured The Schooler for a Holy Joe.

"Hal will ID himself through the intercom and insist on speaking to the Police Commander on duty. It's Frederick Seifert on Thursday nights. He's a twenty-year vet who thinks he's long overdue for a promotion. He'll jump at the chance."

"What chance?" grumbled Jimmy, still swilling java from that speckled blue and white mug. He was Turkish maybe. Turks were addicted to coffee.

Mr. Big ignored him. "Hal will tell Frederick Seifert, breathlessly, that the Fulton Road Mob is coming hard, in full force, that they sent him ahead to talk his way in and take Seifert hostage. At which time Commander Seifert will send his troops into the tunnels that run to the statues outside."

"Why?" said Jimmy.

"I'll get to that," said The Schooler. "Once the Federal Reserve police are dispersed Hal *will* put a gun to Seifert's back and march him downstairs to open the side delivery gate on Rockwell. At which time Jimmy and the boys will drive to the loading dock, gather up the cash from the counting room, wheel it to the waiting vehicle and take off."

Jimmy inhaled the dregs of his coffee and belched. He looked formidable again, head down, chin prowed out like a cowcatcher, his good eye searching the room like a locomotive's rotating head beam. "What I'm hard swallowing is this Seifert sending his boys to tunnels outside the bank. The place is a fort, why leave it?"

"Because Frederick Seifert is a lot like me. He's been waiting for this opportunity a long time."

Jimmy shook a Lucky from his pack and thumbed his lighter. "He in on this?"

The Schooler shook his head. "But if Seifert simply bars the door and calls the cops to come clean up the mess he has blown his big chance."

Jimmy sucked down half his cig in one drag and flicked the hanging ash into his cupped hand. "*What* chance?"

"His chance to be a hero."

"You got it all worked out," said Jimmy, jabbing at me with his burning pill. "'Cept you gotta send the G-man up those steps on 6th Street and trust he's not gonna sell us out."

I could have washed out my socks and underwear in the upstairs sink in the time it took The Schooler to say, "There are no rewards without risks Jimmy."

The Schooler took another pause. Jimmy filled his cupped hand with ash. I examined my fingernails in order to avoid making eye contact with Jesus and the Virgin Mary.

"I believe we can trust Mr. Schroeder," said The Schooler. "He told the truth. He didn't know the previous heist money was counterfeit. In fact he has a big chunk of it stashed in a safe deposit box at National City Bank."

What in the hell? I hadn't been tailed to National City Bank. I had made sure!

"Mr. Schroeder was duped by the FBI just as he was hung out to dry by the OSS. Two years of high-risk service without so much as a letter of commendation. Tsk tsk. I believe we can trust Mr. Schroeder because he feels the federal government owes him a large debt. And he needs our help to collect it."

Jimmy and The Schooler swiveled their mugs in my direction. I met their looks and then some. I was hacked off. That The Schooler's estimation of my particulars was dead nuts on only made me more so. They were waiting on my answer, my affirmation, my pledge of loyalty.

I let them.

Chapter Twenty-seven

The library was a snug room in the left front corner of the brown brick building, on the opposite side of the parlor. It had a bay window and ceiling-high bookcases crammed with leather bound volumes. And a crucifix. I had coaxed the pot bellied stove in the corner to life. It was late, I was dealing solitaire.

I had finally given in and pledged my fealty to The Schooler and his cockeyed plan. He seemed to buy it. Why not? What other choice did I have?

I slapped down card after card on the reading table, finding no joy. What other choice *did* I have? The way The Schooler laid it out made some sense, Frederick Seifert might take a chance for glory. Still, an awful lot of dominoes had to fall in precise order at the proper time. I scooped up my losing hand and reshuffled the deck.

I heard the clocking of soft heels on hardwood. I turned to see Lizabeth standing in the doorway. She wore a sheer, pale green chiffon nightgown over a satin sheath and high-heeled mules with feathers at the toe. She had her hair down.

"The old man's sawing logs," she said, languidly. "May I join you?"

"Sure."

Lizabeth pulled up a chair across the reading table. "There's another deck in that drawer," she said, indicating a round lamp table with a green felt top. I dug it out and handed it over. She side shuffled the deck in her hands. "You ready for some double solitaire?"

I tried to concentrate on the game as Lizabeth's filmy peignoir dissolved in the light from the table lamp. She buzzed through her deck in no time, kinged the aces and said, "Would you like a nightcap?"

What was I supposed to say to that? *No?*

She crossed to one of the ceiling-high bookcases and slid a panel of leather-bound book spines aside, revealing a liquor cabinet. "They took a vow of silence, not sobriety."

"Who's that?"

"The monks. This was a monastery not so long ago."

"Of course. I wondered about all the crucifixes."

Lizabeth handed me a snifter of brandy. "Henry won't let me take them down. He says it's bad luck." She raised her glass. "Here's how."

We clanked and drank. We reshuffled our decks and started over.

"So how does it feel to be a kept man?"

"It stinks. Royally"

"You get used to it. It gives you time."

"To do what?"

"To think, to speculate about things," said Lizabeth, raining cards down on the reading table. "And get really good at solitaire."

She was that. I tossed my deck on the table and raised my hands in surrender. Lizabeth reached down and produced one of her skinny black cigarettes. Did she keep them in her garter belt? I wondered this with a greater degree of curiosity than the question seemed to warrant.

"Got a light?"

I did not. But the way she said it made me wish I had. I searched the drawers of the lamp table, eyed the fading embers in the potbellied stove. "Allow me." I removed the perfumed cigarette from her fingers and returned with a lit cig and singed knuckles.

"Thank you kind sir," said Lizabeth, inhaling deeply, swelling her breasts.

It had grown cold in the room as the fire ebbed. Or so I surmised from the stiffening of Lizabeth's nipples against her satin undergarment. I felt quite warm myself. Lizabeth smiled through a shroud of perfumed smoke.

I took a slug of brandy. Enough of this foolishness. "Why is he doing this? The Schooler. Henry. Mr. Big. This crazy bank heist?"

Lizabeth sat back. "Crazy?"

"Seems that way to me."

Lizabeth flicked her ashes on the floor and crossed her legs. Didn't they have any ashtrays in this place?

"He's a very smart man, my Henry. I've never known him to do anything crazy."

"Crazy's the wrong word then. But it seems like a huge gamble for an old gent with a lot of money in the bank." I paused. Lizabeth smoked. "If he wants to call it quits why not just cash out and sail away?"

Lizabeth lowered her chin and regarded me through long eyelashes that glimmered at the tips. "And be remembered as Henry Voss, king of the vending machines? No, I was wrong when I said that old men only care about money. Henry cares about his reputation. He wants to go out in a blaze of glory."

If Lizabeth was attempting to reassure me about the Federal Reserve heist her words were poorly chosen. Going out in a blaze of glory was not on my to-do list.

Lizabeth leaned forward and clasped her hands on the table, her black cigarette wedged between her fingers. "Was I wrong about young men too?"

"You were wrong about this young man. I've had power. All I want now is a fat wallet and a villa in the South Seas."

"With JJ?"

"Of course."

The ashes from Lizabeth's upturned cigarette had dribbled down onto her alabaster fingers. I reached over and gently dusted them off. Lizabeth curled her index finger around mine.

"I hope that works out for you," she purred.

I willed my hand away from hers but it paid no attention. I heard a soft clunk from under the table and felt a warm foot on my ankle, creeping upwards. Sweat beaded on my upper lip.

"If it doesn't, you let me know." Her toes found my bare shin. "Will you do that?"

I didn't know what to say to that. I was having trouble concentrating. I do know that when Lizabeth got up to go I rose with her and walked her to the doorway. We stopped there.

The sexual tension of that moment could have lit up the Ohio Valley from Akron to Zanesville. I wanted to kiss her, I wanted to kiss her so bad you can't believe it. But I wanted something else even more, difficult as it was to rate anything above drowning myself in Lizabeth's deep lush slightly-trembling purple lips.

I slipped my arm around her waist, resting my hand on the soft saddle of her hip. She didn't pull away. When the blood hammering in my ears subsided to the point where I could hear myself think I said, "The Schooler knew where I deposited my end of the armored car heist, the satchel of money he gave me at Moreland Courts." I steeled myself and peered directly into those oversized aquamarine eyes. "How did he know that?"

Lizabeth didn't appear offended at this crude interjection of business. In fact she leaned in and planted a long sticky wet kiss that stiffened my spine and other places.

Then she clocked off in her high-heeled slippers, saying, over her shoulder, "Who called the taxi?"

Chapter Twenty-eight

I returned to the reading table and shuffled up a deck. Seven up, twenty-one down. I was going to win a hand if I had to stay here all night. Lizabeth had left her cigarette butt on the table, standing upright on its filter tip. I got up and tossed it in the potbellied stove.

There. That was better.

I sat back down. I knew what her parting 'Who called the taxi' meant of course. The Schooler didn't need to have me tailed. All he had to do was call a hackie who was on the pad.

Smart, Schroeder, well done and executed. I slapped a black two on a red three, a red eight on a black nine. I turned over an ace. About time.

The question was why The Schooler cared. My trip to National City Bank told him something important. I cast my mind back to the Moreland Courts. Something hadn't fit. I remembered my excitement, the fat pigskin satchel. And momentary suspicion. The Schooler keeping a big bag of hot snaps on the premises. Why risk it?

There was only one logical explanation. He wouldn't. He *knew*, the son of a bitch knew from day one!

A sharp guy like The Schooler wouldn't have trusted the FBI. He would have had the money from my Society for Savings job checked out right away. He let Jimmy make the announcement, let him have his little moment of triumph, but Henry Voss knew from the get-go that the cash was worthless. He used his paid-for hackie to find out if I was in on the joke. Needless to say, I was not.

So why put Jimmy and the troops at risk in the armored car heist if The Schooler knew it was all funny money from day one?

I slammed my cards down on the reading table, cursed and drained my brandy. I knew why.

All I need is you.

The Schooler had been plotting his grand exit for a long time. When I walked in the tumblers clicked. He approved the armored car heist so that I would maintain my bona fides with the FBI. When I demanded Jimmy's ouster The Schooler refused out of loyalty. That and he needed the big thug to lead the assault on the Federal Reserve Bank. When his on-the-pad hackie called to say that I had deposited my satchel of bogus bucks at National City Bank, Henry Voss knew he had his patsy.

Yours truly.

I got up and warmed my hands at the potbellied stove. I poked at the embers. There wasn't any more wood in the tinderbox so I gathered up my losing hand and tossed it in. The cards smoked and smoldered, then crackled to life in a burst of waxen flame. I soaked up the quicksilver heat and tried to wedge the final piece of the jigsaw puzzle into place. Why did The Schooler wait for Jimmy to tell me about the counterfeit cash?

Jimmy would be an unhappy chappy to know that he had faced the muzzle of an FBI Tommygun just to put the G-man in solid with his superiors. The Schooler must have dropped hints to insure Jimmy made the discovery on his own, *after* the armored car job. Counting up the take maybe, saying, 'I sure hope this is coin of the realm.'

Henry Voss wanted Jimmy Streets to take credit for discovering the phony dough so that Harold Schroeder wouldn't suspect what Harold Schroeder now knew. *Both* The Schooler and the FBI had played him like a drum.

I hunted up that sliding panel in the bookcase. The monks had a sense of humor. The liquor cabinet was concealed behind the collected works of Ludwig Wittgenstein. I poured myself another stiff brandy, tossed more playing cards into the potbellied stove and sat down at the reading table.

Jimmy had been making nice in recent days. I didn't understand why but could be it was simple. The Schooler treated him like a brainless, if loyal, mutt. Maybe Jimmy wanted most what he couldn't get - respect for his smarts.

Had Jimmy staged that silly rescue outside the Theatrical and squired Jeannie and me around town simply to win respect for his wit and guile? If so Jimmy had, in his mind, succeeded. Jimmy didn't know I knew about the staged rescue. And he trumped me with the counterfeit money reveal. In Jimmy's mind he had nothing left to prove to me. He had a lot left to prove to The Schooler.

This was good stuff but I needed something more. That the boss man knew about the funny money in advance didn't figure to be enough.

I sipped brandy. I cogitated till my brain did back flips and my head grew so heavy that my elbows slid sideways and my chin came to a rest on the reading table. I was about to drift off when it snapped my eyes wide open.

A logical inconsistency in The Schooler's plan to rob the Federal Reserve. A logical inconsistency that Jimmy would find interesting.

I checked my watch. It wasn't there. I looked out the window. It was black as pitch. I knew that The Schooler and Lizabeth were lights out and that Jimmy was probably chain-smoking in front of the cavernous fireplace while feeding live baby chicks to Kingdog the wolf. I got up to go see.

Chapter Twenty-nine

Jimmy was sprawled on the couch in the parlor. Kingdog was curled up on a hook rug at his feet. A fire was burning in the fireplace. I should've called Norman Rockwell maybe. Kingdog opened one sinister yellow eye as I approached, Jimmy turned. I gestured with my snifter.

"Want some brandy?"

Jimmy shook his head. He looked groggy, drunk or half-asleep. I parked my carcass in an upholstered chair and nodded at Kingdog.

"He's a wolf, right?" Jimmy didn't dignify this icebreaker with a reply so I tried another. "You think this hare-brained scheme has a holy chance in hell?" Jimmy grunted. "It could work, I'm not saying it couldn't. But I'm a natural born worrier."

I wrung my hands for emphasis. Jimmy's contempt was palpable. A gust of wind shoved smoke down the chimney.

"I didn't know that money was counterfeit Jimmy, I swear. But I'm beginning to wonder if The Schooler knew it all along."

Jimmy blinked his good eye awake at this. He muttered something I took for 'how you figure?'

"I'm not sure. It's just that The Schooler went to some trouble to find out where I stashed my cut from the armored car job. I can't for the life of me think why he would do that. Can you?"

Jimmy sat up straight. He knew he'd been tossed a live grenade.

I made myself comfortable and waited for him to think it through. I pulled up my socks. I took a slug of brandy, trimmed my cuticles and recited the capitols of the forty-eight states.

"He wanted to find out if you knew the jack was no good."

I nodded. "Yeah, makes sense. But you hadn't told him about the counterfeit cash back then, had you?"

Jimmy's clenched jaw answered that question.

"Seems to me like old Henry had a good laugh at our expense, sending us off to rob an armored car full of funny money."

"Who gives a shit? The score he's got lined up'll make us all fat."

"If it works. The bigger question is do we want to trust our payday to a guy who's danced us around the stage like marionettes."

I mimed a puppeteer pulling strings off Jimmy's blank look. He thumbed his lighter.

"Henry's always been square with me. 'Sides, what's he gonna do?" he said, lit cigarette flapping up and down in his mush. "He's one guy."

"One guy with a million bucks in newly-minted cash."

"So what?"

"I'm just wondering why The Schooler wants traceable bills."

I kept him guessing as I nipped at my brandy for a quick minute, then cleared my throat for the big announcement. "The Federal Reserve does more than just distribute new currency to commercial banks. They also collect deposits from those banks - truckloads of used bills, old bills, *spendable* bills."

Jimmy skipped over surprise and fury and went right to grim resignation. "He'll have some mob juice dealer lined up."

"Could be. And the juice dealer will bring friends."

Jimmy's good eye narrowed, his glass eye did not. How did he keep it clean, I wondered. The eyelid never blinked.

"Could be," said Jimmy with some sarcasm. "Now how 'bout you cut the bullcrap and say your piece."

"I'd be happy to."

I explained my objection to The Schooler's plan, how my ugly mug wouldn't be enough to convince the Federal Reserve Police Commander to open the castle gates. If Frederick Seifert knew all about me as The Schooler claimed, then Frederick Seifert also knew the value the FBI placed on my services. As evidenced by my collection of bank bags full of confetti.

"But if I could walk up those steps on 6th Street with a valuable asset in hand, something that would get Frederick Seifert thinking that his time had come...Well then."

"Spit it out already," barked Jimmy. "You're bad as the old man."

I flagged my palms in a peaceable gesture and paused to make sure his outburst hadn't stirred any activity. No upstairs floorboards creaked.

"I want a real gun Jimmy, with bullets and everything. I imagine The Schooler plans to give me a dummy."

I paused. Kingdog yawned. I continued.

"I'll use my real gun to get the drop on The Schooler and march him up the steps and tell Frederick Seifert that I have intercepted a Fulton Road Mob plan to rob the bank and that I have captured the mastermind of that plan, the elusive Mr. Big that his pals at the FBI have been hunting all these years. I believe this approach stands a greater chance of prying open the front door. Don't you?"

Jimmy didn't answer in the affirmative. But neither did he spit in my eye.

"I surrender Henry to the Federal Reserve Police and tell Commander Seifert the rest of the mob is due any second, that the plan was for me to talk my way in, put a gun to his back and force him to lower the drawbridge. I'll suggest he play along, send his troops out those tunnels, *allow* me to put a gun to his back, *open* that front door and *stand* there in plain sight so that the Fulton Road boys will sweep up the front steps only to see the bulletproof doors slam shut and ten members of the Federal Reserve Police pour out of those big statues and round them up from behind, thereby securing Frederick Seifert a place in the pantheon of law enforcement alongside Elliot Ness and J. Edgar Hoover."

Jimmy was listening hard now, trying to keep up. I took a slug of brandy and kept on.

"That's the beauty part, I don't have to get the drop on Seifert. I already *have* my gun in his back and his troops out the door when I let him in on the joke and march him down to the side delivery gate on Rockwell. He opens the gate, you and the boys storm in, we rob the bank."

Jimmy folded thick arms across his chest. "And if it works we've got a million in hot cash and no way to move it."

"You're a smart guy, you'll think of something. Me, I'm taking my dib overseas. The dollar's king, someone'll cash me out."

I watched and waited. I had mentioned my dib. If Jimmy was on board he would ask about percentages. He took his time, muttered something I couldn't make out. I asked him to repeat it. He turned to face me.

"And why would the G-man trust Jimmy Streets?"

I shrugged. "You saved my life."

Jimmy gnawed this comment to the bone. Did he know I knew about the staged rescue? I kept my face straight and my yap shut.

"You'll get your gun before we go," he said after a time. "And we split three ways."

"Who's the third party?"

"The seven gunsels I'm bringing wit' me."

"That's quite a generous offer to the little shavers. But I guess we both have an interest in keeping them happy."

Jimmy bristled. "They'll do as they're told."

"If you say so Jimmy."

"I say so."

I let my breath out nice and slow. I almost felt sorry for the poor dumb Italian Turkish octoroon. He was my puppy now.

"Done."

Jimmy nodded and stumbled up the stairs to bed. Kingdog roused himself and trotted after him. I nibbled brandy and felt quite pleased with myself. Using false gratitude for Jimmy's fake rescue was especially brilliant, if I do say so.

I waited half an hour for deep sleep to settle in upstairs. Then I got up and slipped out the front door. The glacial air slapped me full across the face. I walked down the gravel drive and turned to look. I thought I'd glimmed it when I first arrived but I wanted to make sure.

Yep. A single line drooped down from a telephone pole to the third floor of the brown brick monastery. The Schooler's office. A telephone kept under lock and key. Could I chance it now? Sneak up the stairs and jimmy the lock?

Nah. The humans might sleep through it but Kingdog would be on me in a lick. I would have to bide my time, wait for the right moment. I had an important phone call to make.

Chapter Thirty

I slept late the next morning, best I could tell. I had searched the room for my wristwatch, couldn't find it. What good's a man without a wristwatch?

I kicked off the covers and stretched out my spine, half hoping Nurse Lizabeth would barge in with her tray of ointments. I felt fit as a fiddle but I wasn't above mewling and moaning to garner some female solicitude. The door stayed shut. I heard muffled voices from downstairs.

What a group. Lizabeth was trolling for a new Sugar Daddy, Jimmy had agreed to sell out The Schooler and Mr. Big was in no position to squawk, having initiated the back-stabbing festivities his own damn self. Trust? Loyalty? That and a nickel will get you a cup of joe and two refills at Lulu's Place. Three if you ask nice.

I got up and quick footed across the cold floor to the bathroom, took a shower, shaved and brushed my teeth. My face had healed up some. The cut from Schram was scabbed over and my assorted purple bruises had faded to an ugly yellow-orange. My hair had grown shaggy. I was one tough-looking s.o.b.

I grabbed my socks and boxers off the radiator and slipped them on, enjoying the steamy warmth. Soon, Schroeder, very soon you'll roll out of bed and don a bathing suit and be dressed for the day. Wear one of those Hawaiian shirts to dinner maybe. Or not.

I pulled on pants and shoes and selected a flannel lumberjack shirt from the clothes closet. A Schooler hand-me-down, the sleeves stopped halfway down my forearms. I rolled them up to my elbows and clomped down the stairs, eager to see America's most unlikely homemaker and chow down on a heaping plate of steak, eggs and country fried potatoes smothered in catsup. A wafting aroma quickened my step.

The breakfast room was empty. I poked my nose into the kitchen, I looked in the parlor. Nobody home.

I crossed the entryway and entered the dining room. Jimmy and The Schooler were bent to their plates. The Schooler at the head of the table, Jimmy at the foot. They were flanked by Ricky and Pencil Mustache and five other itchy young men.

"Any chow left?" I said

"Sorry Hal," said The Schooler. "The early bird gets the grub." The young men thought this just about the funniest joke ever.

"Guess I'll go raid the fridge," I said and ankled off. I found an ice pick in a drawer. I ran up the stairs and stopped on the second floor landing, listened for trailing footsteps, then took the third floor stairs two at a time. One of the steps groaned when I put my weight on it. I took the remaining steps gingerly.

The third floor smelled moldy, unused. I followed dusty footprints to a stout door secured with a deadbolt and padlock.

I gave it a go with my ice pick but I'm a deuce with padlocks. There was no way into this room save for a crowbar or a battering ram. Or a key. I took one more stab at the padlock.

It was then I noticed that someone had made a mistake. They'd put an interior deadbolt plate - with easily accessible screw heads - where they should have put an exterior deadbolt plate - with the screw heads covered or removed. All I needed to make my phone call was a screwdriver.

I descended the stairs, marched to the dining room and leaned in. One chair was empty.

"I got time to strop my gums?" I asked.

"Joe's in the can," said one of the punks. "You got all the time in the world."

Laughs around the table. I turned tail and returned to the kitchen. I rifled every drawer and searched every cabinet. Some kitchen, all it had was cooking implements. I grabbed a butter knife, scraped the blunt tip around the inside of a greasy skillet and raced up the stairs. I paused half a breath on the second floor landing, listened, climbed some more, avoided the groaning step and made for the stout wooden door.

I swabbed Crisco below the screw heads and worked it in like a mason with a trowel. I wiped the grease off the knife and plied the tip of the blade. It spun out. I wiped the blade tip on my flannel shirt and tried again. The screw head didn't budge.

I had endured privation, indignity, assault and betrayal in my quest for freedom. No %#?&!% flathead screw was going to stop me now. I torqued the blade till my shoulder burned.

The flathead screw budged. The next three gave up without a fight.

I pocketed the screws, uncoupled the deadbolt plate from the door and entered The Schooler's private office. It held a roll top desk, a fold-up cot and three file cabinets. The telephone was sitting on a small table next to the desk. I removed the slip of paper from my wallet and bent to dial numbers that weren't there. No dial plate. I would have to tippy tap the cradle and hope dear old Edna the operator hadn't wandered off to feed her cat.

I did. She hadn't.

"Number please," said the clipped female voice. I gave it to her. "One mo-ment."

I kept the receiver pressed to my good ear and hoped to hell that Joe was taking his sweet time in the necessary room this morning. I heard raucous laughter from downstairs. A woman came on the line. She sounded just like Mrs. Brennan.

"Is Ambrose there?"

"And who wants to know?"

"Harold Schroeder, ma'am. It's important."

She set down the receiver with a *thunk*.

I was two screws away from having the deadbolt plate back in place when I heard the warped step groan. Whoever was coming to investigate was only half a staircase away. It had to be poor dumb cunning Jimmy stumping up those stairs, wondering where the G-man had got to. I pocketed the screws and tried the door across the hall. Locked. There was another door at the end of the hall but no time to get there. Jimmy was steps away.

I strode down the corridor to greet him, my mind racing. 'Hey Jimmy, I was just'…what? He would notice that unscrewed deadbolt plate and bust me flat. He'd know what I was after in that locked room and check with Edna the operator to find out who. I listened to his final steps on the stairs.

I was dead meat.

I squared my shoulders and approached the dark-haired figure who turned to face me. A dark-haired figure wearing a scoop-necked sweater and a flared skirt.

"Get down there, they're looking for you," hissed Lizabeth. She started back down, calling, "He's not up here!"

Whew.

I replaced the screws in the deadbolt plate and crept down the stairs to the second floor landing. I heard voices in the breakfast room. I couldn't descend that last flight, they would have searched the second floor. I ducked down the hall and into my room.

I grabbed my coat from the closet, crossed to the window, opened it and looked down. A snow-covered hedge twelve feet below. That would hurt. But three feet of snow had drifted against the hedge. It would have to do.

I scooted out onto the sill and closed the window behind me. I crouched down, set my feet on the narrow sill and broad jumped over the hedge and onto the snow bank.

I rotated my ankles, felt for brambles in my keester. A miracle had occurred. I was unscathed.

I shuffled through the drifting snow, keeping an eye out for hungry wolves. I turned the corner to the back of the building. The coast was clear. Now all I had to do was think of some plausible explanation for wandering around in a foot of snow in my street shoes. I slogged to the back door, opened it and entered the breakfast room.

"Where the hell you been?" snapped Jimmy from the parlor. He and two of the young punks were piling into coats and hats. Jimmy had his sawed-off in hand.

"Outside," I said, stamping snow off my shoes.

"Doin' what?" demanded Jimmy, stepping my way.

I summoned my best dopey grin and shrugged. "Communing with nature."

The punks chortled and elbowed each other's ribs. Jimmy's cheeks reddened but what could he say? Whatever I'd been up to I had gotten away with.

Chapter Thirty-one

We were huddled in the library after dinner, Jimmy and me. The potbellied stove was unlit. We could see our breath as we talked.

"You bring the boys up to speed on the new plan?" I said because I knew I should.

"I will when the time comes."

"You got an escape route worked out?"

Jimmy nodded. He nodded and smoked and smoked and nodded. "Who'd you call on the telephone?"

I cleared my throat and tried to think. There was no point denying it, Jimmy had doped it out somehow, followed the one way tracks from above my room to the back door maybe. Shoddy tradecraft on my part. But he didn't know who I'd called. Jimmy wasn't a guy who asked a question unless he had to. I had one shot at this.

"I called Jeannie. You were right about me and her."

Jimmy tilted his head to the right and examined me from an angle.

"I didn't spill anything," I said, looking away, looking down. "Just told her I was coming into some money and I, you know, wanted her to run away with me. I wasn't sure I'd get another chance to call."

I looked up to see how this was going over. Hard as a peeled egg Jimmy Streets held his cigarette two inches from his mouth, waiting on Jeannie's answer to my heartfelt plea. Everybody's a sucker for romance.

"She shot me down," I said, shaking my head sorrowfully. "She's a devoted wife all of a sudden!"

Jimmy nodded and slapped me on the shoulder so hard my teeth hurt. "Broads."

"Yeah, broads."

I stood up and stretched. "You got that gun handy?"

"When the time comes."

I grunted and ankled off. Jimmy wasn't going to make this easy. I went to the kitchen and collected what I needed.

I was jumpy as a hamster when I closed the door to my room. Something was eating me, gnawing at the foundations. I sat on the bed and kicked off my shoes. I got up and paced the room in my stocking feet. The brass band above my right temple started playing, soft but quick.

This better not be an attack of conscience, Schroeder. This better not be an attack of conscience brought on by religious statuary. Not now. You're not an altar boy anymore. You were given a rare gift at a tender age. You were dropped from an airplane into the real world and got to see its inner workings close up. Bloody death and spectacular destruction, celebrated as victory.

Money, Schroeder. Money equals power equals control equals freedom. Go and get your money and leave the rest for later.

This little pep talk calmed me not a whit. I left a trail of garments behind me on my way to a scalding hot shower.

My scattered clothes were missing when I emerged from the shower ten minutes later, my spirits lifted, my insides untangled, a towel wrapped around my waist. Check that. My clothes sat neatly folded on the foot of the bed.

I was glad for the towel. Lizabeth was perched on the side of the bed in her chiffon nightgown.

I was pleased to see her, don't get me wrong. What red-blooded American male wouldn't be pleased to see Lizabeth sitting on their bed in a filmy peignoir, a tray of ointments resting on her lap, Clara Barton meets Lana Turner. But the house was crawling with heavily armed men who might disapprove.

I approached warily. My bed had been tucked and folded into a bounce-a-nickel-off-the covers bunk. Lizabeth dangled my wristwatch from her fingers.

"This yours?"

"Yes," I said, moving closer. "Where'd you find it?"

"Underneath your bed."

"Oh."

I should've looked there maybe. I accepted the dangled watch and hooked it to my wrist. It was 10:26 p.m. Less than 24 to H-Hour. Lizabeth patted the bed. I jumped up and adjusted my towel. Lizabeth set to work on me, stem to stern.

"What happened here?" she said, applying Unguentene to my scabbed over ankles.

"Birdshot," I said.

"Where from?"

"Jimmy's sawed-off."

"He's a wrong number, that one," said Lizabeth. "Scoot over."

I did as I was told. Lizabeth unpeeled the tightly-wrapped bed covers. "Climb in," she said. I did that too. "Give me your towel."

I unwrapped myself under the blanket. Lizabeth folded the towel precisely, absent-mindedly. I shivered on the cold sheets in my nakedness. What was this about?

"Henry won't let me anywhere near him," she said and sat down next to me atop the covers. "Tomorrow's the biggest day of his life and he won't let me near him."

"That's a shame."

Lizabeth kicked off her mules and stretched out. Her toenail polish was dark red.

"I've been thinking about what you said. About this bank job being 'crazy.' I've been having the most awful dreams."

Lizabeth parted her nightgown and reached into her garter belt. "Got a light?" she said, waving a perfumed cigarette.

I wrenched my gaze from her silken thighs to her sea green eyeballs. "Just press it to my forehead."

Lizabeth laughed and rolled over and pulled the covers down to my waist and wrapped me up in a steaming hug. I felt myself responding, felt my hands creeping up to bury themselves in that perfect flesh. My conscience ran up and down empty corridors, looking for an exit from this four alarm fire, screaming, *This is wrong! This is dangerous!*

My hands didn't listen. They were under her nightgown now, coursing up the back of her acutely lithesome legs, past the tender indent of her knees, sweeping upward toward sweet disaster.

Lizabeth's tears doused the blaze in short order. There weren't many against my shoulder, just enough. My hands moved from her thighs to her shoulders. She shook a while. I held her. She shook a while longer.

"It's okay," I said, whispered. "Everything will work out fine."

Lizabeth removed her face from my shoulder. Her runny mascara made her look like an extremely fetching raccoon.

"Will it?" she said. "How do you know?"

"I don't. I just said it because that's what you're supposed to say when you reassure someone."

Lizabeth studied me through half-shuttered lamps. "Then it's not very reassuring, is it?"

We laughed and held each other some more. Tentatively, somewhere between comfort and passion. It had grown quiet downstairs. What was this about?

I held on till my arms numbed. Lizabeth disengaged first, rolling over, head propped on her hand, her blue-veined breasts swelling above the opaque sheath. She ran her finger down the side of my neck and along the ridge of my collarbone.

"I've decided that I like my life the way it is. And you've dodged enough bullets for one lifetime." She leaned over and planted a soft kiss on my bandaged ear. "Will you tell Henry that this Federal Reserve job is too risky, too dangerous?"

Lizabeth's alabaster hand slid down my chest and kept going. "Will you do that for me, Hal?" she breathed.

I snagged her hand by the wrist and sat up.

"Not a chance."

Lizabeth yanked her hand away and strode from the room without a word. I shut the light, put my head down and fell asleep.

Chapter Thirty-two

I woke up a couple hours later, checked my watch and went back to sleep.

When I opened my eyes again it was 2:42 a.m. I got up, opened the door and listened hard. Not a creature was stirring.

I threw on my clothes and stripped the bed, knotting the sheets together. I grabbed two more sheets from the closet and knotted them to the train. This was doing things the hard way but I couldn't risk creeping down the stairs with Kingdog lurking.

I walked the bed frame to the window, tied the train of sheets to a bed leg, opened the window and tested the length of my lanyard. Couple feet short. My flannel shirt was too old and frayed. My blanket was too thick to knot, ditto the bath towels. I looked around, I looked down. My wool trousers were stout as canvas but how to link them to the chain?

Heh heh heh.

I stepped out of my pants and threaded the tip of the bed sheet through the fly and zippered it up snug and tight. I tugged, it held. I opened the window, lowered this raggedy lanyard to the ground and climbed down.

You have not truly experienced cold until you have climbed down the side of a building in northeast Ohio on a wind-whipped night in mid-December in your underwear.

I scissor kicked the side of the building to propel myself over the hedges and dropped to the ground with a crunch. The late night freeze had crusted the snowdrifts with ice. I was so cold I was almost warm.

I removed my sophisticated saboteur's kit from the pockets of my hanging trousers and slogged to the front of the building, my legs on fire. A black panel truck sat parked in the circular drive next to the Packard. I unscrewed the gas cap, inserted the funnel I had filched from the kitchen and poured in the bag of sugar.

I had considered more surefire methods - removing the distributor rotor, cutting plug wires - but the old sugar-in-the-gas-tank wheeze had the advantage of stealth. The truck would start right up the next day, drive a few miles down the lonely country road and sputter out and die.

I emptied every last crystal into the tank, replaced the cap and mushed my way back to the raggedy lanyard hanging from my bedroom window. I had gotten good at the hand over hand rope climb at spy school. Two long years ago. Of course I could put my feet out and walk myself up the side of the building, but where's the sport in that?

I rubbed feeling into my palms and started to climb, Jack Frost nipping at my posterior. I cheated by wrapping my legs around the bed sheets but I managed to haul my carcass up the lanyard and into the window.

I lay there, beached on the window sill - front half in, back half out - and tried to catch my breath. My frozen back half felt warmer than my thawing front half. How did that make any sense? I squirmed inside and closed the window.

I dried off in the bathroom, ran hot water over my hands and face, relocated and remade the bed, mummified myself in sheets and a blanket and shivered myself to sleep.

Chapter Thirty-three

D-day dawned bright and sunny. Melting ice carved channels in the frosty windowpane, the radiator clanked with heat and I stretched out, luxuriating in the warmth, anticipating a long hot shower in my private bath. Came a knock at the door.

"Wake the fuck up."

Jimmy, who else? I got up and splashed water on my face, tapped a kidney and threw on some clothes. I reported to the dining room. Nine pair of eyeballs turned my way.

"The prodigal son returns," said The Schooler.

I apologized for my tardiness and backed into a corner.

"Let's review again," said The Schooler to grumbles and hooded stares at yours truly. I didn't much care. Unbeknownst to themselves the seven punks had been written out of the script.

But Jimmy was still key. I tried to make eye contact with him but he kept his head down. I leaned back against the wall and listened to The Schooler precisely detail a million dollar bank heist plan that would not take place.

The day dragged on endlessly after that. I returned to my room and took a shower. I went to the kitchen and made myself breakfast - liverwurst and onion on pumpernickel, creamed herring on the side. I trailed after Jimmy like a dog, hoping to snag him for a one to one. No joy. He'd had a change of heart, or simply enjoyed torturing me.

And what had Lizabeth been up to since I shot her down? Using her velvet hammer to beat dear old Henry into submission? If so it hadn't worked. And Lizabeth wouldn't be lowdown enough to turn to Jimmy.

Would she?

The day dragged on.

And then, suddenly, it was H-hour. The plan called for The Schooler and me to motor off in the Packard. Jimmy and the boys would follow a few minutes later in the panel truck. We would take different routes. I had been prepped on what and what not to do and when and when not to do it. The only thing I was lacking as I shrugged into my vicuna topcoat in the foyer was the promised gat.

Jimmy was standing ten feet away in the parlor, flanked by the troops. Kingdog the wolf was yipping and yapping, sensing the coiled tension in the room. The Schooler told us to synchronize our watches to 5:08 p.m. He repeated the time line.

The Packard would be parked on E. 4th Street at Superior by 6:40. Jimmy would drive by on Superior by 6:50. The Schooler and I would then walk down the block to E. 6th and climb the front steps of the Federal Reserve Bank at precisely seven p.m. Jimmy would park the panel truck across from the side delivery gate on Rockwell fifteen minutes later.

Lizabeth swept in just about then, dressed in a high-neck navy blue dress with white buttons down the front. The kind you might wear to a high school graduation. Or a funeral. She wished Henry good luck and embraced him tearfully. Then she turned around and took both my hands and lamped me with those sea green orbs. The room got quiet. My palms got moist.

"I hope that we will meet again," is what she said before she kissed me lightly on the cheek. She was gone before I found my tongue.

Was this the Judas kiss? I unhinged my neck and looked at The Schooler. His face betrayed no more emotion than a wall clock. He inclined his head, time to go.

I eyeballed Jimmy, I hiked my eyebrows. He smirked.

My brain boiled with anger and frustration as I followed The Schooler out the door.

Goddamn dumb cunning Jimmy Streets had turned the tables! I had wasted my time sabotaging the panel truck. Jimmy and the boys would not be coming. Jimmy and Lizabeth had conspired to send us off on a doomed mission so that Jimmy could take control of the Fulton Road Mob and Lizabeth could resume her life of leisure and...

It was somewhere around there I felt it. The heavy clunk against my leg as we descended the front steps. I reached into the pocket of my topcoat to be sure. My fingers curled around a gun butt.

The Schooler told me to get behind the wheel of the Packard. He climbed in on the passenger's side and handed me the keys.

Henry didn't trust me. He didn't pull a pearl-handled revolver or anything, just sat angled against the car door, his right hand in the pocket of his topcoat. He was a sharp guy, The Schooler. I fired up the land yacht and wheeled it down the driveway of the brown brick monastery.

We headed west on Mayfield Road, the sunken sun firing red-orange flares on the horizon. We drove through farm country, acres of plowed fields, scalloped like the sea, snow settled in the furrows. A sign said, Chester Township, Geauga County.

The plowed fields went away after we crossed County Line Road. Everything went away. The farm houses, the Sunoco stations, the feed stores, the roadside diners. I saw nothing but great stone posts bracketing long driveways and miles and miles of three-railed horse fences. We passed a discreet sign I had to squint to read.

Welcome to Gates Mills, bird sanctuary.

Rich old birds by the look of things. The Schooler told me to bear left on Old Mill Road. The terrain got hilly and thick with trees. I didn't see an old mill anywhere but we did pass the Chagrin Valley Hunt Club, the hanging sign said as much. The hand-lettered plank below it was redundant.

Private.

We drove on. The Schooler had cooked up a clever getaway scheme. After we'd all boarded the panel truck the driver would wheel it three blocks to an alley off E. 2nd where he would roll up a ramp and into the back of a tarp-covered freight truck that would rumble off, destination unknown.

I took Gates Mills Boulevard southwest to Shaker Boulevard west. Shaker then shaded north to Woodland which proceeded due west till it turned northwest until it became E. 4th which, with an occasional detour, headed due north to downtown.

I needed to get there ahead of schedule so I put the Packard through its paces, passing on the right and crossing on the amber. The Schooler told me to take it easy. I slowed down some and fought my way west, checking my wristwatch every five minutes. If I ever met so much as a third generation descendant of the drunken madman who laid out the Cleveland street grid I would punch him square in the nose.

I got us there. E. 4th and Superior, across the street from the Public Library, down the block from Higbee's and Public Square. I hunted a parking place, and almost flattened a lady jaywalking with a jagged tower of Christmas packages.

"Easy, *easy*," said The Schooler.

I found a spot and curbed the car. I checked my watch. 6:28 p.m. The panel truck was due by 6:50.

We waited. We watched the bustling crowd of holiday shoppers, smiling and rosy-cheeked. The Schooler still had his right hand in his coat pocket. My preference was for that hand to be elsewhere. We waited some more.

A squadrol flashed by on Superior, siren screaming. The Schooler jerked his hand from his pocket as he pressed forward against the dash. The time was now.

"You said something about a gun." No response, Mr. Big was preoccupied. Not a problem. I would soon have his undivided attention. "The gun?"

The Schooler, craning his neck to follow the fading taillights of the squadrol, used his right hand to remove a .38 snub nose from the inside pocket of his topcoat. I knew what that meant. He wouldn't be handing me a loaded weapon with his gun hand.

"Thanks," I said, taking the .38 with my left hand and reaching into my pocket with my right. "But I prefer this one."

As dramatic revelations go this one was a real dud. The Schooler was so intent on the world outside the windshield that it took him a good five seconds to register what I'd said and acknowledge the .44 Special pointed at his gut. Then he deflated like a punctured tire and squeezed his eyes shut.

"Your loyal-as-a-butcher's-dog first lieutenant gave it to me to rub you out."

The Schooler opened his eyes and looked at me. "Why don't you?"

"Because I don't trust the son of a bitch."

"But you trust me?"

"More than I trust Jimmy."

"Why?"

"You don't have anything to prove."

The Schooler smiled, wanly. "What's your plan?"

"Same as yours, knock off the Federal Reserve. Only you're the ticket in, not me."

"Jimmy and the others?"

"They're broken down somewhere in Chester Township."

"And you think two men can do this job?"

"No. I've got three young loogans on ice. That's plenty. These boys are smart, and not trigger-happy. Your getaway plan doesn't change."

"What do you want?"

"Same as the plant heist, 50-50."

"And if I refuse to co-operate?"

I shrugged. "Then I've just nabbed Mr. Big and foiled the biggest bank job in Cleveland history."

I felt kind of bad for the old gent as I watched him nod his head in defeat, his masterpiece in tatters. It was a part of growing up I didn't like. The realization that the elders you looked up to all had feet of clay.

"How in the world did this happen?" said Henry Voss after a time.

"Pride comes before the all," I said. "You were showing off when you announced you knew I'd stashed my cut at National City Bank. You strutted your stuff before Jimmy, God and everyone but you got me to wondering how you knew where I kept my money. And why you'd care."

The Schooler muttered something but I wasn't listening. I was watching the traffic on Superior. The time was 6:49. I kept the .44 trained on him till 6:53. The old sugar in the gas tank trick must have worked. The panel truck didn't show.

We needed to play this out together, Henry and me. So I took a calculated risk and stuck the .44 back in my coat pocket, leaving the Schooler free to plug me. He barely noticed. At the moment I was the best friend Henry Voss had in all the world.

I cranked the ignition and wheeled off, nearly got sideswiped by a speeding taxi, wove my way through traffic like a broken field runner and took a left on Frankfort. We weren't a well-oiled machine just yet.

Chapter Thirty-four

This entire thrown-together-at-the-last-minute criminal enterprise depended on what I saw through the front window of Lulu's Place. I hadn't known the precise time of H-hour when I called Ambrose, just that it was after dark. I told him to park himself and his brothers at the counter and keep an eye out for a wine red Packard.

I took my foot off the accelerator. We glided up to Lulu's Place.

The front window was cloudy with condensation save for a wiped-away square in the middle. I looked through that square and saw what I wanted to see. Three eager young scoundrels looking back.

I double parked. Sean, Patrick and Ambrose tumbled out the door a heartbeat later, Ambrose in the lead.

They piled into the back seat of the Packard, all cowlicks and eyebrows. The youngest brother had a glob of bloody tissue on his chin from a shave he didn't need. Raw assed rookies, eager for action. God help us.

"Gentlemen," I said, indicating The Schooler, "meet the man in charge."

The Mooney Brothers looked from me to him and back again.

"Here's the drill," I said. "You drop us off a block from the front steps. Fifteen minutes later you park across from the gate on Rockwell. When the gate opens you drive to the loading dock. Sean and Patrick jump out and flank up left and right, Ambrose wheels it around and backs up to the dock. He unlocks the trunk and stays put. Do not fire unless fired upon. Got it?"

The Mooney brothers nodded.

"Maintain your positions. If you hear gunfire it means we're dead. Do not go looking for us. Understand?"

They nodded in unison.

"Any questions?"

A quick whispered powwow between the brothers. Ambrose spoke.

"How long do we wait at the loading dock and what do we do if you don't show?"

"As long as you can and run like hell." I turned to The Schooler. "Anything else?"

Henry was facing forward, presumably cursing the day our paths had crossed. And searching the street for a black panel truck.

"You know the layout better'n I do."

The Schooler remained silent, motionless. We waited until he heaved a sigh and turned around to address Sean, Patrick and Ambrose.

"The loading dock is only eight feet wide. There's no room to flank up, no room to wheel around. You have to back into the gate."

So much for my brilliant plan.

"There's a toll gate inside, before you get to the loading dock. A steel arm across and an armed guard in a bulletproof booth. He works for the Secret Service, not the Federal Reserve Police. He doesn't care who has a gun to whose head, his job is to keep unauthorized personnel from entering no matter what."

We waited on the punch line.

"We got to him. But he's expecting a panel truck, not a Packard."

Cripes. This was the first I'd heard of the tollbooth.

Ambrose piped up. "Is the guard lookin' for somebody at the wheel? Someone he knows?"

"No one in particular," said The Schooler.

"Then we tell him the panel truck threw a rod if he beefs us."

The Schooler almost smiled. He liked this itchy young man.

I put the Packard in gear, had a terrible thought and turned around. "You do know how to drive, don't you?"

"Of course," said Ambrose.

"Show me."

Ambrose and I swapped seats. The Schooler gave him a quick briefing on the workings of the Packard. Ambrose put the great beast in gear.

We bounced west on Frankfort, lurched south on W. 9th and jounced east on Superior, Sean and Patrick trying not to pee their pants, The Schooler issuing instructions in a mild voice and me, bracing myself against the back of the front seat as we jerked to a halt at a stoplight on W. 3rd, wondering why I didn't just throw open the door and step in front of a truck.

But I never do anything the easy way.

I checked my watch. There was another unpleasant possibility that I hadn't raised. Jimmy wouldn't stay broken down for long. When the panel truck crapped out Jimmy would know I'd screwed him. He and his bad boys would hijack the first vehicle big enough to hold them and make a beeline for the exit gate on Rockwell. The Mooney boys would have to park elsewhere.

I have always been good in a crisis. Don't laugh, it's true. My foresight isn't always 20-20 but I usually compensate with some inspired improvisation just before the clock ticks down to zero. The clock was ticking. Where the hell was my inspiration?

"Take a left at the next intersection," I said to Ambrose as the light turned green.

The Schooler looked a question at me over his shoulder. The Bank was dead ahead, why the detour? I shook him off, no time to explain.

Ambrose signaled for a left, hemmed and hawed his way through the Public Square traffic and down Ontario and didn't hit anybody. He was getting the hang of it.

"Right on St. Clair," I said and slumped down in my seat as we passed the Standard Building and FBI HQ. We turned right. I sat up a block later.

"And a right here at 9th." Ambrose turned right. Rockwell was one block ahead. "Kill the headlights."

Ambrose hit a switch, the windshield wipers started clacking. The Schooler said the next switch over. The dome light clicked on. The Schooler said to turn it the other way. The headlights dimmed.

"Now slide halfway past this corner and stop," I said, looking hard. No vehicles were parked across from the bank gate on Rockwell.

"Turn right," I said, betting there was an alley off Rockwell.

There was, just past the side delivery gate, other side of the street.

"Here."

We stopped by the alley. "Back in and park behind that dumpster," I said to Ambrose. "Wait for the gate to open."

I pondered what to tell him about the possibility of Jimmy and his punks arriving in a hijacked truck but the answer was obvious. Nothing. There were unknowns in every operation, and the kid had enough to worry about.

The Schooler showed Ambrose how to find reverse. We climbed out. The Packard crabbed its way up the alley. Henry and I buttoned up against the wind and quick stepped up Rockwell to E. 6th.

"What's the play?"

"Your troops are massing up the block for a frontal assault," I said. "You were going to use me as your ticket in but I flipped the switch."

The Schooler nodded.

"And I'll need your weapon."

The Schooler stopped walking, I stopped with him. He dug in the pocket of his topcoat and stood there for a long moment.

Henry Voss could have plugged me there and then, jumped in a cab on Superior and sailed off into the sunset. He could and should have but he didn't. He forked over a tiny elegant seven-shot Beretta instead.

"Nice gat."

We resumed our walk. A gust of wind whistled down the concrete canyon and carried off his remark.

"Say again?"

"Do-you-need-anything-else?"

"Yeah," I said, "I need you to play the part. Look angry, look glum."

The Schooler expelled a fat cloud of steam. "That shouldn't be difficult."

Chapter Thirty-five

The twenty-foot Greek statues were female, laurel wreaths on their heads, holding sheathed swords aloft on either side of the stone steps leading up to the high-arched front entrance of the pink granite building otherwise known as the Federal Reserve Bank of Cleveland. The front door was narrow, a black steel frame punctuated by eight panes of double thick glass. It had no outside handle, just a call box to the right, head high.

I marched The Schooler up the steps with the .44, in my pocket, to his back. I positioned him in front of the door and pressed the call box button. I pressed it again. I stood behind The Schooler and peered through a door pane, saw a cavernous lobby with great hanging lamps shaped like lanterns and a curved white marble reception counter and nobody, not a soul. I pounded on the door. It paid no attention.

"Hey!" cried a voice from the street behind me. I spun around. A swabbie in deck whites had his arm draped around a slender young woman. He was very happy. "You never heard of banker's hours?"

I smiled and nodded and returned to the business at hand, pressing the call box and peering at no one.

The young woman's "Jerry, don't" alerted me. That and Jerry's hundred proof breath. I turned around.

"You din't answer my question mate."

"Sorry, thought you were joking," I said pleasantly.

The call box squawked to life. "Identify yourself," said a hollow voice.

"I asked you a question!" said the sailor, stepping closer, eyes crossed.

"Identify yourself," repeated the hollow voice.

"You deaf or sumpin'?" said the sailor, balling his fists.

I looked an appeal to the slender young woman. She examined her fingernails. I would have to handle Popeye by myself. We had already acquired a small cluster of onlookers, and tossing a uniformed veteran down the steps would start a brawl.

The two-finger lock is simplicity itself. You grab your opponent's ring and pinkie fingers, turn his palm upward and bend his fingers toward his wrist, using your index finger as a fulcrum. The drunken gob didn't like it. He took a swing at me with his left, I ducked. His sailor's cap went flying.

I bent back harder. He cocked his fist for another punch. I was about to snap his fingers clean in two when The Schooler said, in a hearty voice I hadn't heard before, "Shove off mate. This finny ain't worth the chum."

The sailor grinned at this and unclenched his fist. I eased the pressure some. He cocked his head and studied my battered mug. "You got that right mate," he laughed.

I released my grip. The swabbie picked up his cap and stumbled down the stairs, the young woman meeting him halfway, pulling his arm around her shoulders. They tripped off down the sidewalk, happy as clams. I pressed the .44 Special to The Schooler's back once again.

"Identify yourself!" said the disembodied voice.

"I am Harold Schroeder of the Federal Bureau of Investigation and I need to speak to Commander Frederick Seifert." I released the call box button and pressed it again. "Immediately."

No response. Then the microphone keyed on. I waited to hear. The disembodied voice said, "Stand by."

I stood by for several eons of geologic time. Finally a deep angry voice said, "This is Seifert. How do I know you're Schroeder?"

"I'm from Youngstown, I served in the OSS, I was hired by Chester Halladay to infiltrate the Fulton Road Mob," I said to the call box. "I have ID."

"Who's the man with you?"

There was no one on the other side of the door. How had he seen? The Schooler ticked his chin up, towards a black steel frieze above the door, a world globe flanked by American eagles. A tiny lens protruded from the South Pole.

I pressed the call button. "The man in my custody is the head of the Fulton Road Mob, the feds call him Mr. Big. He has ten men waiting two blocks away. They intend to rob your bank."

A disembodied snort from the unseen Commander. "And just how do they propose to do that?"

"Sir I'm happy to explain the details but my fanny is flapping in the breeze out here at the moment and I sure would appreciate it if you could open the door."

A guard appeared on the other side of the door with a ring of keys. An old gent with a shuffling gait, a lifer.

"When the door opens the prisoner enters by himself, hands behind his head," said Seifert through the call box.

"No can do sir," I said back. "He's my collar. Where he goes, I go."

The microphone keyed off, presumably so the Commander could loudly curse my uppity young self. It keyed back on several moments later. Seifert's deep voice rumbled out of the call box as if it came from three stories below which, for all I knew, it did.

"Once you enter both you and the prisoner lace your hands behind your heads."

"Yes sir."

The guard with the ring of keys went to work on locks and sidebars. He yanked open the door, releasing a blast of heat. We shuffled inside and put our hands behind our heads. The welcoming committee consisted of four uniformed officers arrayed in front of the curved white marble reception counter, sidearms drawn. Two more stood behind the counter, sporting carbines. No sign of the Commander. The guard with the ring of keys locked up behind us.

My eyes climbed skyward despite themselves. The lobby of the Federal Reserve Bank made St. John's Cathedral look like Granny's parlor. I felt small. Tiny. Infinitesimal. I had obviously been insane to think this austere principality could be conquered by a ragtag army of five.

I queued up behind The Schooler and looked around, past all the gun barrels trained on my every move. Where the hell was the Commander? The entire loopy half-baked scheme depended on my getting hold of him.

"Do they have explosives?" said the deep angry voice from somewhere to my right. I turned to see. The Commander stepped out from behind a potted palm. Apparently the Federal Reserve Police didn't have a height requirement. Frederick Seifert was barely five foot two.

"No sir. They don't have any explosives, armored vehicles or battering rams. No need to push the panic button."

Commander Seifert approached. No wonder he was grumpy. In addition to being short he was bald and wore thick glasses.

"Then explain yourself!"

I looked him over. Spit and polish top to toe. Wispy strands combed straight back and plastered to his skull, uniform blouse and pants steam pleated, brass buttons gleaming, a see-yourself shine on his oxfords and clear polish on his fingernails.

I skipped the details. How Mr. Big planned to use me as the Trojan Horse to breach the castle walls, how I got the drop on him and flipped the switch. Seifert would want to know what was in it for him.

"Can I check my watch?"

Seifert nodded.

"Okay, it's 7:27. The Fulton Road Mob plans to storm up the front steps in three minutes time. I know, I know. So what?" I spread my stance to lower my height and lowered my voice to draw him close. "Here's what. Why let the Cleveland PD grab all the glory when you, Commander, can round them all up in one fell swoop."

The Commander did not reply.

"I don't have time to explain all the why's and wherefore's. But the mob thinks I'm on their team. They're expecting I've taken you hostage by now. They're expecting to see me standing behind you by an open front door."

The Commander didn't say anything to this either. One crooked eyebrow sufficed.

"Ridiculous, I know, but here's the thing. We've got superior knowledge, why not use it? If you send your troops out the tunnels to those statues and you allow me to stand behind you at the open door, the mob lookout will give the others the go-ahead. They storm up the steps, you slam the door in their faces. Your men pile out of the statues and round them up from behind. Duck soup!"

Commander Seifert's eyelids narrowed to tiny slits but what was left of his eyeballs burned with a fine cold light. He was tempted but not convinced.

There was one more angle I could play. I had grown up with men like Seifert, hard working second generation Krauts, shamed by their ancestry, noses pressed to the glass, on the outside looking in.

"Sir, Chester Halladay and the rest of the country club brass screwed me six ways to Sunday on this operation. You know how they are. But if we can pull this off, well, they'd have to raise a glass in your honor next Friday at Rohr's. Wouldn't they?"

Seifert's eyelids raised up to half staff. I couldn't throw in the closer. This is your last best chance to win that promotion to New York or D.C. or wherever it was Federal Reserve

Police Commanders aspired to go. I wasn't supposed to know about that. And Commander Seifert could do the math.

He took his time toting it up, precious time we didn't have. Jimmy and the seven twerps would be rumbling our way in a hijacked hay truck.

Seifert spoke. "The tunnels haven't been used for years. The entry doors are padlocked, I don't have keys."

Christ, one step forward and two steps back. I was about to give up the ghost and devote my life to serving the poor and destitute when Commander Seifert snapped to and started barking orders.

"Grab the bolt cutters from the maintenance room, machine guns from the weapon's locker! Deploy down the tunnels! Keep watch through the peepholes. When the front door swings shut, jump out and make arrests!"

The squadron of officers looked at their Commander as if he were speaking in tongues.

"Go!"

They went. I used the momentary chaos to return The Schooler's Beretta to his coat pocket. He kept his hands laced behind his head and his eyes downcast, a tiny shrug of his shoulder his only acknowledgment.

I slipped my hand in my pocket and slipped my fingers around the butt and trigger of Jimmy's .44, my pestering brain wondering whether Slopehead was already laying in wait outside the ribbed steel gate on Rockwell. I told my brain to shut its yap.

Timing was key now. I was tempted to stick the .44 in Seifert's belly this instant but that's not the way spies work.

West Point trains soldiers to press the attack when they've got the enemy in transition, scattered, on the run. They teach different in spy school. They teach you to wait for the enemy to take their positions, wait for the enemy to train their weapons on ghostly phantoms in the far distance. At which time you sneak up and shoot them in the back.

I watched Seifert rallying his troops, his skull bright with perspiration, his plastered strands unplastered, his longed-for chance to demonstrate his prowess to the stuffed shirts about to turn around and swallow him whole. I felt bad for him for a moment, maybe two.

Then I pointed at my watch and ticked my head toward the door.

Seifert nodded and strode across the speckled marble floor. He signaled to the keeper of the keys. The old man unlocked the door.

Seifert told him to keep The Schooler covered. The old man unholstered an ancient Colt and held it with both hands.

Commander Seifert stood in front of me and grabbed the door handle.

"My apologies Commander, but I need to ask for your sidearm." Seifert looked up at me, I patted his shoulder reassuringly. "We need to make this look convincing."

Seifert exhaled sharply through his nostrils. I didn't press. This was the make or break moment.

Then he grabbed up his .32 revolver and handed it over, just like that.

Taking a man hostage with his own weapon is pretty lowdown so I was about to pocket his gun and pull the .44 Special when I realized that I hadn't checked to make sure the .44 was loaded. Whoever said there was honor among thieves hadn't spent any time with the Fulton Road Mob.

Frederick Seifert wouldn't be packing an empty sidearm. I didn't intend to use it but you never know. I pressed the barrel of the .32 to the base of Seifert's spine.

"Is that really necessary?" he grumbled.

I placed a restraining hand on the iron door and felt bad for him a third time. "I'm afraid so," I said. "This is a bank robbery."

The man didn't flinch, sigh, curse or fall to his knees and weep. He became, simply, very very still.

I said what I had to say. "I've come a long way to get here Commander, killed a lot of people I didn't particularly want to kill." I jammed the heater hard against his back. "One more corpse won't make a difference."

I couldn't see the keeper of the keys behind me but the back of my neck told me his Colt had strayed from The Schooler to myself. If he was a trained commando like his colleagues I would've been dead by now. But he was just an old man up past his bedtime.

I heard a gun clatter to the marble floor. Henry had disarmed him.

"We're going downstairs and collect the shipment. You can press the panic button the second we leave, there's no need for any heroics. Understood?"

Seifert nodded.

Henry and I marched our prisoners across the lobby, under the steepled ceiling, toward the stairs. We were down one flight and about to turn the corner when we heard slapping shoe leather on stone steps. More than one, coming hard.

I jabbed Seifert with his own gun barrel. "Send 'em back down."

"Return to your posts!" called Seifert to the unseen stair climbers.

Their steps slowed. I prodded Seifert again. "This minute!"

The steps went the other way. We paused a beat, turned the corner and descended another flight. The Schooler led the way.

We turned left into a brightly lit corridor, squinty bright, hospital bright. We approached a room with a floor-to-ceiling glass wall. The currency counting room of the Federal Reserve Bank of Cleveland.

There were two Gorgons at the door. One a dark-haired Latin, the other a strapping Swede with vented short sleeves to accommodate his biceps. Their .45 semi-automatics looked like toy guns in their mitts. These were the stair-climbers, their chests still heaving.

"Weapons on the floor gentlemen," said a calm authoritative voice. The Schooler.

The guards looked to Seifert. He nodded. They very slowly placed their weapons on the floor. "Kick them away." They kicked them away. "Now prone yourselves out."

They remained standing. The Schooler repeated his command. They remained standing.

Henry was a good shot with his elegant little Beretta. He drilled the toe of the big Swede's boot with one shot. The Swede pitched over, howling in pain.

The other guard dropped to one knee. The Schooler put the keeper of the keys on the floor with a nifty leg sweep, stepped forward and stopped five feet away as the burly Latin reached for his ankle gun. "Don't make me kill you son."

The guard froze.

"That's it, that's the way. Now lie down and put your arms behind you."

Henry snatched the ankle gun once the guard was down. He moved over to the wounded guard, talking to him in a soothing voice as he did a quick pat down. The Swede was clean.

I was standing there like a stooge, holding Seifert hostage, watching the Schooler's sure-handed work when I realized we had a fatal flaw in our plan. We had no way to hogtie the guards.

Henry yanked off his belt, a fancy piece of braided leather strips. The buckle hung by a thread. When he bit through it the leather strips shook free.

Problem solved.

I cinched up Seifert in a left-armed chokehold so I could cover Henry Voss as he quickly bound the guards' wrists and ankles. He did the same to the keeper of the keys.

We inched past them and entered the currency counting room. The three clerks wore green eyeshades and gray smocks with no pockets. They huddled against the far wall, terrified. This wasn't supposed to happen. Ever.

The Schooler instructed them to raise their hands. They did. They had little rubber caps on the tips of their fingers.

I surveyed the counting room, hoping to see stacks of spendable bills that smelled of cigarettes and dried sweat. But The Schooler had been right about what we'd find. The big stainless steel tables were piled high with newly-minted currency, stacks of one hundred bills sealed with bank bands, then bound with tape into blocks containing a thousand bills apiece.

Our timing was good. Only one of the thirty or so blocks had been unbound for counting. Twenties. One thousand crisp new twenty dollar bills.

The air in the room crackled with static electricity. The Schooler's eyebrows stood at attention. I kept the gun to Seifert's back as The Schooler issued instructions to the counting clerks in a softly malevolent voice.

"No small denominations. Blocks of fifties and hundreds only. You should have five hundreds and eight fifties."

The counting clerks stood stock still.

"Load the blocks onto the hand truck," said The Schooler patiently, indicating the long flat steel cart against the glass wall.

The counting clerks didn't budge. Henry addressed himself to the youngest clerk.

"What's your name young man?"

"Fran-cis," said the young man as if he wasn't quite sure.

"They call you Frank?"

Frank nodded, looked away.

"Well Frank, here's what I'd like you to do."

The Schooler paused until Frank met his gaze.

"I'd like you to load the eight blocks of fifties and the five blocks of hundreds onto the hand truck and lead us down the hall to the loading dock. Can you do that for me?"

Frank chewed his lip and shuffled his feet.

"I understand your pride in what you do," said The Schooler, gesturing with his free hand, his gun hand steady. "The Bureau of Engraving turns old undershirts and overalls into the world's most valuable commodity, they spin straw into gold. And they trust you to safeguard it," said Henry Voss with fatherly regard. Then his voice hardened ever so slightly. "But it's not worth the life of anyone in this room Frank. Can we agree on that?"

"I...I guess."

"Excellent, now let's get underway."

Frank loaded the blocks of currency onto the hand truck. His fellow counting clerks squinched their mugs at The Schooler with an intense something in their eyes. Defiance, I supposed. But I was wrong.

"Assist him if you like," said Henry.

The other two clerks put their hands down and pitched in, sorting through the thousand- bill blocks on the steel table and heaving them to Frank at the hand truck like gunnery mates pitching shells on the deck of a battleship. They weren't happy about it, but they were a team. They weren't about to let their youngest member take the fall.

Frank wheeled the loaded hand truck to the door. He could have stacked the blocks on top of one another so that we would have had a moment's distraction as we inspected the blocks to make sure they were fifties and hundreds only. But the blocks were laid end to end for easy scrutiny. Fifties and hundreds only.

You had to hand it to The Schooler. The guy knew how to work a room.

Chapter Thirty-six

We formed a procession for the solemn walk down the aisle. Frank and the hand truck in front, The Schooler behind, me and Commander Seifert bringing up the rear. We squeezed past the proned out Gorgons at the door.

"See you soon asshole," said the Latin one to my right.

"Real soon," said the Swede.

I smiled and nodded and checked their leather bindings. Henry knew how to tie a knot.

We made our way down the corridor under the hospital lights. Sweat trickled down my ribcage.

The squadron of officers Seifert had deployed to the tunnels had to know they'd been had. Would they remain at their posts and await further orders like good little soldiers? Or would they come storming down the stairs or deploy to Rockwell to open fire as we pulled out of the delivery gate? Providing we could get the delivery gate open and the loogans hadn't already been bushwhacked by Jimmy and Ambrose was able to bluff his way past the Secret Service agent in the tollbooth, find reverse and back the Packard up to the dock.

Other than that we were all silk.

We reached the end of the corridor. I'm a blue collar boy, I know loading docks. They're loud sprawling places that stink of diesel smoke and sweat. But this loading dock was small and very, very clean. A narrow drive angled off toward the tollbooth and the gate on Rockwell, neither of which we could see from the dock.

The Schooler gave me a quick over-the-shoulder. I had the head muckety-muck at gunpoint. It was my turn.

"Open the gate Commander," I said. "Open the gate and we'll go away and never darken your door again."

"I can't," said Seifert.

I positioned his gun at the base of his spine. "Can't? Or won't?"

"I can't," said Seifert. "It's a two switch system. A release button down here, and one upstairs at the command center. Both have to be activated."

The Schooler's grimace said that this was the first he'd heard of a two-switch system.

"Prove it to me," I said, grabbing Seifert's collar and marching him over to the big square orange wall button to the left of the dock.

He pushed it. Nothing happened. I pushed it and held it down. Nothing happened twice. "Get on the horn to the command center and tell 'em to throw the switch!" I said.

Seifert snorted.

"What's so funny?"

"Lieutenant Commander Rolf Petersen is next in line for my job. This is the best night of his life."

Son of a bitch. This was what the Gorgons meant by *see you soon*. I searched the four walls, six walls, however many there were in this medieval castle disguised as a bank. I saw a fire hose in a glass case. Ah ha.

There was an override, had to be. An override in case of fire. Time to get brilliant Schroeder. Whatever it was wouldn't be hidden or hard to find in a hurry. I searched the ceiling for emergency lights that would kick on in a power outage, saw one above the big orange wall button.

I marched Seifert over to it and explained the situation. "There's an override code for this button. Use it now or we all get dead."

The Commander declined my invitation. I bent down and whispered in his ear.

"I understand that you're eager to die a hero Commander, but I'm thinking young Francis might like to wait a while."

Seifert cursed, and pressed the big square button once, twice, and held it down. The third time was the charm. I heard the distant ribbed steel gate roll open. T'was a sweet and beauteous sound.

I looked at my watch and looked away. I didn't need to know the precise time to know we were behind schedule. The Secret Service agent in the tollbooth knew it too. He wouldn't raise that steel arm if he thought the Federal Reserve cops had time to sniff out the double cross and rush out to Rockwell, blocking his escape route. Could be they were already there. The silence dragged on. The Schooler and I exchanged a quick anxious glance.

Then I heard it, the thrum of an engine. It was low and throaty, idling. A vehicle waiting for permission to enter. Which meant the Fed cops hadn't deployed to Rockwell. Not yet. The question was which vehicle with what passengers?

I squinted my eyes to hear. Muffled voices echoed down the tunnel. No shouts, no gunfire. Just indecipherable conversation followed by a car door slam.

I wrote a term paper on Einstein my senior year in high school. What a headache. What he said, best I could tell, was that if you run real fast time slows down. I wasn't running real fast at the moment but it sure felt that way. It couldn't have been more than five seconds before that vehicle made its appearance, it couldn't have been less than five years.

A wine red Packard backed up to the loading dock.

Sean and Patrick scrambled out and jumped on the running boards, gun hands deep in their overcoat pockets, their eyes darting above the checkered kerchiefs that covered their mugs.

Ambrose moved more deliberately, climbing out in stages, gat in hand, walking to the boot of the Packard with a rolling gait. He wore a black silk scarf pulled down over his nose, eyeholes cut out, tied behind his neck like a buccaneer. Kid was a born crook.

Ambrose opened the trunk.

I nodded to Sean and Patrick. "Unload it!"

They got to work. 900,000 dollars of newly-minted stacked-and-bound Federal Reserve notes, legal tender for all debts public and private, were quickly stowed.

I said, "On the floor, face down," to Francis, "In the back seat," to Sean and Patrick and "You're coming with us" to Seifert.

Sean and Patrick piled into the back seat like kids off to the Bijou, Francis flattened himself on the loading dock, the unseen Federal Reserve cops stayed that way. Not even Commander Seifert squawked, which made me nervous.

The old women in Youngstown had a saying. *Stets hält man den ältesten Wolf an der kürzesten Kette.* 'You keep the shortest chain on the oldest wolf.' Seifert would bear watching.

"You drive," I said to Ambrose. He jumped behind the wheel.

I took a look down the corridor. The Gorgons were still struggling against their lanyards.

"Enjoy the rest of your evening gentlemen!" I called as I marched their commanding officer down the narrow step stairs and into a back seat crammed with masked and giddy loogans.

The Schooler was the last one to join our happy group, Beretta out, backing up, sliding in to the front seat, head and gun out the window as Ambrose wheeled the Packard down the curved narrow drive at a high rate of speed. I braced myself for a collision with the steel security arm and gunfire from the re-deployed fed cops on Rockwell ahead.

The steel arm was vertical, the tollbooth empty. No gunfire commenced.

The Packard breached the castle walls and hooked a sharp squealing left onto Rockwell. No sign of Jimmy and the seven twerps. That I halfway expected. There was another place they could go.

What I hadn't pictured was a street and sidewalk free of Federal Reserve police. They were, apparently, still at their posts. Good little soldiers, their weapons trained on ghostly phantoms in the far distance.

The Schooler and I exchanged another quick and anxious glance. Had we had really pulled this off?

Then we heard the sirens.

Chapter Thirty-seven

"Where'm I goin'?" said Ambrose from the front seat. Yelled actually, the sirens were that loud.

The plan was to drive three short blocks to the alley off E. 2nd and roll up the ramp into the back of the waiting freight truck. But I had other ideas. The Schooler hadn't revealed our final destination, where that truck was headed. If Jimmy wanted in on the party, and he did, then the rendezvous in the alley was his last best shot.

The Schooler told Ambrose to take a right on E. 2nd. Ambrose slowed. We passed a screaming squadrol headed the other way, the cops so intent they never glimmed us.

"Don't turn," I said to Ambrose. "Keep west on Rockwell, and don't spare the horses."

Ambrose punched it good, ignoring The Schooler's angry *Hey*, earning the Mooney Brothers a hefty bonus should we ever get that far.

Another screaming squadrol brodied across the intersection of E. 2nd and Rockwell, behind us, headed east. God bless the bumbling Cleveland PD.

The Schooler and I had to talk, which meant the Commander had to go. He wasn't much use as a hostage now that the local goms were hunting us. And I didn't trust him not to try something stupid. We stopped at the traffic light on West 3rd. I jacked open the door.

Commander Seifert, who was perched on my lap like Charlie McCarthy, lunged for my gun, his gun, with both hands. His left hand grabbed the barrel, pushing it down. His right thumbnail bit into the underside of my wrist as his fingers tried to peel mine off the gun butt.

It was well executed. It might even have worked were it not for my excitable seatmates. Sean and Patrick flew, there's no other word for it, *flew* across the back seat and expelled Commander Seifert from the vehicle and into the middle of Rockwell Avenue.

He staggered, blinking, to his feet. I felt bad for him one last time.

We roared off at the green. When I looked over The Schooler was measuring me for a coffin.

"Jimmy and his itchy young men are hiding in that alley, have to be," I shouted. "Wherever we're going we need to get there without the truck."

The sirens swelled to an operatic chorus, Ambrose sped west. Rockwell became Frankfort. We passed Lulu's Place, clusters of people on the sidewalk asking what's all this, and entered the Warehouse District. That was the plan maybe. Wheel into the abandoned plant that Jimmy had hauled me to when I first met The Schooler. Lie low, wait for the heat to cool.

"It's close, right?" The Cuyahoga River was now just three blocks away. And Frankfort didn't cross it.

"It's not a place you would expect," said The Schooler, turning away from me, surveying the chaotic street calmly.

"Where then?"

"Whiskey Island," said The Schooler to no one in particular. "We go tonight."

I didn't have time to ask go where and on what because Frankfort came to a screeching halt and us with it. The Schooler told Ambrose to turn left on West 9th, then said "Hold up!"

A big dark sedan with a red light on the dash took the corner on two wheels, headed east. The car had the seal of the City of Cleveland on the door and two guys in suits in the front seat.

Christ, they had everybody out. The driver raked us with a look and said something to his passenger.

"Go, go, go, go," I said.

Ambrose launched the Packard south on West 9th, sideswiping a southbound taxicab in a shower of sparks. The dark sedan hooked a U and gave chase. Ambrose leaned on the horn and straddled the centerline. Oncoming cars ducked for cover.

And there we all were. Me, The Schooler and the Mooney brothers, tearing into the teeth of traffic, a ragtag band of bank robbing bandits pursued by a couple of Cleveland building inspectors. It was almost funny.

And a positive knee-slapper when Ambrose, at Henry's instruction, raced ahead of a lumbering flatbed and Sean and Patrick leaned out the window to shoot out its tires and Ambrose used the shuddering, sideways skidding flatbed to cover his high speed, hair raising, horn honking expedition across the six-way intersection in front of the Detroit-Superior Bridge that climaxed in a hairpin right turn down dark narrow twisty Columbus Road.

No big dark sedan followed. My heart resumed beating. Sean and Patrick whooped and hollered. Ambrose told them to shut the feck up. The Packard wound its way down into the netherworld beneath the span, passing snow-capped mounds of anthracite and square brick buildings so soot-blackened they existed only in silhouette.

"Take a right on Canal and follow it around to Center," said The Schooler.

"Where's Canal?" said Ambrose.

"Here."

Ambrose turned right and followed it around. The bleating screaming squadrols wouldn't find us down here, I thought. We were home free.

But then we Midwesterners are optimistic to a fault.

Chapter Thirty-eight

A distant burn-off pipe cast a faint hellish glow on the Flats as we approached a narrow, red steel pivot bridge. A bridge used by ore trucks headed east to the steel mills, a bridge used by I-beam and ingot haulers headed west to the docks. It was pivoted in the right direction, across the river. It held no traffic.

Once we crossed the bridge it was a straight shot down Center Street to Whiskey Island. We would pass just below Mrs. Brennan's rooming house, repository of my one priceless possession, a creased and spattered photo of the All American girl next door.

"Stop here," said The Schooler at an unmarked cross street that fronted the pivot bridge. He studied the span intently, I couldn't say why. There was no roadblock in sight, save for the standard crossing gate at the far end. And tempus she did fugit.

I looked behind. Headlights, a few blocks backs, closing fast. I looked ahead. Nothing but asphalt.

"Go for God's sake."

Ambrose tromped it. The Packard jumped up off its back axle and rocketed onto the narrow span, spewing a vapor trail of gravel, ice and iron ore dust. The Schooler cursed and ducked his head under the dashboard.

The bridge was clear, likewise Center Street on the far side. What had the Schooler seen that had him cowering on the floorboard?

Maybe it was what he hadn't seen. There were only a handful of bridges across the Cuyahoga, a handful of choke points. They had everybody out by now. Off duty jailers, bailiffs, high-ranking desk jockeys and every Treasury, Secret Service and FBI agent in town. The Schooler had his head under the glove compartment because he hadn't seen a road-block.

I told Ambrose to slow down. I hung my head out the window and squinted against the wind, saw a shack-sized pilot-house on the far side of the bridge. I wiped grit from my eyes and looked again. The guard gate was down.

I looked behind. The following headlights were gone, possibly laying in wait back at the bridgehead. We weren't going to back up and find out. We had to cross a bridge at some point.

I told Ambrose to slow down some more, looked to my right and saw two very eager young loogans who were likely to blow my head off by mistake if gunfire commenced.

"Heads down, both of you."

Sean hesitated. I grabbed a hank of hair and did it for him. Patrick took the hint and scrunched down.

It was up to Ambrose and me now, the Gold Dust Twins. I readied Commander Seifert's little .32 caliber peashooter and felt heft against my hip. Jimmy's .44 Special. I whipped it out. I was a two-gunned hombre now.

We approached a lone man in the pilothouse at 20 mph. Ambrose took one hand off the wheel and reached into his pocket.

"You drive, I shoot."

Ambrose returned his hand to the wheel. "You're no fun."

We closed to within twenty yards of the pilothouse.

"Ease up, slow down," I said and settled back in the leather seat of the Packard touring sedan like a well-fed nob headed home to his lakeside manor, his chauffeur at the wheel.

The pilothouse door kicked open. A man in dark clothing stepped out, swinging a Kerosene lantern. He was not in uniform.

"Pull up just shy, make him come to us."

The man with the lantern was unarmed. But the man who followed behind him held a semi-automatic M1 carbine, the kind with a thirty round clip.

God bless the bumbling Cleveland PD. That the M1 wasn't ripping us up one side and down the other meant the bridge tenders didn't have an accurate description of the getaway vehicle.

The man with the lantern approached. I yearned for a newspaper. A portly lakeside nob would have folded up his late edition of the Plain Dealer impatiently before he inclined his head out the back window and said, "Is there a *problem?*"

I used my best hoity toite accent, somewhere between Boston Brahmin and the Court of St. James. I'm not saying it was convincing exactly but the lantern swinging man slowed his rapid gait. I piped up before he got too close, keeping the battered right side of my face in shadow.

"Who are you? Are you a police officer? Never mind," I said with a dismissive wave. "I'm hosting a dinner reception for the Lithuanian Ambassador." I checked my wristwatch. "In twenty minutes time. If I'm late I'm holding you personally responsible."

This stopped the man in his tracks. He raised his lantern to look at me. "You're hostin' the *whosie-whatsie?*"

"The Lithuanian Ambassador, his Excellency Klaus von Heeberling. He's going to stand at the head of the table, raise a glass of champagne to his host and *I'm not going to be there!*"

The poor slob didn't know what to say to that. He turned to look at the man with the carbine. The man shrugged.

I grabbed my wallet. "Now open that gate, and here's ten dollars for your trouble."

Lantern man snatched the sawbuck quicker'n you can say *huh* and told his pal to hike the gate.

"Shall I drive on sir?" said Ambrose, brightly.

"By all means driver," I replied.

The gate popped up and we motored west down Center Street. I wanted to duck down just in case the gatekeepers had a change of heart but how would that look? I remained rigidly upright. No shots were fired. Ambrose gave the great beast its head.

"Klaus von Heeberling?"

"Best I could do on short notice."

I looked to my right. Sean and Patrick were still bent over on the back seat, giggling like schoolgirls.

Chapter Thirty-nine

I got a bad feeling in the pit of my stomach when I saw that we had another bridge to cross, a short two lane cantilevered span from the north end of the Flats to Whiskey Island. But we crossed the bridge without incident. Apparently the authorities weren't concerned about Whiskey Island, didn't think much of our chances to make a daring escape across a frozen lake. I tended to agree with them.

Henry directed Ambrose to turn left off the bridge and onto a vast expanse of snowy silt. I had been here before, the dock-side meeting where I'd laid out the plans for the armored car heist. I recognized the Hulett ore unloaders along the canal to my right. I didn't recognize the set of rickety conveyor belts that climbed the mountains of sodium chloride to my left.

How do you not see a salt mine?

Spies are supposed to be observant. Yet I had managed not to notice that the FBI's sting op was unfunded, that Mr. Big was a non-existent phantom, and that the cops and crooks had superior knowledge in these matters and were laughing up their French cuffs at yours truly. I had come a ways since then, made the best of some bad situations. But the sight of those mountains brought me up short. Anyone who doesn't notice a salt mine had better look again.

We rumbled across train tracks and motored west to the tip of the island, past the dock I had visited with Jimmy, Kelly and The Schooler. We drove another hundred yards and parked by a big rusty corrugated shed that stood on wood pilings above the lake.

I looked, I spied, I wore my eyeballs to a nubbin searching for signs. If there was a lonelier place than Whiskey Island in mid-December I hadn't seen it. I was looking for Jimmy of course. I couldn't believe we had actually given that cunning Cro-Magnon the slip. We piled out of the Packard and awaited instructions.

"You three come with me," said Henry to the Mooney boys. He climbed steps and unlocked the shed. The brothers followed him inside. I was left alone with a wine red touring sedan and $900,000.

I had to look. Not that I would have jumped behind the wheel and raced off with enough geetus to buy an entire tropical island much less a villa on a spit of sand. It wasn't that. I simply wanted to know if The Schooler trusted me.

The car keys were still dangling from the ignition.

I would call it Schroederland maybe, or *L'ile de Hal*. And I would be a very benevolent despot, overseeing my kingdom from a bejeweled deck chair, the regal Miss Jeannie by my side, a staff of eager lackeys poised to cater to our every whim.

Maybe next time. I returned to the rear of the Packard, stamping my feet to keep warm, eyes sweeping the perimeter. I heard a wrenching angry squeal that sounded like a big rusty hinge. This was followed by a *shuck shuck shuck shuck* of metal on metal.

I shifted over to see the front of the shed propped up like a garage door, and what looked like a wide steel sluiceway tailing down from the boathouse to the lake. A launch ramp for a boat. Okay. Provided The Schooler had a 10,000-ton destroyer tucked inside that shed. Even a landlubber like me could see that Lake Erie was a block of ice.

The Schooler and the Mooney Brothers trooped down the side doorsteps a moment later and joined me at ground zero. The trunk of the car.

I liked the Mooney brothers, Ambrose especially. It was pleasant to see a young man so well suited to his chosen profession. Kid was a born crook. And therein lay the problem. I didn't *think* he would turn on me, but if he made a play his brothers would back him in a blink. And Ambrose, I noticed, had his gun hand in his pocket. I did likewise and backed up two steps.

The Schooler, oblivious to such concerns, stood with his back to the boys and asked, over his shoulder just before he popped the trunk, "What's your arrangement with these gentlemen?"

"No particular arrangement."

The Schooler opened the trunk and grabbed a block of fifties. "Fifty thousand okay?"

Sean and Patrick shivered with glee. Ambrose kept a stone face. I answered for him. "Fifty thousand's okay."

The Schooler walked over to Ambrose though his brothers were closer. He handed him the tape-wrapped block of currency. Ambrose had to remove his gun hand to accept it. His stone face cracked and fissured in several places.

"It's hot," said The Schooler. "*Don't* try and move it for at least six months. Are you listening to me?"

Ambrose nodded dumbly, his eyes locked on the block of one thousand fifty dollar bills that he held in his own two hands and was his to keep. His brothers drew closer and clustered to his right, moths to the flame.

The Schooler continued. "Drive off the island and head west..."

The gun blast was loud as a howitzer.

It came from close by, from the direction of the shed. Sean and Patrick pitched over on their faces, their legs cut out from under by a carom shot off the frozen silt. Ambrose dropped the block of fifties and spun on his pivot foot to confront the attacker, his gun hand digging deep.

The attacker rushed forward and laid him out with a shotgun butt to the forehead.

I had my weapon in hand by this time. The one in my right pocket, the .44 Special that Jimmy had given me. I pointed it at the attacker's head and clicked and clicked and clicked.

Jimmy smiled and swung his pig snout sawed-off in my direction. I said my goodbyes.

The Schooler directed his Beretta at Jimmy's midsection. "You don't want to do that Jimmy."

"Why not?"

Jimmy wore a simian grin that ran up both sides of his face and squeezed his beaked nose down to his chin. He sure looked like he wanted to do it.

I still had Commander Seifert's gun in my left coat pocket. The Schooler either noticed the drift of my hand or read my mind. Anyhow he signaled, through a squint or a gesture or whatever mysterious way he made his wishes known, that I should stand down, that he would take care of it.

Sure thing. It beat drawing a .32 peashooter left-handed against a scattergun. I kept my arms at my side and waited for The Schooler and Jimmy to decide my fate.

Sean and Patrick lay face down, groaning, semi-conscious. Ambrose was out like a light. Judging by the fat round blood spatters on the frozen silt Jimmy had graduated to buckshot.

I didn't feel much of anything at the sight of the Mooney Brothers bleeding at my feet, just the remote and icy calm that the smell of blood and cordite conjured in me. I'd seen a lot worse. Saw a kid outside Freiburg get his jaw blown clean off, nothing left of his face but a blood-pumping hole and two bright brown eyes, alive and bright with agony.

All Ambrose had was a concussion, worst case a fractured skull. Sean and Patrick had multiple surface wounds, worst case a severed artery. They were lucky. Lucky that Jimmy didn't shoot to kill, lucky this wasn't Hamburg or Cologne or Dresden. Quality medical care could be had in Cleveland, Ohio in December of 1945.

I stood still as a cigar store Indian. Jimmy kept his sawed-off on me. The Schooler kept his Beretta on Jimmy. Not a word passed between them. I filled in the blanks best I could.

Jimmy: Why defend this traitor?

Schooler: You gave him the gun.
Jimmy: It wasn't loaded.
Schooler: You knew that, I didn't.
None of this was spoken. All The Schooler said, finally, was, "Trust me."

Jimmy slowly lowered his shotgun. Why he didn't call The Schooler's bluff, why Jimmy didn't blow me to pieces then and there I couldn't tell you. But I had a moment's chance to yank the .32 and blaze away at his big ugly hawk-nosed head and I didn't do that either.

The Schooler gestured at Ambrose with his gun. "Get him up. We need them out of here."

I didn't see why. If and when the coppers searched Whiskey Island the long steel boat ramp would tell them all they needed to know about our escape route.

I bent to Ambrose, scooped up a handful of frozen snow and rubbed it on his face. I scooped up some more and stuffed it down his shirt. His eyelids fluttered but remained closed. I slapped him hard across the face. "Snap to it, ya dumb Mick!"

Ambrose came to. Jimmy put a foot on the kid's right elbow, dug down in Ambrose's coat pocket and removed his gun. Ambrose propped himself up on his elbows, not sure what was happening but sure he didn't like it.

Jimmy put the barrel of his shotgun in Ambrose's face. Ambrose bared his fangs.

"Help me out here Jimmy," said The Schooler, rolling Sean over on his back. Jimmy trotted off without a backward look. He and The Schooler hauled the two brothers by feet and shoulders into the back seat of the Packard. I saw a large pool of coagulating blood on the frozen silt. Somebody had a serious wound.

I dove into the back seat to assess the damage. Patrick, the gangly youngest brother, had a puncture wound in his right thigh, just below his crotch. I pulled his pants down to his knees and used my handkerchief to stanch the bleeding. The wound soaked through it pretty quick so I pulled off his belt and cinched up a tourniquet.

Middle brother Sean blinked woozily to life and asked what was what. I looked him over. Not too bad, his bloodstains were below the knee.

"Keep a compress on his wound, hard as you can, and keep his leg elevated."

"Okay. What's a compress?"

"A towel, a handkerchief, use your coat if you have to, just don't let him bleed out!"

I climbed out of the back seat to see Jimmy and The Schooler removing blocks of money from the trunk and Ambrose tottering on two legs. I went to him, braced his shoulders and walked him to the Packard.

"You'll attract too much attention in this heap, I was you I'd ditch it and hotwire something." I helped Ambrose into the driver's seat, leaned over and keyed the ignition. "Now *go.*"

Ambrose tried to shake off the cobwebs, winced at the effort. At minimum he had a concussion. But a fractured skull and a massive brain hemorrhage wouldn't have kept him from saying what needed to be said.

"Not without our dib."

Jimmy and The Schooler were carrying the unloaded money to the boathouse. The blood-spattered block of fifties remained where Ambrose had dropped it. I transferred the .32 from my left pocket to my right hand, then walked over and picked up the block of fifties. It didn't weigh five pounds.

Jimmy stepped down the stairs just about then. He registered his disapproval by cocking his scattergun. I had an odd thought as I carried the block of cash to the Packard, my back braced for an imminent blast of buckshot.

I had witnessed every type of weaponry imaginable during the war. 500 pound frag bombs, 88 millimeter cannon, fifty caliber machine guns, mortars, howitzers, GI pineapples and Kraut potato mashers. But I had never once encountered a shotgun on the battlefield. Shotguns were for hunting grouse. There was no glory in being killed by a shotgun. It was, in fact, an insult.

I opened the passenger's side door and turned to face Jimmy on the steps. The Schooler was clanking and clunking around inside the shed. Jimmy waved his sawed-off in my direction.

"They get fifty gees and they go away," I said to Jimmy as I dumped the block of currency into the front seat. "They earned it."

Jimmy's hiss was like a plume of cigarette smoke in the frozen air. He curled his lips to say something vile that Ambrose didn't wait around to hear. The Packard shot backwards.

Jimmy raised his shotgun to his good eye, like you needed to aim a sawed-off shotgun. I whipped out the .32 and sighted down my arm at Jimmy's big ugly head.

"This one's got bullets Jimmy. Trust me."

Ambrose spun half a donut on the frozen silt, straightened out and wove his way east toward the cantilevered bridge. Jimmy shifted the pig snout sawed-off from the Packard to myself.

The Schooler ducked out of the boathouse at this commotion and stood in the doorway. He had no visible reaction to the Mexican standoff between Jimmy and myself. He said "Stop this nonsense" and went back inside.

Jimmy and I remained in place, guns pointed at each other's heads. The Schooler was correct. The situation was nonsensical in the extreme. But I was determined beyond all reason not to be the first to blink, not to surrender to the iron will of this one-eyed grouse-hunting s.o.b.

The Schooler's shouted "Hurry *up*" broke the spell. Jimmy lowered his sawed-off and, cursing, went back inside the shed.

I took a last look around the perimeter. Where the hell had the bastard come from?

Then I saw it. Under the boathouse, painted white, crusted with ice. You had to look twice to see it. A rowboat, bottoms up. How Jimmy knew to come to Whiskey Island and hide himself under an overturned rowboat was a question for another day.

I put the .32 in my pocket and climbed the steps to the shed. It was The Schooler's show now. Jimmy and I were just along for the ride.

Chapter Forty

I had expected to find a broad beamed diesel scow inside the corrugated shed, something bulky and muscular. But the boat that sat up on a V-shaped dry dock frame was a sleek 30-foot Chris Craft cabin cruiser with dual props. The *Tin Lizzie*. The kind of boat Pepper Pike nobs use for sport fishing on weekends. Summer weekends. The Schooler had obviously taken leave of his senses.

"I need a volunteer," said Henry. He was holding a ten-foot aluminum pole topped with a large hook, held it upright at his side like a scepter. "One of you has to trust the other one for a few minutes. Any takers?"

If this wasn't the easiest decision I ever made it was a close second. Ditto Jimmy.

"Such mistrusting young men," sighed The Schooler, fishing out a quarter. He flipped it, caught it and slapped it on the back of his hand.

I called heads.

It was, of course, tails.

"Jimmy and I will climb aboard," said The Schooler and gestured toward the bow. "Your job is to pull the chocks."

The *Tin Lizzie* sat on two horizontal crossbars. The one underneath the bow was lower than the one underneath the stern. Wooden chocks were wedged between the front crossbar and the hull. Removing them would send the boat plummeting down the scooped steel ramp.

The Schooler continued. "After the launch you unhook the launch ramp from the shed wall - use the crowbar - lower and seal the front wall and close and lock the side door. Go to the edge of the bank and use the boathook to slide down to the lake

- it's only eight feet or so - then pole your way out across the ice to the boat. Keep an eye out for gray spots. Once you reach us grab the stern with the boathook."

I considered these instructions for a moment. "This is a joke, right?"

"We'll pull you aboard once you're done."

"Gee thanks."

Sirens crisscrossed in the distance, one getting louder, one fading away. The Schooler handed me the ten-foot boathook and climbed aboard the *Tin Lizzie*. Jimmy followed. I didn't see his smirk exactly but I could feel it.

I positioned myself at the bow of the boat. The Schooler had thought this through, sort of. The chocks on either side of the hull were attached to ropes that had been twined together. One good yank would release the chocks simultaneously, launching the boat. What The Schooler had not adequately considered was the fate of the yanker. What I was staring up at was no ordinary boat hull. It was shiny steel and serrated at the prow like a carving knife.

"Let's launch!" said The Schooler.

I looked behind me. The open front wall was only six feet away. Not enough space for me to flop back and avoid a serrated appendectomy. I would have to be nimble. Whatever happened to smacking the bow with a bottle of champagne?

I gave the twined rope a mighty tug, the *Tin Lizzie* lurched forward. I staggered backwards, caught myself and dived left.

The Chris Craft wobbled from side to side as she cleared the dry dock cradle and nosed down the jerry rigged launch ramp. I turned to watch her progress. She was heavy in the stern, which kept her serrated bow from slicing the jerry-rigged launch ramp in two, but the scooped metal ramp was barely wide enough to hold her. She would have to gain speed to avoid yawing over.

She did. The *Tin Lizzie* bucked and humped and *dove* down those last few yards below the bank and busted a gash in the frozen lake, busted it fat and wide. I watched The Schooler fire up the inboards, watched the twin screws churn slushy water. Jimmy and The Schooler were all aces, they could motorboat off to points unknown while young Harold waved a tear-soaked hankie from the bank.

Where the hell was the damn crowbar? The Schooler said there was a crowbar. I searched left, I searched right, stepped on something hard. There it was.

I pried up the hooks that fastened the launch ramp to the lower lip of the open wall. The ramp clattered to the frozen ground below. I unhinged the front wall and let it slam shut. I crossed to the side door, picked up the boathook, shut the light, shut the door, snapped the padlock closed.

I stopped to scoop snow over the pool of clotted blood outside the shed, then trotted to the lake bank. The *Tin Lizzie* had already plowed a twenty-yard long channel through the ice.

I looked down from the bank. The shoreline was only eight feet below, as promised. Unfortunately it was a jagged pile of boulders. I leaned down and probed at the pile with the butt of the boathook, trying to find a pivot point, looking to pole vault myself over the rocks and onto the ice. The pole found a crevice with some play in it.

I looked up. The Chris Craft continued to plow north in the moonlit dim.

I dug the boathook into the crevice. It bit, leaving me with a pole vault handle approximately ten inches long. I sat down on the bank. That got me another foot or two of pole. I gripped it with both hands and pushed off with my feet.

The pole swung out towards the lake and came to a stop at 90 degrees straight up. I clung to my perch like a flagpole sitter. I shifted my weight to the seaward side, braced a leg against the pole and pulled on the hook with both arms. The boathook drooped over like a licorice whip, depositing me deftly on the icy lake.

I yanked the pole from the rocks and duckwalked north along the carved channel, keeping an eye out for gray spots, whatever they were, determined to walk all the way to Canada if that's what it took to get my dib. I could barely see the *Tin Lizzie* furrowing through the ice field ahead. Goddamn Jimmy Streets. What else? Goddamn Jimmy Streets had his sawed-off to The Schooler's head.

Then an amazing thing happened. The distant thrum of inboard motors changed pitch and the *Tin Lizzie* buzzed backward at a rapid clip.

I put my foot on the neck of the boathook and straightened it out best I could. The Schooler put the engine in neutral when he got close and drifted back in my direction. I snagged the stern with the boathook and prepared to board.

The Schooler pointed toward shore. "The launch ramp!"

"Huh?"

"We need to grab the launch ramp!"

Sirens swirled from nearby, the cops were climbing all over the West Side. Now seemed an inappropriate time for housekeeping.

"Go back!" said The Schooler.

I shimmied back toward the shoreline on the silvery ice as the boat backed up beside me. We reached the head of the ice channel that the boat had dug. The front end of the launch ramp was submerged.

"Pry it up," said The Schooler. "Use the boathook."

I tried my damndest but I had a lousy angle and no way to brace myself. Sirens carved bright loud circles in the frozen air. Why was this so all-fired important?

The Schooler grimaced. "Get on board!"

I heaved the spindled boathook into the back of the boat and minced my way along the edge of the ice channel. The Schooler handed the boathook to Jimmy and issued instructions.

Jimmy stood at the stern and dug down in the water. He reared back as the boathook snagged the launch ramp.

I inched closer and planted my feet to climb aboard. That's how I learned what a gray spot was. It's a thin sheet of ice with slush underneath. I gulped air as my head went under.

I'm a good swimmer under normal circumstances. Not so good in frigid water wearing a topcoat and leather shoes. I backstroked and frog kicked best I could but the sodden coat dragged me down like an anchor. I struggled to shed the damn thing, fumbling at buttons as I sank. For the second time in an hour I said my goodbyes.

It was under twenty feet of water, standing at the bottom of Lake Erie, that I stripped off and discarded my $90 vicuna topcoat. Broke my heart. I swam to the surface and gulped air.

"Hoist him up," said The Schooler. Jimmy reached down and offered his hand. I took it.

I shivered on the deck as The Schooler put the inboards in gear and motored north through his pre-cut channel. Jimmy stood heroically on the stern holding the boathook in both hands, dragging the long metal launch ramp off the lake bank and into the ice channel.

The far end of the launch ramp snagged on something just before it reached the lake. Jimmy lost his footing and fell forward over the gunwale. I jumped over and cinched my arms around his waist, God knows why.

We held fast. Jimmy, his face lashed by icy prop spray, arms extended, gripping the boathook like grim death. Me, soaked to the skin, legs splayed for leverage, clutching Jimmy's backside to my crotch.

We held fast and reeled in the long shiny sea serpent. When its silvery tail finally submerged The Schooler told Jimmy to unhook. The launch ramp sank quickly. Jimmy and I uncoupled and stood as far away from each other as possible.

The *Tin Lizzie* picked up speed. The channel would scab over with a crust of ice by daylight. And Jimmy, The Schooler and yours truly would vanish without a trace.

Chapter Forty-one

"I've made a study of bank robbery," said The Schooler, at the helm of the *Tin Lizzie*, half a mile offshore. Jimmy and I stood on either side of him, studiously ignoring each other.

I was ignoring Jimmy anyway. His good eye was probably drinking in the spectacle that was Harold Schroeder. Having stripped off my waterlogged clothing and toweled off, I was now clad in Schooler hand-me-downs. A sailor's watch cap, ill-fitting gloves, a long sleeved shirt I had to tug past my elbows, a sweater vest, highwater pants and a windbreaker I couldn't zip closed. Oh, and leather bedroom slippers and white socks.

"Robbery is easy," said The Schooler, standing on the bridge, peering through the windshield at the icy lake. "You can control events inside a closed space. It's the getaway that'll kill you."

We had been making slow and steady progress through the harbor ice and Henry was well pleased. Harbor ice was generally thicker than lake ice, or so he said. All I knew about ice came from chunking it off the sidewalk. One patch breaks up easy, the next patch breaks your back.

"You use roads, they put up roadblocks. You use public transportation, they stake out the depot. I thought a small plane on a private strip might solve the problem until radar came along."

The Schooler had been studying this for a long time. Radar had been around since before the war.

"I've always liked boats, motorboats. An eighteen-foot speedboat with a hundred horsepower Evinrude can outrun a

Coast Guard cutter on a flat lake. But Lake Erie never stays flat for long."

I looked down from the bridge, at the vast moonlit ice field arrayed before us and said, drolly, "It looks pretty flat at the moment."

The Schooler's smug smile said *that's entirely the point.*

"The Coast Guard doesn't have a way to pursue us?"

"They have an iceboat. The *Mackinaw*, just commissioned, magnificent ship. Ten thousand hp diesel, welded hull, no rivets. And bilge pumps that shift water in the ballast tanks fore to aft."

"What does that do?"

"Lets the captain rock the vessel front to back if he gets stuck. But the *Mackinaw* clears shipping lanes, it's not a pursuit vessel."

I gestured at the frozen harbor. "So where the heck is it?"

"*She* is clearing the Toledo-Detroit channel at the moment. We've got Cleveland harbor all to ourselves."

Lucky us. "This ice thick enough to support a car?"

"Sure."

"Then what's to keep the coppers from sending a buncha squad cars after us?"

The Schooler's grin was wry, one-sided. "Their lack of imagination."

I returned his grin. "I thought iceboats had to be big."

"Not, it's all about hull design, and plenty of horsepower." The Schooler looked down from the bridge at the arctic seascape. "That's the theory anyway."

I bounced a look off Jimmy. He made brief eye contact before he looked away. *Theory* was not a word we wanted to hear at the moment. Jimmy said as much.

"You haven't tried it the fuck out?"

The Schooler's face glazed over. "What's that?"

"This tub. You been hammerin' at it for months. I know all about it."

The Schooler shrugged. I asked the question. "How did you know all about it?"

"I looked into it," said Jimmy. "Got suspicious when the old man didn't have a tan this last summer. It meant he wan't out snaggin' walleye with his high hat pals. I looked into it. I figure there's only one reason a man puts a one-inch steel skin on the hull of a fishing boat."

Well. That explained how Jimmy knew to go to the boat shed. What it didn't explain was how he got there.

The Schooler, one hand on the helm and the other on the throttle, answered Jimmy after a time, explained why he hadn't tried the boat the fuck out. "You can't take a big stakes gamble with nothing at stake."

The impenetrable circularity of this statement brought me up short. It sounded like Jap poetry. But I took his point, I think. Ike didn't get a dress rehearsal for D-day. You can't do a dry run on a secret mission.

I turned to look at the distant shore. The city of Cleveland was nothing but a fog of misty lights and the Terminal Tower. We were a million miles away. I spun around when Henry jumped up off his captain's chair and said, "Oh *screw*."

I thought it some trick of the light at first, an optical illusion, an icy blue mirage forty yards off the bow. It didn't belong there, that was sure. The Schooler worried the helm and goosed the throttle. We churned closer.

"What *is* that?" I said.

"I don't know," said Henry Voss. "I know about windrows and pressure ridges. But I have no bloody idea what that is."

Jimmy clambered forward and perched at the stem of the prow. I shook my head in wonder. A five-foot wall of ice extended east-west as far as the eye could see.

I'm not a big believer in divine retribution, the hand of God reaching down to smite the wicked and all that. It seemed to me God had been asleep at the switch the last five years. Still.

If what we were looking at wasn't a sign from above my name isn't Harold Martin Schroeder.

A long perfect glistening blue wave. Concave, frozen and curled at the tip.

Chapter Forty-two

"I can't make sense of it," said The Schooler.

He had throttled back and sat in the captain's chair, staring down from the bridge at the sculpted wave. "A windrow looks like a tumbled down wall, broken blocks of ice piled up by the wind. A pressure ridge is a hump. Tidal currents cause ice plates to fissure and overlap. It makes a hump in the ice, a foot high, maybe two. Nothing like this."

I couldn't make sense of it either and I didn't care to. This wasn't a field trip.

The Cleveland PD might be Keystone Kops chasing their tails but Commander Seifert had told the full story to the feds by now. Plump-fingered Chester Halladay would be climbing the walls when he learned about the first-ever robbery of a Federal Reserve Bank, a robbery aided and abetted by an operative he recruited. Once the roadblocks and stakeouts came up empty search planes would be launched. Or had been already. We didn't need to waste time trying to make sense of an ice formation. We needed to get busy busting through it.

That's what I told myself. What I did was continue to stare at the perfect rolling frozen wave ten yards off the bow. The base, like the lake, was thick and gray. The wave tapered gracefully as it swept upward, however, and crested in a curl as clear as Steuben glass. The moonlight painted it a pale and shimmering blue.

I had seen a great deal in my twenty-five years but I was unprepared for this. So I did what any red-blooded can-do American would do, I concentrated on the mechanics. If the icy blue mirage could be made sense of then it wasn't an evil portent from on high now was it?

"We had a lot of snow early in the week, a lot of wind the last few days," I said to Henry as Jimmy monkeyed his way back from the bow, swinging from cleat to grab rail. "If one of the whatchamacallits, a pressure ridge or window…"

"Wind*row*."

"Right. If one of those was already in place wouldn't it act like a snow fence? The ones you see along the highway, keep snow off the road?"

Jimmy joined us on the rear deck. "It's solid, top to bottom." The Schooler swore a blue streak.

I continued. "The whatchamacallit collects the windblown snow, the temp falls, the snow freezes. The temp rises, more snow falls and drifts against the snow fence. The temp falls, the snow freezes. And so on."

"That doesn't explain the wave formation," said Henry.

"But it explains how you can have a five-foot wall of ice on a frozen lake. Once it's in place the onshore wind does the rest, shapes and chisels it. Hell's bells it's nothing but a frozen snow drift!"

I looked to my audience for acknowledgement of my brilliant bit of deductive reasoning. Jimmy put hands in his armpits and attempted to stamp feeling back into his feet. The Schooler said, "I should've installed a bow prop."

The hell with 'em. God was not conspiring against me. It was only Lake Erie and Chester Halladay, and I could lick them any day.

"The ice on the other side of that wall should be thin, right?" I asked. "Just like the snow on the lee side of a snow drift."

"Presumably."

"Then all we need to do is bust through and we're home free."

The Schooler roused himself from his funk. "Here's what we need to do."

You wouldn't think it possible to work up a sweat standing on a frozen lake at night in single digit temperatures but you'd be wrong. It was boathooks again, but The Schooler had replaced the hooks with a new attachment, a big-toothed saw with a sharpened tip.

Funny joke on ol' Hal. I thought The Schooler had rescued me from Jimmy's sawed-off because he valued my smarts. Turned out he just wanted another swabbie, deckhand, ice hacker, whatever it was Jimmy and I were as we balanced on slick lake ice and stabbed and sawed at the sculpted wave with ten-foot aluminum poles. This was not easy to do in bedroom slippers.

We were stabbing and sawing because The Schooler had made a mistake. He had neglected to ironclad the hull all the way up to the gunwales. If we were to breach that five-foot wall it would be at the point of a big-toothed saw.

Jimmy stood to starboard of the hull, I stood to port. The plan was to cut a notch in the frozen wave large enough for the cabin cruiser to pass through. Jimmy was sawing away at a furious pace, I took a more measured approach. The ice below my feet was spider webbed with cracks. I wasn't taking another dip in Lake Erie no matter what.

Then I heard the far off drone of an airplane.

I notched the saw and used the ten foot pole like a towline to pull myself across to the frozen wave. I straddled it, unscrewed the attachment, set down the pole, grabbed the big-toothed saw in my gloved hands and got busy.

My saw strokes were short and quick, no handle to hang on to. Jimmy's strokes were longer, using the full length of the blade. Long and strong beats short and quick every time so I pushed down on the blade with all my weight. The plane droned closer. It was flying slowly, searching.

Jimmy and I were hard at it, neck and neck with about two feet of ice to go when our captain yelled, "Back on board!"

We looked up and saw why. The plane banked and turned, about a mile away. It looked like a twin engine Grumman Goose, there was no mistaking that squat high-winged profile. It was conducting a spotlight-sweeping grid search of the lakefront. The area it was searching was Whiskey Island.

Jimmy punched at the notch in the frozen wave with the butt of his pole before we shuffled along the ice and climbed into the back of the boat. The notch didn't budge.

The Schooler nudged the bow of the *Tin Lizzie* against the sawed notch and gently throttled up. He couldn't gun it for fear the icy wave would tear open the bow above the steel skin. The Schooler reversed engines and tried again. And again.

"Not working, we need to raise the bow," said The Schooler. "If we haul the ballast in the hold up to the stern we might…"

We looked skyward as the Grumman did another bank and turn. There wasn't time to rebalance the cargo load. The Schooler removed an anchor from a stow box on the main deck and clipped the end of the anchor chain to a metal ring on the stern. He handed the anchor to Jimmy.

"Toss it high, *on* the ice, as close to our wake as you can get."

Jimmy reared back and let 'er rip. The anchor landed on the ice, to the right of the channel the boat had carved. It landed and lay there in a heap. None of its prongs had bit. Henry Voss turned to us, full face.

"An extra twenty gees to whoever climbs out and plants that anchor."

"I'll go," I said. "But I'll need some better shoes."

It wasn't just the promise of an extra twenty thou that returned me to the frozen surface of Lake Erie in white socks and Jimmy's shoes - they were one size too big but perfect for ice walking with their rippled soles. It was basic geometry.

You can kick a sphere from here to Sandusky, you can stomp a rectangle flat. Only a triangle wants to stay put and be itself. Jimmy needed The Schooler to get his payday. I did too. The Schooler needed us to help him get where he was going and back him up when the exchange was made. We were a triangle now, Euclid's indomitable structure.

I dug two anchor prongs into the ice and pressed down with my foot to make it fast. I gave The Schooler the go sign, he nursed the throttle forward. The anchor chain grew taut, the Chris Craft sat back on its haunches. I heard the search plane bank and turn.

If I remembered rightly the amphibious Grumman Goose carried up to five passengers. Five armed-to-the-teeth G-men would be my guess.

"Go, dammit!"

The Schooler counted down. Jimmy unclipped the anchor chain from the stern on three as Henry throttled all ahead full.

The armored bow of the *Tin Lizzie* leapt up and busted through the notch in the frozen wave, smashing it to smithereens and surging into the thin ice on the other side, free and clear.

I minced forward on the slippery surface, keeping an eye out for gray spots. I leaned myself against a section of the sculpted wave, watched the Chris Craft tear northward, listened to the throbbing drone of the Grumman Goose and waited to see if Euclid was right about that triangle.

Chapter Forty-three

I wasn't left to freeze to death on Lake Erie. Euclid was right about the triangle.

The *Tin Lizzie* reversed engines after crashing through the sculpted wave. I wished for a camera. Were I fortunate enough to survive this screwy adventure no one would believe this part of the story.

The Schooler cut the inboards, the cabin cruiser drifted back through the notch in the wave. I cringed when I saw Jimmy pick up a ten-foot pole but he had, thoughtfully, unscrewed the spear point saw. I grabbed the pole, pulled the boat close and lunged for the gunwale. Jimmy, in another thoughtful gesture, snagged me by the back of my belt and dumped me face first on the deck.

I stood up and shook myself off. "Nice slippers."

Jimmy ignored me, he was staring skyward. The twin-engine Grumman was no longer crisscrossing Whiskey Island, the search plane was now circling in a tight pattern. They had found something of interest.

The Schooler cranked the throttle, the *Tin Lizzie* took off. I used my newly acquired ripple-soled shoes to secure my balance. Jimmy sloshed around on the sloppy deck and fell on his butt.

The Grumman was still a half mile off and we were running without lights. They hadn't seen us, but they were examining something under that thousand-watt spotlight. Only one answer to that question. The G-men had spotted the narrow channel we had carved in the ice.

The Schooler gripped the helm for dear life as the cabin cruiser bucked and galloped. The ice was scattered here, free-floating plates that offered hit and miss resistance to the steel hull.

The good news was that we weren't leaving much of a trail, what with the scattered ice. The bad news was that the Grumman was no longer circling in a tight pattern. The twin-engine amphib was now buzzing straight up our icy trail.

I huddled in a corner and attempted to keep the contents of my stomach where they belonged. This was something I knew well, hunkering in a bunker, waiting for the devastation from above. Jimmy did not. He reached into his coat and palmed his nickel-plated .45 as he watched the Grumman sweep closer. He was ready to do battle.

Hardee har har.

The Grumman Goose had wing-mounted machine guns if memory served but the feds wouldn't use 'em. They didn't want the *Tin Lizzie* at the bottom of the lake. Chester Halladay would want a clean capture of the bank robbers and their ill-gotten gains. The ill-gotten gains anyway. Halladay would not be overcome with grief if the bank robbers in general and Harold Schroeder in particular weren't around to answer embarrassing questions.

The pilot would swoop down low to let the G-men squeeze off short submachine gun bursts through the slid-open hatch, targeting the inboard motors and anyone dumb enough to remain up top. Hiding below decks would keep me alive for a minute but then what? Once the *Tin Lizzie* was disabled the pilot would land the Grumman, the feds would board the boat and some hotshot G-man would top me off as I cowered in the head.

I watched the Grumman bearing down and thought of another airplane, a lone B-24, and a farmhouse outside Heilbronn, swallowed up in flames. My death would not be so heroic as Alfred and Frieda's but damned if I was going to die in the toilet.

I stood up and walked to the stern and held on to a grab rail. I looked up at the starry sky.

"Beautiful night, isn't it?"

Jimmy turned to face me. "What're you, nuts?"

"That's entirely possible."

Ah, but it was a beautiful night. Made even more so by a sudden warming wind from the north.

I had become a halfway decent meteorologist in my two-year overseas employment, accurate weather reports being critical for bombing runs. Spikes in temperature were usually accompanied by incoming weather systems. Clouds, big fat beautiful low-scudding clouds. When the mercury was really surging ground fog would rise up to greet them. If we could buy ourselves another fifteen minutes we might be able to escape under cloud cover. But one man's fifteen minutes is another man's eternity. Ask Einstein you don't believe me.

The Grumman Goose reached the frozen wave a mere two hundred yards to stern, but they no longer had a clearly carved ice channel to follow. Continuing due north would put us square in the crosshairs.

"Change course, ninety degrees!"

The Schooler didn't argue. He pinned the wheel to the left and leaned into the turn.

I clutched the grab rail on the stern of the *Tin Lizzie* with both hands and watched the furiously boiling wake.

Chapter Forty-four

Our course correction worked. The Grumman Goose continued north. And then the clouds rolled and the mist rose and the *Tin Lizzie* was swallowed up in heavenly vapor. The Grumman Goose kept its noisy vigil but they were flying blind. So long as the weather front kept us company we were snug as a bug.

"Free and clear on the high seas mates!" said The Schooler in his hearty sailor voice.

I echoed the sentiment with the only maritime expression I knew. "Anchors aweigh!"

Jimmy laughed at me, like he was an old salt from way back.

Truth was I had never understood why anyone would voluntarily abandon the feet-on-the-ground security of terra firma in order to be cooped up on a sea-tossed tub. My only nautical experience came from troop shipping over to Liverpool with a boatload of GIs. I wasn't in uniform and I wasn't permitted to say why. The OSS had warned me against fraternizing, which was a strange word to use for a young mope stuck on a passenger ship with a couple thousand other young mopes just like himself, scared, lonely, seasick. *Fraternize* is what you're not supposed to do with the enemy.

The clouds rolled and the fog swirled. The thrum of the twin engine Grumman grew faint. I drew a full unhurried breath for the first time in six hours.

The Schooler continued west at full throttle, which meant we weren't bound for Canada. Good, too obvious. And too far to go before dawn. Where else? Port Clinton? Sandusky? They'd have their PDs and Coast Guards on hot standby as the teletype Paul Revere'd its alarum from post to post. Where else could we reach before dawn?

"Gimme back my shoes," said Jimmy all of a sudden. He was squared up on the rear deck, raring to go.

"Why should I be the only one who looks ridiculous?" I said, lightheartedly.

"Gimme the fuckin' shoes!"

So much for the lighthearted approach. "Come get 'em tough guy."

Jimmy doffed his topcoat. I removed my windbreaker and assumed the position. Jimmy was a handful, no question. But if I couldn't handle a guy wearing bedroom slippers on a slippery deck it was time to hang up my cub scout beanie.

"Stow it, you nitwits," shouted Henry.

"He won't give my shoes!" said Jimmy.

"What's wrong with your shoes Schroeder?"

"They're frozen!"

"Then set them on the engine block and give Jimmy back his pair," said the long-suffering headmaster.

"Okay, on one condition," I said to Jimmy. "You tell me how you got to the boathouse." This wasn't much of a condition. Jimmy was dying to tell me about his clever subterfuge.

"You made a phone call."

"Yeah I did. How'd you know that for sure?"

"I din't," said Jimmy, "you told me."

Sumbitch was right about that. All Jimmy knew for certain was that I was AWOL for a short bit of time at the brown brick monastery. He'd called my bluff and I bit, saying I had phoned Jeannie.

"You din't go through all that bullcrap just to call your lady friend," said Jimmy. "You called for reinforcements, feds or crooks. Neither case was I getting behind the wheel of that panel truck."

"If you knew that going in why didn't you rat me out to the old man?"

"If you called the feds the deal was dead, nuttin' I could do about it. But if you called in a new crew, well, I do what I did."

Let the new hires risk their necks. Hide yourself under a rowboat in hopes the new hires got lucky. Then ambush them with your sawed-off.

The *Tin Lizzie* buzzed through the scattered ice, the clouds rolled and the fog swirled. I asked the question again.

"How did you get to the boathouse?"

"In an Alfa Romeo roadster. Lizabeth's car."

"You swiped her keys."

"She drove me herself," said Jimmy with a lurid grin.

The Schooler was standing at the helm, the seat of the captain's chair bracing his lower back, grinning, talking to himself, in his glory. I nodded my head in his direction.

"You want to say that a little louder Jimmy?"

"Gimme back my shoes!"

I did so, taking my sweet time, then shuffled my slippers down to the cabin to retrieve my soggy brogans. I opened the bulkhead door.

My knees buckled and my head swam. Heat. The cabin was *heated*. I had stripped off my clothing in this very room, I would have noticed. Unless I was too frozen. Or the heat hadn't kicked in yet. And how does a cabin cruiser heat itself anyway?

I flopped down on the narrow bunk and fell dead asleep.

Chapter Forty-five

I woke up on the floor of the cabin about four hours later. 3:40 a.m. The *Tin Lizzie* was no longer slicing through icebound Lake Erie like a hot knife. In fact we seemed to be moving backwards at the moment.

Then we reversed gear, shot forward and smacked into something, hard. The hull of the ship shuddered and groaned. We backed up and did it again. No wonder I woke up on the floor.

Jimmy banged in. "Wake up Sleeping Beauty."

"And you must be the handsome prince."

"It's boathook time, funny boy."

I climbed to my feet and followed Jimmy up to the rear deck. We sat on the gunwale and held fast as The Schooler put the iceboat through its paces, backing and ramming, backing and ramming. We had outrun our warm front. The night was clear and bright with stars, and cold as a banker's smile. I looked to see what The Schooler was trying to bust his way through.

Plates of ice had fissured and overlapped. The obstruction wasn't nearly as tall as the sculpted wave but it was a damn sight wider. The *Tin Lizzie* backed and rammed once again, then sat back on its scuppers, exhausted. I looked again. The boat had only carved a small vent in the windrow or pressure ridge or whatever it was.

The Schooler looked down at us from the wheelhouse. Jimmy handed me a boathook pole with the big-toothed saw attachment. I stood up and sat down.

I'm a trooper, I'm a super-duper double trooper. But Jimmy and I weren't equipped to do the work of a 10,000 hp diesel iceboat with bilge pumps that move the ballast fore to aft. I said as much.

"You're the genius Henry. Dazzle us."

The Captain of the *Tin Lizzie* took this challenge with a snide smile. He bent to his stow box and removed what looked like two leather bridles.

"And I suppose we're the horsies."

The Schooler did a hearty pirate version of his flat clipped laugh. *Herr herr herr. Herr herr herr.*

Turned out the bridles were safety harnesses - you clip 'em onto the hand railing so's you don't fall off the boat when you snag a big one. Jimmy and I shrugged into them. The Schooler positioned us amidships with our boathooks, saw attachments removed. Jimmy was starboard, I was port. Then he backed the Chris Craft up the channel a good thirty yards.

"Poles at the ready gentlemen," called The Schooler as he gunned the engines.

I raised my ten foot pole up high like I knew what I was doing. We motored forward at a stately pace. If Captain Bligh intended to blast his way through the jumbled ice plates he had better pick up the pace.

He did. Ten yards shy of impact The Schooler redlined the inboards, raising the serrated bow of the *Tin Lizzie* just enough to ride the carved vent up and onto the thick mass of ice.

"Pole, you worthless buggers, pole!" shouted Henry in his hearty sailor's voice.

We poled. We dug the boathooks into the starchy ice and oared the boat forward with all we had. I counted six full strokes before the cabin cruiser ground to a halt.

"To the cutwater!" crowed The Schooler.

I unclipped my harness and followed him to the prow of the boat. Jimmy was already there. The Chris Craft was teetering on a precipice of ice plates. All we needed was a shift in the cargo load to get us over the hump and into the thinner ice below.

Jimmy, the big hambone, climbed over the bow and hung from the handrail like a grotesque figurehead. Henry and I did our bit by jumping up and down, but it was Jimmy's triumph when the *Tin Lizzie* slowly, finally, slid down to the other side.

Just as the prow dove into the thin ice the hull shuddered and made a long loud wrenching sound. It came from the stern, starboard side. The Schooler clambered back to inspect the damage. I held fast to the handrail and understood about boats.

I've always been a car guy. My best ever was a deuce coupe Ford. I tinkered with it, spent money on it, took it out on the weekends. But I didn't sit up nights worrying about it, it didn't have a *name*. Then again I didn't have to worry about an untimely burial at sea if the oil pan sprang a leak.

El Capitan surveyed the hull and gave us a thumbs up. Untimely burial at sea postponed. He climbed back onto the bridge, throttled forward and ground his way through the brittle harbor ice.

And harbor ice it was. Smudgepots of light glimmered in the distance, dead ahead. We were approaching our destination. An island.

Chapter Forty-six

An island. A place for this weary landlubber to rest his bones. A place for this sorry backstabber to sort things out.

I had double crossed both The Schooler and Jimmy Streets and lived to tell about it. I assumed The Schooler would forgive and forget, given how things had rounded out. Then again I had messed with his masterpiece.

And I had committed the cardinal sin with Jimmy Streets. I had tried to chump him, which meant I thought he was stupid. The wheel had turned in his favor but Jimmy wouldn't forget. The moment he glommed his share of the laundered money our ironclad triangle would pull apart.

Or sooner. If I'm Jimmy why wait for the mob juice dealer to show? Why not clean house with my sawed-off and get in the wind, find a way to launder the newly-minted money my own damn self?

Come to that if *I* were me why wait for the money broker? I was the one who said *and the juice dealer will bring friends*.

It grew colder on the rear deck as the cabin cruiser ground its way toward the island. The racket was ear-busting in the dense air. Jimmy Streets sat across from me on the portside gunwale and pretended he wasn't freezing his miserable ass off. His performance was unconvincing, something to do with the tiny icicles hanging from his eyebrows. We passed an ice-bound bell buoy and set it rocking side to side. Its clapper made a sound no louder than a hiccup.

The Schooler piloted the boat north, abreast of the island, away from the smudgepots of light. The ice thickened. We were barely making three knots, and were about to lose the cover of night.

I looked to the east. Jet black. I blinked ice from my lashes and looked again. Jet black with deep purple underneath. I dug ice crystals from my ears and listened for twin-engine aircraft. All clear.

The cabin cruiser plowed on, the Ancient Mariner at the helm. How he kept himself unfrozen and alert after all these hours I couldn't tell you. A point of negative light came into view. A tip of landlocked darkness circled by icy starshine. It looked like the tip of a peninsula. Where the hell were we?

The *Tin Lizzie* was laboring mightily now, making little headway. The Schooler consulted a navigation chart, throttled back to neutral and joined Jimmy and me on the rear deck.

"The channel gets shallow here. It's solid ice to the shoreline."

I let Jimmy ask the dumbass question for once.

"So whatta we do?"

The Schooler looked amused. Amused, ruddy-cheeked, bright-eyed and very pleased with himself.

"We gather up our ill-gotten gains and walk across the frozen lake to shore."

Jimmy and I executed a perfect vaudeville turn - to Henry, to the shoreline, back to Henry. The shore was a quarter-mile distant and the twelve blocks of cash were a bulky load.

The Schooler ticked his head. We followed him down to the cabin.

He threw open a closet, we grabbed the loot. The stack reached our foreheads. The Schooler pulled the bunk mattress off its box and removed the contents underneath. A kid's sled with a pull rope.

Jimmy and I tottered up to the rear deck and dumped the cash. The Schooler dropped the sled on the ice. Jimmy grabbed his sawed-off from a stow box.

"Over you go," he said.

Over we went. The Schooler handed down the twelve blocks of cash three at a time. We piled them on the sled. He handed me a roll of tape, I secured the money blocks to the Flexible Flyer.

The Schooler returned to the helm and backed up the *Tin Lizzie* twenty yards or so. I figured he was going to get a flying start and shoot her across the ice as far as he could, then haul her in from shore with a rope and winch. But Henry killed the engines and went below decks.

The boat shivered her timbers and lurched slightly to port. She shivered again and lurched slightly to starboard. She settled lower in the water as The Schooler climbed out and walked forward to join us, carrying a gunnysack. His shoes made a squishing sound.

"Ballast plugs," he said by way of explanation.

The *Tin Lizzie* wallowed from side to side as she descended, struggling against the inevitable, every wallow pulling her lower. I watched The Schooler's mug for signs of distress but he was stolid as Abraham on the mountain.

The boat sank stern first, her serrated steel prow rearing up angrily before she was sucked under. Wherever the hell we were, we were here to stay.

The ice burned through the soles of my shoes. I looked down. Check that, I was still wearing The Schooler's leather bedroom slippers. My spit-shined brogans had gone down with the ship. Shit oh dear, it was going to be a *long* walk to shore.

"What do they call this place?"

"Kelleys Island."

We started towards the shoreline. Three dark figures crossing the frozen lake in the purple dawn. One pulling a kid's sled piled high with blocks of cash, one carrying a shotgun at his side, the other slipping and shuffling behind, trying to keep up.

I imagine we made quite a sight.

Chapter Forty-seven

The three-story Victorian flanked by cedars had seen better days, years, decades. The roof sagged, shutters hung from loose screws and all the windows were boarded up. The chimney looked solid though, that's all I cared about.

Jimmy, The Schooler and I picked our way up the stony shoreline. I knew my feet weren't frostbitten because I felt the painful outline of every pebble.

This too shall pass, Schroeder. Soon, very soon you'll stretch out your weary dogs in front of a roaring fire, a snifter of cognac in hand. The Schooler thought of everything, which meant he had stockpiled foodstuffs for our arrival. Wisconsin cheddar, Westphalian ham, plump squab we could roast on a spit. I struggled up past the rocky shoreline and sat myself down on a fallen log.

Jimmy stopped and looked contemptuous, something he did well.

Screw him. I was simply taking a breather, a moment to rest my weary dogs. The Schooler leaned against the high-stacked sled. Now that he was a landlubber again he looked as beat down to the ankles as I did. We took a breather.

A knife-edged gust of wind and visions of a crackling fire got me up again. We trudged through shin-high snow to the front of the house. A long boat dock jutted out from the craggy tip of the peninsula. It was covered in virgin snow. So were the front steps of the Victorian. We were alone.

Jimmy climbed the snowy steps and put a shoulder to the front door as I unwound the tape from the sled. We played pitch and catch with the blocks of cash as The Schooler sat with his back to us on the bottom step.

"That's the crop," I said when we were done. "Henry?"

The Schooler slumped over sideways and lay there in a heap.

I scrambled over to him and put my finger to his carotid artery. I felt a pulse and thumbed open his eyes. They were bloodshot.

"What happened?"

"You fell asleep." I said. "You okay?"

The Schooler took a deep draw of arctic air, sat up and shook himself back into order. "Never better."

I helped him to his feet. He took the snowy steps slowly. I picked up his gunnysack, it was heavy, bulky with stuff. Cheddar, ham and squab no doubt.

"This was our drop off point," said Henry Voss. "We ran bonded booze from Canada. It arrived on commercial fishing boats, it shipped out on pleasure craft, sailboats mostly. Coast Guard didn't bother them much."

We were seated on cane-backed chairs in the parlor of the Victorian at 6:45 p.m. The sofa was too moldy and spring sprung to sit on and, no, I wasn't toasting my weary dogs in front of a roaring fire for fear the smoke would announce our presence. Two kerosene lanterns were our only source of heat. That and a bottle of 20-year-old Armagnac from the gunnysack.

"They knew what we were up to, the island folks, but they let us be. They hated the feds. They were wine growers, Prohibition put them out of business."

I nodded and took another bite of bologna on a hardtack wafer. I'm not an expert on these matters but bologna and vintage Armagnac seemed an odd pairing. The only other goodies in the gunnysack were three fat oranges.

I asked a question. "Was this when Teddy Biggs ran the show?"

"No, Teddy didn't take over till '36."

"You said you'd tell me all about it sometime."

Jimmy sat on a turned around chair, arms folded over its cane back, half asleep, the bottle of hooch dangling from his hand. The Schooler said his name, Jimmy passed the bottle. Henry took a quick pull.

"Teddy Biggs died eighteen months after he took the reins. Drowned, on a fishing trip to Canada."

"Were you there?"

"Yes I was."

"You give Teddy Biggs any help?"

"No. And no. Teddy didn't need any help falling overboard, and he didn't get any help when he tried to climb back on."

"What happened then?"

"I came home and told the boys he fell off a boat and drowned. They didn't believe me, they figured I clipped him and most were glad to see him go. I wasn't next in line but Teddy's successor celebrated himself to death in short order so I took over," said The Schooler. "Teddy was a lone wolf, nobody outside the gang noticed he was gone. The FBI still doesn't know."

"How can that be?"

"You've worked for the government Schroeder, you know how they are."

I did indeed. Factual reality was a poor cousin to the revealed truth that resided in some bureaucrat's file cabinet. If it was typed on a form and filed in a drawer it was true, everything else was just rumor and speculation.

"When's the juice dealer get here and what happens after?" demanded Jimmy, suddenly, furiously, awake.

"The juice dealer gets here when he gets here and what happens after depends on you."

"Which means what?"

"It means," said Henry so softly I had to lean in to hear, "that the size of your dib and your ticket off this island depends on how well you behave. Both of you."

Jimmy didn't much like the sound of this and I wasn't crazy about it myself. Neither one of us figured we'd be where we were now. Sitting in the drafty parlor of an old house on Kelleys Island, waiting for the headmaster to tell us what to do.

"Who's to say this juice dealer's not gonna show up with a buncha goons and top us off?" said Jimmy, jumping up, spittle down his chin. "He ain't gonna come alone!"

Not a twitch, not a ripple disturbed the downy surface of The Schooler's mug. He stood up. "There are blankets in the closet," he said and wandered off to a room by the kitchen and closed the door, leaving the bottle of Armagnac on the floor.

Jimmy seethed. I drank. I forget the rest.

Chapter Forty-eight

I woke up with a skull-bender at 3:36 a.m. I was wrapped in army blankets on a moth-eaten rug in the parlor. Jimmy was elsewhere. I counted the blocks of cash stacked against the front wall. All twelve were present and accounted for

I had heard of Kelleys Island as a kid. Nice resort, good fishing, dead in the wintertime. Were there permanent residents? The Schooler said something about island folks. How did they provision themselves, get back and forth to the mainland?

I sat upright. My headache accompanied me. I rolled my head around on my neck, stretched and took some deep breaths. I did it again. I felt like shit.

They would cross to the mainland by ferry in summer, by car or sled when the lake was frozen solid. Seemed like we were betwixt and between at the moment. The harbor ice was solid enough to hold a vehicle but I wasn't sure about the ice further out. I would need a vehicle big enough to haul me and $300,000, one third of the take. I'd wanted half originally but things had changed. And I'm a pig not a hog, I could scrape by on three hundred grand. I imagine a dollar bill goes a long way in Fiji.

Jimmy and I were going gun to gun as soon as the juice dealer money exchange was made. I would deal with that when the time came but Jimmy didn't figure to wait that long. He would try something sooner rather than later if he thought the money broker and friends were set to take him out.

Of course I was the genius who put that idea in Jimmy's head in the first place.

I couldn't plug Jimmy in the back, I wasn't that kind of rat, and The Schooler might object. But I could yank his tripwire maybe, needle him, taunt him into pulling his piece in the presence of Mr. Big. I'd have no choice but to defend myself.

I let this idea marinate for a minute. I liked it. It was ju jitsu, using your opponent's hard-charging aggression against him. But it would be tricky to execute, the jibe mild enough that The Schooler wouldn't suspect what I was up to yet raw enough to prompt Jimmy's gun. Something personal. Something Jimmy didn't know I knew. Tricky, hell, it was damn near impossible.

What did I know about Jimmy's background? Not a ding-dong thing. What did I know about his weak spots? He hated being pegged as stupid. But calling him a dunce was way too obvious.

I jumped to my feet at an enormous rumbling *SHRUNNK*. I dug for my gun and took inventory.

Nothing but wind. Wind strong enough to shake an old three-story Victorian to its foundations.

I relaxed and walked the floor, arms swinging freely, enjoying the cold for once. I did have a few clues to Jimmy's background. I knew he liked strong coffee, bebop, garlic...and something else.

Oh yeah, the Westside Market. When I followed him inside he bagged some ethnic specialty from a booth called...some name that sounded rude, like a sound you'd make when you stuck your tongue out. Blah, blugh, ba...*Baleah*. Baleah Meats. It had sounded familiar, a name I'd heard before.

I sat down on my pile of blankets and rolled my head around, hoping to shake the marble loose. I didn't push, I didn't strain. It would come to me. Eventually. The wind rattled the boards on the windows so hard they whistled a tune. I pulled a blanket around my shoulders and kept still.

I remembered. An older boy in high school, Something Baleah. He had a nickname he didn't like...

The Count. The kids used to ride him something fierce. 'Watch your neck, here comes *the Count*,' they'd say in a Bela Lugosi accent. Whatshisname Baleah would go batshit. Want to get a rise out of some mope? Insult his background, insult his *grandparents*.

Jimmy was Romanian, that was good. I rolled myself up in army blankets and fell asleep.

I woke up ten seconds later. Where had Jimmy got to? We had both nodded after Henry retired to his private den. We didn't leave the parlor because that's where the geet was.

Two possibilities. Jimmy had gone outside to reconnoiter a means of escape. Or Jimmy had crept into The Schooler's den and caved his head in.

Nah. He would have stove mine in first.

I went back to sleep. My eyes popped open some time later at the sound of heavy footfalls on the front stairs. I feigned sleep as Jimmy shouldered open the front door. He looked defeated, he looked miserable, he looked like W.C. Fields in that movie where he opens the cabin door and says, '*Taint a fit night out for man nor beast!*'

Jimmy wiped icicles from his eyebrows and chin. He shook himself dry and slumped down, his back against the blocks of cash. His good eye closed. But his glass eye kept watch.

There were, apparently, no readily available escape routes from Kelleys Island. Nice of Jimmy to do the legwork.

Chapter Forty-nine

We were sitting at a round table in the kitchen, if you can call a room with no icebox and bare cupboards a kitchen. It did have an old wood-burning stove we were forbidden to use. The time was 12:08 p.m. and Henry, Jimmy and I were dining on bologna and hardtack with melted snow chasers. The pipes were frozen. We melted the snow by cradling glasses of the stuff between our thighs. We were that parched.

"Sir, Henry, Mr. Big," I said, "Are you as hungry for some good eats as I am?"

The Schooler chewed and swallowed. "My apologies for the grub, it's an old superstition of mine. Best fishing trip I ever took somebody stocked the galley with bologna, hardtack and oranges. Turns out walleye like bologna better than night-crawlers."

"Learn something new everyday." I said and turned to Jimmy. "I don't know about you, but the first chance I get I'm going to take my ill-gotten gains and have me a serious feast. One of those soup to nuts meals like Grandma used to make, you know, takes two hours to eat it all."

Not a flicker of interest.

"I'd start with a big bowl of liver *knödel* soup - don't laugh, it's delicious - then a cucumber salad to 'wash the tongue' as *Oma* used to say."

Jimmy dug out a Lucky, tossed it high, thumbed his lighter and caught the cig in his craw as the flame erupted. He held them apart, the flame and the cigarette. "What's your point, G-man?"

"No point," I said pleasantly. "Just killing time."

White winter sun leaked through the splintered plywood window board. Jimmy lit his cigarette. I kept my yap shut. Time passed.

The Schooler picked up the slack. "And what's the main course?"

"That's what I'm trying to decide. You can't go wrong with sauerbraten and red cabbage, or beef goulash and noodles. You know, been simmering on the stove all day, so tender you don't have to chew, just kind of mush it around in your mouth before you swallow. But it's not a serious *feast*. You know?"

I shut my yap some more. Jimmy was sucking that cigarette like a hog teat and there was a slight glimmer in his good eye.

"And what's a serious feast, Krauthead?"

"*Krauthead*, that's funny. How many Jerries you kill Jimmy? I lost track myself."

Jimmy didn't answer. All he did was suck that burning dinch into his mouth, chew and swallow.

Well. There's something you don't see everyday. Henry endeavored to break the tension. "So what's on the menu?"

"*Spannerferkel mit kaiespaetzle.* Spit roasted baby pig served with dumplings cooked in cheese and butter, fresh-baked Bavarian rye on the side. You know, to sop up all that good juice."

More yap shutting, more silence, more contrails of frigid wind about the ankles.

"I don't eat Kraut food," said Jimmy after a time.

"No?" I said, stretching out my legs, slipping my gun hand casually into my pants pocket. "What do you eat?"

"*Ciorba de burta.*"

"What's that?"

"Tripe sour soup."

"Sounds interesting. What's the main course?"

"Two courses."

"Okay."

"*Gulas de inima* and *creir fiert*. Heart goulash with mashed potatoes and calf brains cooked in lemon butter."

"Ahh, organ meats. I didn't know you were Romanian."

Jimmy raised his chin. I slipped my finger through the trigger guard and placed my left hand on the table. "Your family Gypsies?" I said. "Or vampires?"

Jimmy didn't go for his gat. He didn't lunge across the table, toss a chair or throw a glass at my head. He didn't curse my name or my parentage, didn't even say *nice try asshole*. What he did was laugh, loudly.

And then he went for the jugular.

"When I grow up I wanna be a G-man, and go bang bang bang bang bang. A rough and tough and rugged he-man, and go bang bang bang bang bang…"

The Schooler smiled at Jimmy and upbraided me with a look. Nice try asshole.

I pulled an army blanket over my head and shoulders and went outside. Goddamn stupid cunning Jimmy Streets had out-maneuvered me once again. I pulled the blanket tighter and looked around. The bare trees on the shoreline were gnarled, permanently hunched against the prevailing wind.

I shuffled down the front steps in my bedroom slippers. A red fox was burrowing in the snowy front yard. He poked his head up at my approach, took a quick sniff and bounded off. Can't say I blame him.

I circled north, past the long dock that elbowed out into the lake, past the jagged shelves of shale along the shoreline, past the frozen beer bottles on the bank above the shore. They looked like recent additions. *Erin Brew* was still bright red. Someone had been here not so long ago. Which meant there was a passable road nearby.

How did I know for sure? How did I know that our beer drinkers didn't trudge through the wooded thicket to the shoreline? Because people take roads no matter what, they take roads seeded with land mines and booby traps, they take roads bristling with Gestapo checkpoints. People take roads even when they're not hauling cargo, even when the alternate route is a stroll through sweet-smelling wheat fields, even *then* they will take a road.

I didn't take roads. Not after my last jump. I reported all the troop movements, supply shipments and weather data in my little personal patch of Germanic hell outside Heilbronn. It was a strategic spot, a crucial juncture of road and rail. The OSS got valuable intel from yours truly. But I didn't take roads. It's why I didn't have any letters of recommendation in my jacket. It's why I'm still alive.

I shuffled along the bank, wincing across the rocks and the mussel shells, turned inland and made my way through a stand of trees, wind-ripped branches hanging by a thread. The road approached the back yard of the old Victorian from the south then curved west. A passable road with recent tire tracks. It beckoned to me.

I could shuffle my bedroom slippers down that snowy path to the local village and radiotelephone the FBI. If they didn't have a radiotelephone they'd have a radiotelegraph, something this old brass pounder knew well.

Operation concluded Stop Roll up suspects and contraband far N/E corner Kelleys Island Stop Suspects armed and extremely dangerous Stop Logged by MUTTON.

MUTTON is my FBI code name, don't ask me why, but it beat the hell out of my OSS handle, which was POODLE.

I stamped my feet. They hurt. That was good, it meant they hadn't turned black and died.

You're not going to shuffle your way off this island and back into the good graces of the FBI, Schroeder. The risen Christ couldn't pull that off. You're a prisoner in what spies like to call a 'controlled environment' until Henry Voss says otherwise. So's Jimmy. You're both just along for the ride.

I looked around. I noted the caved-in garage behind the house. I shuffled back toward the house, pulling my army blanket poncho tight, sidestepping the pointy shells. If Jimmy and I were captives on this island so was Henry.

That didn't scan. What if the money broker didn't show? Henry would have a way to call for help if things didn't go as planned.

I stopped and examined the old Victorian. Unlike the brown brick monastery no landline drooped down from a telephone pole to the top floor. I shifted my gaze down one. And again. If it existed, if The Schooler had the transmitter he had to have, it would, most likely, be hidden in the basement.

Chapter Fifty

The basement windows weren't boarded up but they were half covered in drifted snow. I approached one at the back of the house and scooped it clear. It was a standard frame and sash and it was locked up tight. An easy, five second job with the knife I didn't have, the knife my spy school instructor instructed me to carry at all times. All I had was Commander Seifert's service revolver.

I removed my army blanket poncho, folded it over the gun, pressed it against the bottom sash, shivered like a son-of-a-gun and waited for a noisy gust of wind. There's never a noisy gust of wind around when you need one.

When it did come it was so quick I missed it. I waited some more, my teeth chattering like bones in a dice cup. Some day soon this will all be over, Schroeder. Some day soon you'll be toasting yourself to a golden brown on a white sand beach. Or pushing up daisies. And either one will be an improvement.

The next gust was a nice long howl. I busted the window-pane with the butt of my pistol, sprung the latch and opened the sash.

I dropped down into the murk. I listened for sounds from upstairs. Footsteps, very faint. The basement had a plaster ceiling, I could make a little noise without being overheard. An old walnut bar with a brass foot rail stood against the left wall. Past the bar, in the far corner opposite the staircase, was a small walled-off room. I went there.

The gods were smiling, the door to the small room was un-locked. They were grinning ear to ear in fact because the small room also had a grimy window that permitted enough light to search the interior. I found a barrel of nails, a big tackle box, three rods and reels plus two canvas beach chairs and a deflated inner tube.

I tried to picture it. Two hairy-legged armbreakers wearing sunglasses and shoulder holsters reclining on the rocky shore as Teddy Biggs splashed through the summer surf on an inner tube, taking potshots at the skirling seagulls overhead. Fun!

The small room also contained a cedar chest, one of those long low cabinets that grannies use to store lace doilies and tablecloths. It was piled high with hip waders and girlie mags. I cleared it off, lifted the hinged top and saw a beautiful thing. A 150 megahertz Motorola with a modern handset and a telescope antenna. It would have a range of at least five miles, good enough to reach a telephone relay station on the mainland.

All I needed now was a power supply. I dug down and found it, wrapped in old newspapers. A twelve volt battery.

I lifted the battery and the transmitter from the cedar chest, closed the lid and set them on top. I connected the battery to the transmitter and flipped the power switch. No juice. I removed the battery caps and checked the cells. Bone dry. That was good, that was something I could do something about.

I returned to the busted window, scraped up a handful of snow and packed it into the battery cells. I listened for raised voices from upstairs. Jimmy wouldn't like it that I was out communing with nature once again. I clicked the power switch. No juice.

Shit. Time to get brilliant, Schroeder. What do you know about twelve volt car batteries? They're lead, they're alkaline. They need a shot of acid to get them going.

I went to the well-stocked bar and stepped behind. I searched the shelves and cabinets. A bar stocked with booze was a bar stocked with mixers - tonic water for the Gilbey's, Coca Cola for the Bacardi. But the only mixer I found was a bottle of soda water for the Chivas Regal. No help, wrong pH.

The Schooler thought of everything, he'd have something handy. I searched some more until the obvious thought occured.

I returned to the small room with a bottle of Chivas Regal, opened the bottle and served the battery a liberal portion of the golden nectar of the peat bogs. I waited. The transmitter's vacuum tubes hummed to life.

While I didn't care for it personally, I have to give credit where credit was due. Scotch whisky is an excellent proxy for battery acid.

Chapter Fifty-one

I held the fired-up-and-ready radiotelephone transmitter in hand. All I had to do was extend the antenna, get on the blower, contact the local telephone relay station and place a call. That's all I had to do. Provided I knew who I wanted to call.

I did know of course. I wanted to call Jeannie.

There was a grimy piece of tape on the back of the handset with writing on it. *Lorain TelCo*. And a phone number.

I unfurled the radiotelephone antenna and dialed. I heard a *brrrt brrrt* sound, like a European phone ring. An operator answered.

"Mr. Voss, is that you? I haven't talked to you in ages!"

I said I was, indeed, Henry Voss.

"You don't sound like yourself!"

"Been down with a cold, I...sorry, I've forgotten your name."

"Velma."

"Velma, of course. Great to hear your voice. How have you been?"

I listened to Velma's laundry list of complaints patiently because I didn't want to tell her I had an urgent phone call to make and tempt her to listen in. She went on and on, I clucked sympathetically until she ran out of steam. I asked her to connect me to Pappas Deli in Cleveland.

"Right away Mr. Voss, nice to hear from you again!"

"And you too Velma."

Jeannie answered on the second ring. The connection was clear but hollow.

"Pappas Deli."

"You have take-out?"

"Yes we do."

"Cause I could sure go for a Westphalian ham and Swiss on rye."

"Hal?"

"It's me."

"You okay? You sound a million miles away."

"I'm fine. I'm calling to say goodbye."

"Goodbye? Where're you going?"

"I'm not sure."

"Holy cats Hal, I've got a customer here."

"Sorry to bother you."

"Hold on a minute, *don't* hang up."

I held on. I felt stupid. I listened to Jeannie ring up a sale in the background.

"Hal?"

"I'm here."

"Where the heck are you?"

Could I tell her? I wanted to. I wanted someone to know where I breathed my last if it came to that.

"Operator? Operator?" No answer. "I'm on Kelleys Island."

"Why?"

"That's a good question and a very long answer."

"Are you in danger?"

"That's not why I called."

"Answer me!"

"Could be, but it's not anything I can't handle. I just wanted you to know that..."

Jeannie put her hand over the mouthpiece, probably telling her husband that it was just a girlfriend calling to yak. I hoped she'd be quick, I'd been out communing with nature far too long.

When Jeannie came back on the line her voice was hushed. "Do you need to get out of there? Because the Sunday paper just had a write-up on Kelleys Island, the hardy folks there, the *year-rounders*."

"That's nice."

"Listen to me! They have a taxi service that crosses the lake in old Model A's with the doors stripped off, you know, so they can bail out if they start to sink."

"I don't think the ice is thick enough to cross."

"They said there's a pathway from Marblehead, all marked out. They use tree branches for curbs."

"You're kidding."

"It was in the *paper*."

"I'll be damned."

"Can you get away?"

"I don't see how."

Jeannie paused a moment. "What if I come to you?"

I laughed. "That's nuts JJ."

Jeannie placed her hand over the mouthpiece again. I waited. I looked out the window. A hulking figure was tracing my footsteps along the snowy bank, shotgun in hand. I had two minutes at most.

Jeannie came back on the line. "I'm coming out there," she said, whispered, *hissed*. "I'm coming out there 'cause you're too stupid to save your own hide and....let me finish...and...and because I owe you one."

I hadn't thought of it in that way before but it made some sense. Jeannie and I were engaged when she up and married the first gink who asked her because she was ticked off that she didn't receive the love letters I was forbidden to send. She did owe me one.

"What about your husband?"

"What about him?"

"You'd have to leave right away."

I waited. No objection. I continued.

"I'm in an old Victorian at the tip of a peninsula, northeast corner of the island, *northeast*. It's almost one now. What's Marblehead from Cleveland, two hours? Another hour across and, shit, I dunno, let's say five-thirty. There's a road to the back of the house, a caved-in garage, but don't get that close. I'll wait for you there, the garage, five-thirty. If I'm not there, *go home!* Tell the driver you're...you'll think of something, I gotta go."

A belch of static bounced down the line. I could almost feel Jimmy's hot breath on my neck but I held on.

"Is that all?" said Jeannie, dryly.

"No. You might want to pack some sandals and a sarong."

Dead silence. I had offended her.

Always with the wisecracks, Schroeder, when are you going to learn? It was probably just as well this time though, dragging JJ into this catastrophe was stupid and plain wrong. I was about to say so when Jeannie said "I'll see you at five-thirty" and rang off.

Well. Well now.

I lowered the telescope antenna from the opened window, closed the window, unhooked the battery from the transmitter, rewrapped the battery in the old newspapers and returned it and the radiotelephone to the cedar chest. I closed the lid and re-piled the crap on top.

I closed the door to the small room and got behind the walnut bar. I ransacked the cabinets. I had seen some highball glasses somewhere...oh yeah, on the bar sill, right in front of me. I poured myself a double VO, set another highball glass on the bar, bit my drink and waited.

Jimmy dropped down through the back window a few moments later. "What's your pleasure?" I said in a jolly bartender voice.

Jimmy's good eye followed the muzzle of his sawed-off in the general direction of my head.

"I'm pouring Bacardi rum, Gilbey's gin, Seagram's VO and Chivas Regal." Jimmy didn't indicate a preference. "Bacardi Dark it is," I said and poured two fingers. "And put down that grouse musket. You're not gonna shoot me, not here."

I slid the glass across the bar. Jimmy lowered his shotgun and approached. I kept my hands where he could see them. Jimmy grabbed the glass and drained it. "Where *am* I gonna shoot you, G-man?"

"I dunno Jimmy, that's your call. But preferably in the foot."

That coaxed a greasy smile from the old gypsy vampire, which I counted as a personal victory.

"Got any soda water?"

I opened the bottle and set it on the bar. Jimmy poured soda water into his empty glass, dug out his glass eye and plopped it in the tumbler, where it fizzed.

Well. There's something you don't see everyday.

I made my pitch. "Jimmy, you said Henry's always been square with you. Me too, for the most part. I know what I said about the money broker bringing friends and all that but I'm thinking..."

Jimmy triangulated me with his good eye and an empty black socket that looked like a bottomless portal to hell. Any hopes I had of talking him back from the precipice disappeared down that hole.

Jimmy drizzled rum in the glass of soda water, stirred it around with his finger, retrieved his glass eye, polished it on his shirttail and plugged it back in its socket. It was off kilter.

"You got sumpin' to say, say it."

"Okay." I crossed my arms and made a face. "You got your eyeball in sideways."

Chapter Fifty-two

Jimmy grabbed the bottle of Bacardi, I grabbed the bottle of VO. We trooped up the staircase to the first floor. The door was locked. Jimmy knocked, The Schooler answered.

"I'll take those," he said. "I need you two halfway sober."

We surrendered our bottles and followed Henry Voss to the icy kitchen. He had a game of solitaire laid out on the round table. He placed the hooch bottles on a nearby counter where we could see them, a very mean thing to do.

"What did you two talk about down there?"

"Well, I said that, despite our past differences, we had to link arms and pull together to get through this thing."

"And Jimmy agreed with you?"

Jimmy had a Lucky out, lit and in his maw in the time it took to turn my head in his direction. Cigarette smoke is blue when lit and gray when exhaled I noted absent-mindedly.

"Yeah I did," said Jimmy with a squint. "I told the G-man I'd keep an eye out for him."

This bit of drollery from Jimmy Streets was so unexpected that it took The Schooler and me a moment to take it in. Then we shared a hearty guffaw. Jimmy didn't join in exactly but he did snort smoke at short intervals.

The Schooler scooped up his game of solitaire and handed me the deck of cards. "Maybe you'll have better luck."

A thought occurred. I needed a way to kill the afternoon while keeping Jimmy's mind off his twelve gauge. I sat down and shuffled. "Seven card anyone?"

Jimmy grabbed a box of kitchen matches off the wood burning stove and dumped them on the table. "You in?"

The Schooler shook his head. "Five card then," said Jimmy, divvying up the matches.

Two-hand, five card, now there's some excitement. Raking in a two dollar pot with a pair of treys. "What stakes?"

"Hundred dollar minimum," said Jimmy, pushing a stack of matches my way. "We'll settle up later."

Uh huh. The only settling up later we'd do would be at the point of a gun. But the high stakes were good, it meant Jimmy took this as his last chance to add insult to injury, to demonstrate how all-fired smart he was before he blew my head off.

Fine. Jimmy would concentrate on bulldozing me off the table while I cursed my luck and waited for the right moment.

I pushed out a hundred dollar ante and dealt one down to Jimmy, one down to me, one up to Jimmy, one up to me. I'm an indifferent poker player, I enjoy the banter around the table more than I do the game. No doubt Jimmy was just the opposite. He peered at his hole card as if it contained atomic secrets.

Killing Jimmy and The Schooler was the percentage play of course. A .32 is plenty lethal at close range. But this wasn't war, this was commerce. And I had enough blood on my hands. I would have to conk Jimmy out, then hold The Schooler at gunpoint. And there would be no going back inside once I backed out the door with three blocks of hundreds.

Tough shit. Were it humanly possible, Jeannie would be waiting nearby that caved-in garage at five-thirty p.m. Me too. I wasn't going to leave her hanging this time.

Jimmy had a queen of diamonds showing. I had a four of hearts. His bet. He pushed another hundred dollar matchstick into the pot. I saw Jimmy's hundred and raised him one. He hesitated, staring at my four. Poker is a simple game, the only thing that makes it interesting is the bluff. And I had nothing to lose but matchsticks.

I dealt an eight of spades to Jimmy and a queen to myself. "An Ada from Decatur and a bitch of hearts." I'm no good at poker but I know the lingo.

I checked my watch. 1:38 p.m. Way too early. Time to put my pride in my back pocket and lose a few hands. I wanted Jimmy sitting back and relaxed for now, head down and hunched over later on.

Jimmy was a good poker player, I didn't have to try very hard to lose. Okay, I didn't have to try at all. I ran out of wooden matchsticks at one point. Jimmy dredged up a soggy matchbook and tossed it over. I tore out the paper matches and piled them in front of me. Jimmy had taken the winner's habit of high stacking his chips one annoying bit further. He had built a long cabin with his wooden matches.

Time passed quickly. The next time I checked my watch it was 4:51. Time for Mr. Jimmy to bend to the task at hand, bend down nice and low. The Schooler was sitting off to the side, buffing his nails with an emery board if you can believe that. Riding herd on his itchy young men.

"Okay Jimmy, I concede. You're the king of five card. Now how 'bout some Down the River?"

"Suit yourself."

I shuffled up the deck. Jimmy cut the cards. We hadn't set any maximum on wagers. My plan was to bluff Jimmy into submission. Down the River, with three hole cards, makes a bluff harder to detect. I slid another glance at my watch. 4:56.

I looked up. Jimmy was waiting on me.

I anted up and dealt. Two down, followed by one up, high card bets first. Jimmy had an ace of diamonds. I had a nine of clubs.

Jimmy had only two facial expressions, bored and angry. Bored was bored and angry covered everything else, from defeat to elation. Jimmy looked bored as he checked his hole cards.

I hiked my eyebrows as I looked at mine. He bet a hundred off his ace. I threw in two soggy matches. Jimmy called, I dealt him the two of hearts. "Deuceball." I dealt myself the four of clubs. "The devil's bedposts."

Jimmy bet one hundred, I bet three. I hadn't bluffed him all afternoon, not seriously. My bet said I had two clubs in the hole to go with my two showing. A five-card flush is a dead lock in a two-man game. I didn't have any clubs in the hole but that was beside the point.

Jimmy called my bet. I dealt two more. A six of spades to Jimmy, a queen of spades to me.

Well now, a face card. Could be I had three of a kind. One up, two in the hole. I waited on Jimmy's bet.

One hundred. I called and raised him three. Jimmy carefully removed the top matchstick from each wall of his log cabin. I dealt two more. Five of diamonds, seven of hearts. No obvious help to either faction. I kept a calm and confident demeanor. This bet would be my last chance to bluff Jimmy off the table before the final hole card showdown.

Jimmy looked at his cards, looked at my cards, looked at me and checked. Give him credit. Only Jimmy Streets could make the harmless ritual of tapping the table look like a death threat.

I pushed all ten remaining paper matches into the pot. I kept a calm and confident demeanor. Jimmy, legs still stretched out under the table, counted out ten matchsticks.

This contest of wills was completely stupid of course. I would have a perfectly good opportunity to crease Jimmy's skull if he leaned forward to gather up the pot. But I didn't want that to be Jimmy's parting memory of Hal Schroeder.

"Bring it here," said Jimmy.

I dealt. One down to him, one down to me. We peeped our hole cards. I had drawn another four. I had two grand on the table and a pair of fours to back it up.

Jimmy didn't have much showing but he didn't need much. Almost anything beats a pair of fours in seven card. Provided you're willing to pay to see them.

"I need another pack of matches."

The Schooler handed me a small waterproof cylinder with a screw top and said, "We need to wrap this up."

Uh oh. That meant the money broker was due soon. I unscrewed the cylinder and dumped six long gold-tipped matches on the table. "There they are, my five hundred dollar chips."

Jimmy tapped the table. I took my time rolling out the gold-tipped matches, all six of them. Would Jimmy call a $3000 bet?

Yes he would.

I reached my right hand into my gun pocket, slid my finger through the trigger guard, behind the trigger, and got nervous. A .32 revolver wasn't much of a cudgel against Jimmy's thick skull. The butt was hollow, better to use the cylinder, smash it into his temple. If that didn't take I'd have to shoot him. There wouldn't be time to subdue Jimmy while The Schooler dug for his Beretta.

I leaned forward. I used my left hand to turn over my hole cards and expose my puny fours.

Jimmy surveyed my hand for the longest time. He looked perplexed, defeated. Angry. But, despite my silent pleadings, he didn't lean forward. *Dammit.*

Then he did something unexpected. Jimmy threw his hole cards down on the table, grabbed the bottle of rum off the counter and stormed out the front door.

Guess I wasn't the only one bluffing.

I gathered up the cards. If The Schooler followed Jimmy out to the lake I could grab my dib and escape out the basement window.

But Henry Voss didn't co-operate. Best he did was stand on the snowy porch and call after Jimmy.

I glanced down as I absent-mindedly gathered up the deck. A tiny alarm bell sounded in the lower chambers of my skull.

Chapter Fifty-three

"Jimmy won't stay away long," said The Schooler as he closed the front door. "Not if he knows what's good for him."

"That's the question, isn't it?" I said, still at the kitchen table, shuffling the deck of cards into order. I put the cards down and crossed to the parlor.

"I insulted Jimmy, tried to chump him. If I walk away in one piece with my fair share, Jimmy loses. And Jimmy can't lose."

"Jimmy has worked for me since he was ten years old, I raised him from a pup. He'll come around."

Such paternal concern. Such filial devotion. Of course it hadn't kept Jimmy and Henry from selling each other down the river when given the chance but, still, it was a sweet and tender thing.

"Maybe he won't shoot *you*. But soon as Jimmy gets his dib he's in a duck blind and I'm a redwing mallard." The Schooler didn't argue the point. "Which is why I would like to take my share and go."

"I can't let you do that."

I yanked my .32.

The Schooler looked disappointed at this crude breach of etiquette. "You'll freeze to death out there," he said after a time.

"Hell, I'm freezing to death in here!"

The Schooler laughed his mirthless laugh. *Heh heh heh.* I felt a pang for the old gent, decided to throw him a bone.

"I'll take whatever dib you say is mine."

Two hundred and fifty was his answer.

"Done." I backed up to the wall of money and removed two blocks of hundreds and one block of fifties, keeping my gun leveled. Henry Voss made no move for his Beretta. Gunplay wasn't his strong suit, guilt was. I felt a complete shit while collecting fifty grand less than I thought I deserved.

"You going out that rear window you broke?"

I nodded. The old man didn't miss much. He opened the door to the basement. I grabbed up an army blanket. He wished me luck. I took the steep stairs one at a time. Henry Voss locked the door behind me.

I made my way across the basement, one quarter of a million dollars clutched to my chest, the half-empty bottles winking at me from the old walnut bar. I used my blocks of cash to bust out the jagged shards of the rear window but I needed a satchel to hide my loot.

I searched behind the bar, I searched the little room. Not even a paper bag. I eyed the big tackle box, dumped the contents on the floor and crammed the cash inside. It didn't want to fit, I had to sit on the box lid to snap it shut.

Hip waders, right in front of me on the cedar chest. Perfect. I sat down and pulled them on over my bedroom slippers.

I climbed out the open window with a minute to spare, 5:29 p.m. I crunched through the snowfall, a swashbuckling figure in thigh-high rubber boots, two-days' growth and an army blanket shawl. Jeannie would swoon at the sight of me. I hid myself on the far side of the garage. I set down the tackle box and shivered and stamped my feet and kept a lookout.

Had Jimmy got wind of my call to Jeannie somehow, used the poker game as a pretext to storm out and intercept her? Nah, there was no way he could know she was coming. No way in hell.

When I checked my watch again it was 5:44.

I would give Jeannie ten minutes more, I thought, then had a good laugh at myself. And just where do you intend to go once those ten minutes have expired, Mr. Schroeder? I considered my options. That killed two seconds.

I looked down the road, hopefully, unseeing. It was dark now, and the snow was coming down like sleet.

I eyed the dubious shelter of the caved-in garage. It was then I heard the distant thrum of a twin-engine airplane. Had to be the money broker, he was due.

I stood there in abject misery for another five minutes. In that time the twin-engine circled high overhead and dipped its wings. It was all white, pontoons under the wings, not an airplane I knew the name of. It droned away and droned back, on approach for a landing on the frozen lake.

Jeannie didn't show.

I shook myself like a wet dog, picked up my cash-crammed tackle box and trudged back across the backyard, not sure what I was up to but certain I would think of something.

I reached the back corner of the old Victorian and took a look. The airplane, lights blazing, was slowly taxiing up to the pier. Where was The Schooler? This was his moment of glory, the dramatic conclusion to his masterpiece. By rights Mr. Big should have been standing on the end of that pier with a big pile of dough and a triumphant grin.

I didn't see him. Which meant The Schooler was still trying to round up Jimmy. Or Jimmy had found him and The Schooler was now deceased. Jimmy wouldn't like it that Henry had let me skate.

I watched and waited. The white plane approached the dock and shut its engines. It was a big sleek pricey-looking job, with bright nav lights mounted above the hatch. The hatch remained closed.

A minute passed. Nothing happened. Then the side hatch of the snow white plane popped open and a man leaned out and lashed the plane to the dock pilings. He had a big gun slung over his shoulder.

The man stepped out onto the pier, cleared away snow with his foot and extended his hand behind him. A woman inside the cabin took his hand and stepped out. A tall woman wearing a white fur jacket and matching hat. She stood on the end of the pier with her hands on her hips. I couldn't see her face with the bright light behind her but I knew who it was. Lizabeth.

"She's a sight to behold, isn't she?"

My heart leapt to my throat and attempted to squeeze itself out through my ears. I whipped around. "Where did you come from?"

"The basement," said The Schooler. "I'm surprised you're still here."

"Me too. Where's Jimmy?"

"He's hiding. He does that sometimes."

"How come?"

"Well, he was already teed up about the money broker. And if he saw you sneak out the basement window he may have reached a wrong conclusion. Jimmy tends to have a gloomy outlook on life."

"Yeah, no shit."

"That's why I need you to walk down that pier with me, arm in arm."

I checked the road by the caved-in garage one last time. "Let's went."

The Schooler grabbed up his lumpy gunnysack. "Where's yours?"

I hoisted my tackle box. The Schooler laughed his flat clipped laugh and led the way down the side of the house under the shelter of snowy cedar branches.

"You leave Jimmy his dib, inside?" I asked.

"Of course not."

"Then could be Mr. Jimmy's standing on the front porch right about now, looking to blow our heads off."

The Schooler didn't comment. But he did stop just before we reached the front corner of the house. "Jimmy? Jimmy, we've got the money. We've got the money and we're going to walk down the pier and we want you with us! Jimmer?"

Little Jimmer didn't answer.

"He's not there," shrugged Mr. Big and walked out into shotgun range.

I waited five seconds and followed. The porch was empty.

We hurried toward the pier, The Schooler striding forward with spring in his step, me walking backward, tackle box in one hand, gat in the other. No Jimmy, no-where. Henry stopped by a little fishing shack at the head of the pier. Jimmy's duck blind? No, the door was padlocked.

It was then that The Schooler had his moment of triumph. At the head of the long pier, on Saturday, December 15th, 1945, 6:18 p.m. He held up his gunnysack in the bright wash of the nav lights, the gunnysack formerly filled with stale bologna and hardtack wafers, the gunnysack currently containing $600,000 of freshly minted currency.

Lizabeth waved and clapped her gloves together. They made a hollow sound. *Pock pock pock puck.*

We waded down the snowy pier to the waiting plane. No goons jumped out to mow us down. No Grumman Goose full of G-men swooped down from the sky. No Jimmy, no-where.

The Schooler and Lizabeth embraced. She lamped me over his shoulder. I looked elsewhere.

A small man wearing a bowler hat and a pince-nez appeared in the hatch door. The money broker. The Schooler greeted him and opened his gunnysack. The small man grabbed a block of cash and ducked back inside.

The man with the big gun took his place. He held it at quarter arms, a Bren machine gun with a short stock. Nasty weapon. The man was forty or so, ex-jarhead by the look of him. A soldier of fortune.

We waited for a time, The Schooler, Lizabeth and me. I kept an ear out for airplanes and an eye peeled for Jimmy. The snow slackened, the wind picked up. The money broker returned and gave The Schooler a deferential bow. The cash had passed inspection.

Henry Voss turned to me and said, "We're headed north. Care to join us?"

Lizabeth stood next to him and hiked her eyebrows above those beautiful sea green orbs. A thunderous shotgun blast rent the air and echoed out over the lake.

Chapter Fifty-four

The soldier of fortune pushed The Schooler and me aside as we turned to look for the source of the gun blast. Another hired gun, a younger version, jumped out of the airplane and joined him at the end of the pier.

The Schooler told them to lower their weapons. They ignored him.

The blast didn't hit anyone. It was more along the lines of an announcement. It came from the direction of the fishing shack at the head of the pier. Jimmy yelled something that the wind carried away.

I didn't get the timing. Jimmy should have made his move long before Henry and I were about to step aboard a seaplane under cover of ex-Gyrencs with Bren guns. It made no sense of any kind, which flanged up my neck hairs. That he had waited till now meant something.

The wind settled for a moment. Jimmy piped up again. "I'm not going down that pier! Bring it here!"

Bring it here. Bring it here. Bring it here.

That's what Jimmy said when I dealt his last hole card. What he said when…oh Christ.

Two jacks! That's what had set my alarm bell dinging. There were *two jacks* in Jimmy's discard pile on that final hand. I had glimmed them for an instant when I gathered up the cards, too distracted by Jimmy's tantrum to pay attention. He had thrown that final hand as an excuse to storm off! Only one reason to do that. Jimmy knew I had help coming, and he wanted to greet them before I did.

How could he know that?

Shut up, Schroeder. How was a question for later on. What mattered now was that Jimmy Streets, unless I was very much mistaken, was standing behind the fishing shack at the head of the pier with his pig snout sawed-off pressed to Jeannie's head.

Holy Mother of God.

The Schooler picked up his gunnysack, pushed past the Gyrenes and proceeded down the pier. I picked up my tackle box and followed. Father Sullivan said salvation is many choices well made. Damnation, on the other hand, can come in an instant.

I didn't care. I didn't care who got hurt, maimed, killed or mutilated, myself included, so long as Jeannie stayed safe. We closed to within shotgun range of the shack.

The Schooler was blathering on. Jimmy, this is foolish, Jimmy, you have nothing to fear, Jimmy, Jimmy, Jimmy.

THINK, Schroeder. DO something!

I opened the tackle box, grabbed a block of fifties and tossed it next to the shack where he could see it. "You win Jimmy, my dib's all yours." I tossed another. "Just let her go."

Jimmy didn't answer. The Schooler eyed me like I was nuts.

"Show yourself and I'll toss the rest. Two hundred and fifty gees!"

That Jimmy had Jeannie meant he also had the car she came in. He had a means of escape. He was sitting pretty!

"Jimmy listen to me, you're the champ, I'm the chump! You've got me outgunned and outmaneuvered. Collect your winnings!" I said. "I won't stop you, how can I?"

Jimmy Streets stepped out from behind the shack, holding a bound and gagged Jeannie as a human shield. She looked frightened, and very angry.

Jimmy pointed his shotgun at The Schooler and me and said, "I want it all."

This was it then. Jimmy's answer to The Schooler's well-considered master plan. We were not all going to come to a meeting of the minds here and walk away in one piece. This was war.

I tried. I got behind Henry and put my gun to his back. "Sure, I'll toss it all over. Just let Jeannie go. You've got a sawed-off, I've got a .32. You don't need her."

But The Schooler had heard enough. The fucking ingrate he had raised from a pup wasn't going to piss all over his masterpiece.

Jeannie gave me a heads up with a flick of those bright brown eyes.

Down, to my right.

The kindly headmaster who preached reasoned dialogue and thoughtful deliberation was fumbling in his pocket for his Beretta. He was slow, out of practice.

It cost him.

Chapter Fifty-five

The Schooler took a full load of twelve-gauge buckshot in the chest and throat. I know about the throat because I heard him gurgling. I took a few myself, standing behind him.

They were caroms mostly, left cheek and shoulder. They stung like hell. That was good, I wasn't in shock.

Henry clutched at his throat as his knees buckled.

I held him up, braced my left arm across his chest to protect myself from the second shotgun blast. But The Schooler's soul left his body right about then. He grew heavy, my left arm too slippery with blood to hold him up.

Jimmy didn't look so good when he saw it. His long time mentor-protector-father figure face down on the pier, his body haloed in bloody snow.

Jimmy pressed his sawed-off to Jeannie's temple and yelled something I couldn't hear. The blast had deafened me. Jimmy's jaws jacked up and down furiously.

I tried to make sense of it. He had one shell left in his shotgun. Why mess with Jeannie? Why not just finish me off?

I glanced back at the seaplane. The hired guns were down on one knee, locked and loaded and ready to do business. That was why Jimmy hadn't finished me off. He didn't want the soldiers of fortune to have a clear shot.

Me neither. Not with Jeannie in his grasp.

"Hold your fire!" I yelled, screamed, *shrieked* at the hired guns. I couldn't see their faces with the light behind them, just the shiny barrels of their Bren's. They held their fire.

All was not lost. Jimmy had a hostage but I did too. My tackle box and The Schooler's gunnysack, $700,000 all told.

I didn't care about the money, I cared about that last remaining twelve-gauge shell. Jimmy was sure to use it one way or another. My job was to make sure that shell had my name on it, not Jeannie's.

I dug into the gunnysack and came up with a block of hundreds. I tore off the tape and held it up and said, "Come get it dumbshit!"

I let the wind carry many thousands of dollars out over the frozen lake.

Jimmy, crazy-eyed, jammed the snout of his sawed-off to Jeannie's temple. Her eyes got big. This wasn't working.

The ringing in my ears subsided. I heard rushing wind, and the distant thrum of a twin-engine search plane. The dreaded Grumman Goose.

The snow white seaplane fired up its engines at the end of the pier. Jeannie and I locked eyeballs. She saw what Jimmy saw. She knew what I knew. With the hired guns piling back on board the plane I was target practice for Jimmy Streets.

I gave Jeannie a winsome goodbye smile. She sneered at me.

Jeannie was a tomboy, had always challenged me at everything from beer chugging to a foot race down the block. The only constant was her little girl countdown before the contest.

Ready, set, go!

Jeannie gave me a big wink with her left eye.

"You win Jimmy."

Then her right eye.

"I'll have to trust you." I threw the gunnysack at Jimmy's feet.

Then her left eye.

"There's the rest of ..."

Jeannie dropped to her knees on cue. Jimmy clutched at nothing for a half a second. Half a second too long as it turned out.

I would have to write a nice thank you note to Commander Seifert. His .32 caliber revolver was well maintained. I put four of six in the kill zone, the target area of vital organs above the waist.

Not that Jimmy noticed.

My first round banged off his orbital bone and tore into his brain, blowing his recently cleaned and polished glass eye to smithereens.

Epilogue

And that's how I came to have all these overturned shot glasses lined up on the bar. Drink one, another one takes its place. It feels good to be a hero I must admit. I was plain jealous of those uniformed GIs parading around with all that fruit salad on their chests. Stupid, but I was.

How's come I'm not in jail? I told the FBI I had been playing along, biding my time till I could finally get the drop on both Jimmy and Mr. Big. They didn't believe a word of it but my version made them look a lot less stupid than the truth. Louis Seltzer and *The Cleveland Press* took the story and ran with it. I got my beat-up mug on the front page. **FBI Spy Shoots Fed Bank Crooks!**

It's New Years Eve. I'm at Otto Moser's on E. 4th, a smoky old joint with lots of playbills and autographed portraits on the walls. John Barrymore. Helen Hayes. No spit-roasted squab on the menu but the corned beef is first rate. Ol' pegleg Wally is drinking with me, basking in my reflected glory.

It's getting close to midnight now. I can't see the wall clock and I no longer wear a wristwatch but the crowd is buzzing and the waiters are raking in the silver. They stack it up behind the bar here at Otto Moser's, no cash register. Wally tells me it's a tradition started by the man himself. He died in '42, of p-neumonia. We down a shot in his honor.

I no longer wear a wristwatch because, best I can tell, my watch is the reason Jimmy and The Schooler are dead. Jimmy caught me checking it once too often toward the end of our poker game. Why do that unless I was meeting someone?

I'm not crying in my beer about Jimmy. We fought World War II to defeat guys like him, half smart thugs who got too big for their britches. But I feel bad about The Schooler. Worse than bad, he was an honest crook.

Here is what I've concluded. Loyalty isn't for saps, trust is. Loyalty is based on something - your track record. Trust is pie in the sky.

The Schooler walked down that pier trusting that I wouldn't plug him in the back and Jimmy wouldn't plug him in the front. A sharp guy like The Schooler should've known better. Neither one of us had earned his loyalty. The Schooler's death was his own damn fault.

Which brings me to Alfred and Frieda. I was loyal to them because they rescued me and held me from harm. I told them what was coming. They remained inside their farmhouse and entertained the assembled *Panzertruppen* on piano and violin in order to drown out the drone of the B-24s. I didn't kill them. They chose to be heroes.

I'm not a real hero of course, not even close. But if people want to slap you on the back and buy you a round then I guess you've gotta let 'em.

Lizabeth?

She got away. The white seaplane made it back across that dotted line in the middle of Lake Erie before the Grumman Goose could hunt it down. I don't imagine she's in any dire straits. Lizabeth makes friends easily.

The Mooney Brothers?

I called their phone number. The girl who answered said the family had moved away, wouldn't say where. Back to County Cork if they knew what was good for them. And yes, she said, all three boys were alive and kicking.

And Jeannie? Does the hero get the girl?

What can I say? Our timing is plain lousy, Jeannie's and mine. Our first reunion took place while I was helping Jimmy beat the crap out of her husband. And our last reunion was a long embrace at the head of a pier littered with shit-smelling corpses. I told Jeannie how I felt about her and she returned the favor. But we took the hint. Jeannie and I weren't meant to be.

They pass out horns and party hats, must be about time. Wally dons two hats, on either side of his head, like horns. He's having a great time. We down a shot to 1946.

I try to get into the New Year's spirit but old questions tug me back. Why did the FBI pick me of all people? And fail to back me up once they did? The counterfeit cash I could chalk up to Chester Halladay trying to be clever, or cheap. But sending Wally in a '39 Hudson when I had a good chance to shag the mob's weekly take to Mr. Big, well, it stunk to high heaven. Smelled like the whole operation had been a sham from the start.

The why of that is beyond me at the moment.

The crowd whoops, hollers and sings "Auld Lang Syne." I think about that hoary old elevator operator in the Standard Building, the one with the oversized Adam's apple, the one who pointed his bony finger at me and said, *You'd best go home.*

And here I am, in Cleveland, Ohio. The best location in the nation.

"A Despicable Profession,"
Book Two of the American Spy Trilogy,
will be published sometime in 2009.

To be placed on our notification list
please visit
www.bluesteelpress.com

Blue Steel Press
Chicago

1972456

Made in the USA